MY LOVE
MY LAND

A heartbreaking and powerful WW1 saga

JUDY GARDINER

Revised edition 2023
Joffe Books, London
www.joffebooks.com

First published by Hachette Digital
in Great Britain in 1980

This paperback edition was first published
in Great Britain in 2023

Cover art by Jarmila Takač

ISBN: 978-1-80405-749-0

For F.G.G. with love

PART ONE

CHAPTER ONE

At seven o'clock on the morning of Tuesday, 4 August, 1914, Germany invaded Belgium.

Slowly the giant army moved through the drowsy summer countryside to the winding river Meuse, raising clouds of white dust with its endless columns of chugging motor-wagons and horse-drawn artillery. At the head rode a company of Uhlans, the cold-eyed spike-helmeted Prussian Lancers. Seeing them, village women snatched their children in from play and hid with them behind locked doors. Events were to prove that their fears were more than justified.

Leaving the small frontier town of Visé a smoking ruin, the Germans opened their attack on Liège. The town fell on Friday, 7 August. Only the encirclement of military forts held on, grimly firing back shell for shell until one by one they were silenced by the great siege guns.

Inexorably the Germans continued on their way westward and then swung south, effectively smothering Belgium in their progress towards France. Time and again the hastily mobilized Belgian army fell back in defeat. On 14 August, the French launched a desperate offensive in the Ardennes, the lovely area of rich farmland and wild, tree-covered hills with their secret caves and small close-knit villages. But nothing could stem the enemy advance, and on the following day the war came to Dinant, the little town that over the centuries had spread itself along either bank of the Meuse in the shelter of the hills.

As the shells screamed back and forth and the houses collapsed in rubble the people of Dinant took shelter in the caves nearby. Sections of the 148th French Infantry were trapped and finally bayoneted in the ancient stone fortress that overlooks the town, and by Sunday the twenty-third it was all over. During the bombardment nine hundred and fifty houses had been destroyed, and in the massacre that followed six hundred and seventy-four Dinantais were shot.

On Monday, 17 August, in a cave some eight kilometres from Dinant the woman Thérèse Aubel sat apart. As oblivious to her fellow refugees as she was to the war outside she sat with her chin in her hand, staring blindly through the gloom.

She was staring at the farm. Remembering without emotion the rough cart track that wound through the coppice of goat willow to the grey stone outbuildings that sheltered the house where she and Henri Aubel had spent the fifteen years of their marriage. It was a good marriage. Childless, but good even so. And they had worked. Two hardy peasants toiling side by side in the fields as they hand-ploughed and sowed, weeded and harvested.

It had taken over a year to save enough money for a cow and they had strained their resources to the limit to buy the white heifer who was to be the founder of the herd. But Flavie had amply repaid the expenditure, dropping strong lusty calves and giving rich milk in abundance. People spoke of the Aubels' luck but few people spoke of their single-minded determination, their capacity for hard work. And no one spoke of the love they had for the soft crumbling soil, the warm winds that swept down over the forests and the small farm with its cows and fat chickens scratching in the sun-drenched yard. No one spoke of it because probably no one knew; Thérèse and Henri Aubel would have been embarrassed to speak of such things, even to one another.

But with the coming of war, everything changed. Late in July when the corn was deep gold under the hot blue sky Henri volunteered for the Belgian infantry and Thérèse stood at the end of the cart track, watching him walk away down the road that led to Namur. At the bend in the road he turned to look at her for the last time and she began to ran towards him, stumbling over her long skirt, her sabots clacking.

There was nothing to be said. They could only stand there holding on to one another before returning to their customary good sense and making the best of a bad job. War was a huge and largely incomprehensible affair ordered by people better-born, better-educated than they. As the weather was organized by the hand of God himself, so were wars directed by the superior intelligence of Kings, Kaisers and such like, who presumably knew what they were about.

Henri Aubel was thirty-six, and his wife a few months younger. Goodbye was a difficult word for them to say.

In the half-light of the cave, Thérèse retraced the memory of those last few days. News of the Germans' coming had reached her from the village, together with rumours of their behaviour in the towns they had already taken; looting, plundering, ransacking shops and stripping farms of their livestock. A woman who had a sister in Liège had heard even worse. Innocent civilians had been shot by the Uhlans and some had even been used as targets for bayonet practice.

While remaining sceptical of the more blood-curdling tales, she nevertheless thought seriously about the probable arrival of the enemy. It seemed only too logical that they would help themselves to anything they wanted, particularly in the nature of food. Feeding a vast army of men and horses must of necessity constitute a serious problem of organization and the simplest method of solving it was obviously to steal from other people as they went along.

Alone at the farm on Saturday the fifteenth she became aware of a sound like the distant rumble of thunder. Outside the kitchen door she shaded her eyes and stared up into

4

the peerless sky. The weather showed no sign of breaking. During the afternoon the rumbling grew more insistent, and after the evening milking she drove the cows into their stalls in the shippen and slipped the heavy iron bolt on the door. Slowly and very thoughtfully she made her way down through the bottom meadow, across the slab of rock that spanned the stream, then set off through the woods, climbing the tortuous path that led to the summit of the high plateau opposite the farm. Coming out on to the clearing where the rock face dropped steeply towards the winding Meuse she looked towards Dinant. It was burning.

For a long while she stood motionless, watching the billowing smoke and the shells exploding like brief yellow stars. Now and then the smoke clouds would roll back for an instant and her eyes would search for a reassuring landmark; the bridge, the dark full-bellied spire of the church of Notre Dame, the school, the Hôtel de Ville. But if they were still standing, they remained hidden from view. The roar of German howitzers echoed and re-echoed along the valley and blended with the rumble of falling masonry.

When at last she turned towards home there was no feeling left in her. The beauty of the evening sunlight slanting through the silver birches left her unmoved and she took no notice of the family of deer who stood flicking their tails in a clearing.

The sun was low when she reached the farm. Slowly she went into the silent kitchen, and standing on a stool reached Henri's gun down from the wall. Carefully she loaded it and went out again, walking across the worn cobbles to the shippen and unbolting the door. She stood on the threshold with the gun held in her square-cut peasant hands, breathing in the warm animal smell and meeting the look of gentle enquiry they turned on her.

Flavie, as matriarch of the herd, should be the first to go.

The woman Thérèse walked across to her, patted her white shoulder and pressed her face fleetingly between the animal's eyes. Then with a quick movement thrust the muzzle of the gun against the place where her mouth had just touched and pulled the trigger.

Without a sound Flavie sank slowly to her knees. A single bead of blood appeared on her forehead, swelled and then trickled through the white hair towards her nostrils. She shook her head once, as if troubled by something beyond her comprehension, and then died while the other cows looked on uneasily.

Stony-eyed, Thérèse Aubel walked the length of the shippen, entering each stall in turn and pulling the trigger against each forehead. When she had finished the acrid smoke was stinging her eyes. She wiped them on her sleeve before going across to the well and dropping Henri's gun down into it.

In the chicken house the birds had already settled to roost. Closing the door behind her she continued with the grim task of annihilation, wringing each neck quickly and expertly. When at length she left there was total silence.

Twilight lay thick inside the house and she stood in the kitchen for a moment, listening to the uncanny stillness. Even the bombardment seemed to have stopped.

Lighting the oil lamp she carried it slowly through the rooms; the storeroom, the dairy, the prim parlour where she and Henri had never had time to take their ease. Beneath the bowl of wax flowers was their wedding photograph, the two of them standing nervously to attention in their unaccustomed finery.

The bedroom was airless under the hot slate roof. She leaned her elbows on the windowsill for a minute, following with her eyes the familiar line of the hills that rose opposite. The hills and valleys of the Ardennes were in her blood, as they were in Henri's; since small children they had known every step and stone of the wild luxuriailt area in which they lived, and the farm itself seemed to encompass everything in the world that mattered. But now? Now the old familiar way of things had vanished abruptly, and no one could fore-tell what the future had in store.

Except for one thing. The Aubel farm at St Louis les Bois would yield nothing to the Germans when they arrived.

Taking a large china jug from the kitchen she went out to the barn and filled it with paraffin. Back in the house she walked upstairs and tipped it over the bed. Returning, she refilled the jug and poured the contents over the stiff horse-hair chairs in the parlour. The next jugful was reserved for the kitchen; the scrubbed oak table, the huge armoire and the wooden rocking chair that had belonged to Henri's father.

Six times she refilled the jug, then turned her attention to the shippen. The cows lay motionless in death and she covered their bodies with straw before sprinkling them liberally with paraffin. When she had poured the last jugful over the chicken house she stood resting for a moment, wiping her hot face on her forearm and calculating the distance from the shippen to the haystacks.

The flames would reach easily. After weeks without rain everything was tinder dry and a mere spark would be sufficient to start a blaze.

She lit a screw of paper and pitched it inside the shippen. It landed on a bed of straw and she stood listening to the soft sound of crackling. The flames began to spread, leaping joyously towards the roof as they found the paraffin.

Back in the farmhouse that smelt of death she returned to the parlour and before setting fire to it picked up the wedding photograph and thrust it down the neck of her blouse. The flames leaped swiftly, rising higher in their clear yellow beauty, stretching out welcoming arms to one another before joining together in one vast conflagration.

Smiling grimly, Thérèse Aubel walked away.

* * *

In contrast to the breathless summer heat outside, the cave exuded a damp chill. The earth floor had been beaten hard by dozens of anxiously pacing feet and from somewhere behind the rock face came the faint tinkle of a waterfall.

Many people had been in the cave for three days, and after the initial relief at escaping from the bombardment, nerves were becoming frayed. Families were asking one another *What next?* Hidden deep in the mountainside it was difficult to tell what was going on, and as the food, hastily snatched from threatened homes, began to run low, there was talk of taking a chance in the open.

But no one went. Wives forbade their men to go, fathers forbade their sons. Torn by doubt and uncertainty they remained in the cave, soothing the fractious children and speculating endlessly on the conditions outside.

An old woman with thin hair pulled back from a bony forehead sat on a small promontory of rock with her arms linked round a feather mattress, and tried to remember why she was there.

Sometimes the clouds of confusion would clear and disclose fragments of the past few days, but the more her mind tried to sort them into some form of coherence the more the reason for what had happened eluded her.

The most persistent memory was of her eldest grandson banging on her door and shouting to her to leave her home at once. Outside the gate were his horse and cart piled high with household chattels.

It was then the confusion had started, but while the urgency in his white face prompted her to instant obedience some primitive force within her urged her to take her feather bed and the little statue of the Virgin. Because of the war she would go wherever he said, but he must understand that of all her possessions her bed and her statue of the Holy Mother were the most vital, and that they must go with her, to the ends of the earth if necessary.

Together they dragged the billowing mattress downstairs and out to the cart. He helped her up beside him, and with the statue held reverently on her lap she had sat staring at the thick brown reins linked through his strong fingers.

That was her most persistent memory. The most vivid was the way he lay half-spilled out of the shattered cart, the reins still threaded through his fingers and his blue eyes staring up at the sky. The horse was dead too, a blood-splashed tangle of entrails lying in front of a wild cascade of household goods; a kettle, a bundle of firewood, a flowered chamber pot. And as if it had suddenly awoken to the horror of the situation her grandson's alarm clock began to shrill hysterically, slowly revolving in the roadway with its broken face upturned to the brassy sun.

She had no recollection of guns or soldiers, merely her grandson's abrupt departure from life into death, and for a moment or two it was impossible to believe that she was not dead too. Then looking down at her hands she saw that she was holding no more than a fragment of the holy statue. The rest of it lay in senseless little pieces round her feet.

With a cry of anguish she bent to retrieve them, then turned again to her grandson. Already the blood was congealing on his blue workman's blouse and it came to her again, much more forcibly, that he was dead.

She must find a priest. Urgently she looked about her but the country road was empty of human habitation. The only living thing was the crow that sat regarding her from the top of a telegraph pole. It appeared unmoved by her predicament.

With mounting agitation the old woman ran a few steps in the direction they had been travelling, then changed her mind and ran back to the cart. Rummaging hastily in the jumble of belongings she found a clean white cloth. Unfolding it she laid it over her grandson's dead face, crossed herself, then once again set off at a hobbling run.

A dozen paces further on she hesitated again, struggling painfully between the dire necessity to find a priest and the possibility of losing her feather mattress. She stood by the wreckage of the cart, her lips working, then abruptly began to tug the mattress clear. Panting, she rolled it up as well as she could and hoisted it on to her back. The effort made her dizzy and she staggered, then she righted herself and hurried away on the desperate search for a priest who would administer Extreme Unction to her grandson.

Somewhere across the fields the shelling started again. Seen in retrospect it became more and more difficult for her to remember what happened next. She had only confused memories of empty roads that suddenly became filled with endless columns of marching men with rifles on their shoulders, with sweating horses dragging guns and heavy ammunition wagons. Once an aeroplane, a queer box-kite affair, flew low overhead, frightening her so much that she cried out and fell on her knees, the mattress rolling off her back and on to the road.

And then she would be alone again. A bewildered black-clad figure whose frantic running had long since degenerated into a snail-like creeping, bowed beneath an almost intolerable weight of goose feathers.

Sometimes she forgot about her grandson's death and would be troubled only by the inexplicable need to find a priest, then as time wore on the thought of the priest faded from her mind as well. She became a young girl again, living in the old stone cottage with her father and mother. Her father's name was Emil. Or was it Gustave? No, Gustave had been her husband's name.

Letting the mattress slip to the ground for a moment she would slowly straighten her aching shoulders and look round the burning August emptiness to see what had become of him. He was a good man, Gustave. But no, not Gustave. His name was Emil . . .

Somehow she found her way to the cave, creeping silently along in the wake of a large and loudly lamenting family with their possessions piled in a wheelbarrow; dazed and exhausted, she was now only aware of the sudden blessed cool, and of the unknown woman sitting on the rock nearby who offered her a drink of water from a tin mug. With her cheek resting trustfully against the mattress's striped ticking, she slept.

Two boys woke her, standing in the green-tinged gloom in front of her and chanting, 'Grand'mère, Grand'mère, let's have a turn in your bed . . .'

Startled, she leaned forward, striving to see their faces more clearly, and with a gasp of delight recognized her eldest grandson.

'Gustave—' she cried, 'what are you doing here? Why are you not at school?'

Confused, the boy shuffled his large boots and muttered that he wasn't Gustave. His companion began to titter.

'Gustave,' repeated the old woman, nodding her head violently, 'come here and tell me why you are not at school. Your father will surely beat you.'

The boy turned sheepishly away but the old woman shot out her little claw hand and grabbed his sleeve.

'Gustave,' she said, 'I fell asleep and had a terrible dream that you had grown to be a man and that you were dead!'

Twisting strenuously in her grasp the boy managed to release himself. Abruptly his fear of her turned to hatred.

'My name is not Gustave and I am not your grandson,' he said, standing just out of her reach. 'You are a stupid old woman and you ought to be in a madhouse.' Glancing rapidly to one side he saw that his companion was listening admiringly. 'You are mad,' he repeated. 'You are a mad old woman and you ought to be locked up!'

The shock of his words made her catch her breath and she began to cough. Her mattress slipped sideways and one end of it lay on the dirty floor. Contemptuously the boy took a running kick at it, then reeled as a woman's square-cut peasant hand reached out and clouted him on the ear.

'Mind your manners,' said Thérèse Aubel quietly, 'before I box the other one.'

* * *

Clothilde Toussant, aged forty-five, genteel spinster-dressmaker of Dinant, sat grimly upright on the lid of her sewing machine and tried hard not to imagine what it would feel like if a bat flew into her hair.

Three days of terror during the course of which she had seen her home collapse in a choking cloud of rubble should, she considered, have made her immune to such comparatively mild horrors as bats in the hair, but unfortunately this was not so. Having been of a nervous disposition all her life, the new agonising fears engendered by war had merely overlain the homely ones of bats, mice, thunderstorms and runaway horses. They had not annihilated them.

The noise in the cave had increased considerably. Fractious and hungry, children were becoming unruly; tense with anxiety, parents were scolding them with unaccustomed harshness. Slaps sharp as pistol shots rang out with ever increasing frequency.

Rigid with distaste, Clothilde Toussant averted her eyes and turned her thoughts towards the curé of her church. Or at least, the church she had had until a German shell sent it crashing down, filling the little square with its broken stone.

Time and again she searched the wan faces in the cave for Père Joseph, but there was no sign of him. She had no means of knowing whether he had taken refuge in one of the Dinant caves or whether he was dead. She prayed for him, her eyes closed and her lips moving soundlessly, and was comforted by a strange feeling of reassurance. He was not dead. Neither was he hiding in a cave like lesser mortals. He was somewhere outside in the heat of battle, alleviating the suffering, succouring the needy and consoling those in distress.

Père Joseph was the greatest, the saintliest man living, and she loved him with the full force of a young girl's innocent, tremulous love.

Abruptly someone sat down on the other end of the sewing machine and sighed loudly. Somewhat affronted, Clothilde opened her eyes and saw a young woman in a long full skirt and a torn white blouse with leg-o-mutton sleeves.

'I have such hunger I could die,' she said simply.

'So has everyone else,' retorted Clothilde.

'Yes,' said the girl, 'but there are certain times when some people feel hunger more than others.'

'I personally have never been a large eater,' said Clothilde, a shade more conversationally. 'But on the other hand my poor Maman thought nothing of consuming a whole pigeon pie when the fancy took her.'

'Is she here?' asked the girl idly.

'Alas no, she died during the winter of 1904, although one feels perhaps that one should offer thanks that she has been spared the suffering of the last few days.'

'Someone told me that my mother was killed on Saturday,' said her companion. 'We used to live at St Louis les Bois.'

'Oh, my poor child,' said Clothilde, distressed. Her thin dressmaker's fingers began to make small rapid pleats in the front of her skirt. What will you do now?'

The girl shrugged. 'I shall manage,' she said. 'For women, there is always one certain way of earning a crust or two.'

'There is domestic service,' offered Clothilde, 'but of course it is somewhat difficult to forecast whether things will ever be the same, after what has happened.'

The girl shot her a brief, amused glance which Clothilde failed to interpret. They lapsed into silence.

'Where do you come from, Mademoiselle?' the girl asked at length.

'I come from Dinant. I am — was — a dressmaker there.'

'Dinant?' repeated her companion. 'Then how do you come to be nearly nine kilometres away?'

Suddenly confused, Clothilde Toussant bent her head. In the dim light she could feel her cheeks burning with shame at the memory of the weeping, whimpering woman snatching up her sewing machine and running as fast as she could away out of burning Dinant. The sewing machine was both heavy and cumbersome, but fear had given her almost maniacal strength and she had climbed the narrow winding path up out of Dinant scarcely aware of her burden. She had only been aware of the screaming shells, the sudden vicious bursts of machine gun fire, and then the lone French dragoon who had appeared from nowhere and offered, in return for certain specific favours, to carry her luggage.

13

The dragoon with his heavy moustache and unfamiliar accent had been the most terrifying thing of all. Shaking, she had walked on, trying to ignore him and trying not to break into a run. And he had deliberately walked his horse closer to her so that his knee, pressed against the rhythmically creaking saddle, was almost touching her cheek. The hot smell of horse flesh and human male made her head reel, and in desperation she dropped the sewing machine and bolted like a hunted animal into the bushes at the side of the road. She heard him roar with laughter.

Crouched on her hands and knees behind a screen of gorse she prayed that he wouldn't come searching for her, and had let out a long shattered sigh of relief as she heard the hollow ringing of hooves continuing away up the road and into the distance. But even so she was afraid to move, and had remained for a long time in the parched and rustling grass, sick with disgust at her own cowardice and at the circumstances that had enforced such extraordinary indignity upon her. Even as a little girl, games of hide-and-seek had filled her with nervous apprehension, and she had hated to feel dirty or dishevelled.

But the thought of her sewing machine finally drove her forth. Hoping against hope that the French dragoon hadn't carried it off in mean retaliation for her obvious antipathy, she was overcome with relief to see it standing in the road where she had left it.

Anxiously she examined its fine mahogany case, its ornate brass handle and lock, the key to which hung round her neck on a ribbon, together with her pince-nez. She could find no sign of damage. With a little prayer of thankfulness she picked it up and hurried on, striving with all her might to put as much distance as possible between her and the fiery furnace of Dinant.

Two hours later she reached the cave, where she sat brooding between bouts of prayer on the twin horrors of war and male animalism. Time passed with agonising slowness.

'What am I doing so far from Dinant?' repeated Clothilde Toussant, raising her head. 'At the time of the bombardment I — I happened to be visiting friends in this area.'

'Ah yes,' said the girl. 'I understand.' Again they fell silent.

They wanted to talk, to draw comfort from one another, but they seemed to have so little in common.

* * *

'Forgive me, my friends,' said a voice, 'but do either of you recognise the old woman sitting over there with the striped mattress?'

Sunk in apathy, Clothilde and the girl looked up with a start. The girl gave a little smile of recognition.

'Are you not Madame Aubel, from the farm?'

Thérèse gave a brief nod, then glanced down at Clothilde.

'This,' said the girl politely, 'is Mademoiselle—'

'Toussant,' said Clothilde. 'I am called Clothilde Toussant.'

'Mademoiselle Toussant from Dinant,' said the girl, 'here is Madame Aubel from St Louis les Bois. And I,' she added, turning to Clothilde, 'am Yvette Mazy. My mother kept the café in St Louis les Bois.'

Impelled by a strange feeling of inevitability the three of them shook hands gravely and unsmilingly, quite unconscious of any incongruity between their formality and their squalid surroundings.

Thérèse was the first to break the spell.

'The old woman over there,' she said, inclining her head. 'No one seems to know her, and she calls all the time for someone called Gustave.'

Clothilde and Yvette looked across the cave to where a beam of pale greenish light illuminated the old black-clad figure rocking itself slowly to and fro, its broomstick arms linked protectively round a bulging feather mattress.

They shook their heads.

'Someone will have to look after her,' Thérèse said with a sigh, 'and I have a suspicion that it is going to be me.'

'What will happen to us all, Madame?' asked Yvette, shifting to a more comfortable position on the sewing machine. 'It is not possible that we stay here for ever.'

Thérèse said, 'What happens to us will be largely governed by what we decide to do. I for one am going to leave the cave, and if no one else is prepared to befriend the old woman I shall have to take her with me.'

'When are you going, Madame?'

With a hint of sardonic amusement Thérèse replied, 'I have few preparations to make. I can leave at very short notice.'

'May I come too?'

'I suppose so,' said Thérèse indifferently.

'I could help with the old woman, that is if you are really going to take her.'

'I shall take her.'

'Where shall we go to, Madame?'

'Who knows? Wherever it is safe.'

'Your farm?'

'My husband's farm,' said Thérèse abruptly, 'has been destroyed.'

'I would be happy to think,' said the girl, 'that the same fate had befallen my mother's café, along with my mother herself.'

'That is no way to speak of your home and family.'

'I have no home,' said the girl, looking suddenly older. 'And I have no family. Or none that I care to think of as such.'

Thérèse grunted. Then asked her how old she was.

'Sixteen. Seventeen after Christmas.'

Thérèse Aubel subjected her to a long thoughtful stare. 'You may come,' she said at length, 'although the good God alone knows what is in store.'

'May I—' said Clothilde in a pinched little voice, 'come too?'

'That will make four,' said Thérèse, frowning.

'I have my sewing machine, and I — I . . .'

Abruptly Clothilde Toussant averted her head. Once again the huge misery of war broke over her like a wave and shattered into a thousand icy drops of sub-misery; the fear of bats, the discomfort of cold feet and an empty stomach, the spinsterly squeamishness that prevented her from availing herself of the dark corner that had by general consent been set aside for sanitary purposes.

Choked with a hopeless self-pity she sat fighting the tears that threatened to spill down her cheeks and on to her neat handmade blouse. She was afraid of the shelling and of all the man-produced misery outside the cave, but she was even more afraid of the sordid loneliness within.

'So be it,' said Thérèse. 'Perhaps it might be well for us to stay together now that we have met.'

Standing up, the girl Yvette helped Clothilde to lug the sewing machine over to the other side of the cave where the old woman still sat mumbling and rocking with her arms round the mattress.

'Grand'mère,' said Thérèse slowly and distinctly. 'Come with us. We are going to find a new home and we will look after you.'

'Home?'

'Yes,' said Yvette, brushing back a long strand of fair hair, 'we are going to find a nice house away from all the bombardment and the war and we are going to commence life all over again.'

'Gustave . . .' said the old woman. 'I dreamed that he was dead. I was trying to find a priest.'

'The good God is taking care of Gustave,' said Thérèse. 'He has no need of a priest.'

'Where is he?' demanded the old woman.

'Not far away, my old one.'

'Who is Gustave?' whispered Clothilde. Thérèse shrugged.

'If you think of going outside,' said a small pale man in a cap, 'I beg you not to. The Uhlans are waiting there and they are going to murder us all.'

Clothilde gave an involuntary gasp and her hand flew to the high-boned neck of her blouse.

'Who told you that, Monsieur?' asked Thérèse, eyeing him briefly. She began to re-roll the old woman's feather mattress into more manageable proportions, soothing her anxious protests as she did so.

'I heard from someone who has been outside, Madame. All lined up with their lances they are, ready for when we go out.'

'No one has been outside,' interrupted Thérèse, but the man, intent on some hideous vision of his own, took no notice.

'Have you not heard how they used the little babies in Liège for bayonet practice? Little helpless babies torn from their parents' arms? — and all that is nothing to what they did to the women . . .' The man shuffled a few steps nearer and Clothilde wondered whether she was going to faint.

'Be silent,' said Thérèse. 'You have no conception of what is happening outside.' Brushing him contemptuously away she finished re-rolling the mattress, then helped the old woman to her feet.

'Come along, my old one,' she said gently. 'We four are going home now.'

* * *

Suddenly swept by a fresh agony of fear Clothilde hung back. It was all very well to dismiss the man's warning as nonsense, but how could one be sure?

Gripping the handle of her sewing machine she remembered the lazy insolence of the French dragoon; the way he had mockingly appraised her meagre body and then ridden his horse closer and closer to her until all the world had become suffused with the stench of sweat, the rhythmic creak of leather and the soft jingle of spurs. And if a Frenchman, one of Belgium's allies, had had the effrontery to behave like that, who could possibly say what the Uhlans themselves might not do? Certainly not this Madame Aubel with her sabots and work-roughened hands who appeared to take everything so calmly.

With nerves strained to the uttermost limit she took one tentative step outside the shelter of the cave and stood well behind the other three.

The sunlight struck their bodies and temporarily blinded them. Stumbling closer together the four of them stood motionless for a moment, gulping in the scent of sun-baked earth and listening to the lazy churr of grasshoppers. There was no gunfire. Neither were there any Uhlans.

While Grand'mère fussed about with her mattress Thérèse and the young Yvette remained motionless, their eyes closed and their faces upturned to the sun. Like two plants they seemed to be absorbing the life-giving rays, soaking them up and drawing them deep into their hungry bodies. Clothilde too stood motionless, praying to the Holy Mother of Sorrows to deliver them from all the perils which lay ahead.

Yvette with her ropes of long fair hair and cheap clothes stood with her hands folded in front of her.

'When is the baby due to be born?' Thérèse asked quietly.

'Sometime next month, Madame,' she replied.

Instinctively Clothilde twitched her skirt out of contact with her, and with an oddly dignified little gesture the girl raised her hand, unadorned by a wedding ring, then let it fall again. Fascinated and revolted, Clothilde found her gaze riveted to the swelling barely discernible beneath the girl's long full skirt.

Pregnant and unmarried and sixteen years of age. And to think that she had innocently made friends with her and allowed her to sit on the other end of the sewing machine.

Thérèse was in the act of gathering up Grand'mère's mattress when Clothilde took one step back towards the cave and said in a high chill voice, 'I have changed my mind. I will not be coming after all.'

Thérèse straightened up and stood staring at her without speaking. Yvette turned away.

'Why not, Mademoiselle?' Thérèse enquired at length.

Once again swept by uncontrollable emotions of misery and fear and outraged prudery, Clothilde tightened her grip on her sewing machine.

'I am not accustomed to the company of harlots,' she said.

Yvette swung round, her hair flying. Her face was alight with incredulous anger.

'And I, on the other hand,' she burst out, 'am unaccustomed to the presence of soured old virgins!'

As swiftly as she was able she ran behind Clothilde and stood in the entrance to the cave.

'Go on—' she cried, waving them away. 'Go on — I have no need of you! Go and find a home and be old and prim all on your own. I hate you — I scorn you — and I have no *need* of you!'

Weeping, she dragged her torn leg-o-mutton sleeve across her eyes and the pale man in the cap peered hungrily at her from the gloom.

'For the love of heaven calm yourself,' called Thérèse. 'The Mademoiselle meant no harm.' She looked meaningfully towards Clothilde, who obstinately averted her face.

'Go away — go *away!*' cried the girl. She waved her fist at them.

With her lips drawn into a pale thin line Clothilde picked up her sewing machine and started to walk off with as much dignity as possible. Longingly she thought of Père Joseph, and wondered whether she would ever feel sufficiently spiritually clean to enter his presence again.

For a long moment Thérèse stood looking at the convulsively sobbing Yvette, then without a word shouldered the feather mattress, and, steadying it with one hand, reached into the front of her blouse with the other one.

'Here,' she said to Grand'mère. 'Carry that for me and promise not to lose it. It is all I have left.'

Pleased, the old woman took the Aubels' wedding photograph in her speckled brown hands and began to follow Thérèse trustfully down the long stony track.

The weather had remained unbroken during their incarceration in the cave and larks rose up singing from the ripe corn. From among the trees on the other side of the Meuse came the soft intermittent rumble of gunfire, but the sound was no more disturbing than a warning of distant thunder.

'Where are we going, Madame?' ventured Clothilde in a small voice. With her shoes already worn thin on the flight from Dinant, the sharp stones made her feet very sore and she had to stop with increasing frequency in order to shift the sewing machine from one hand to the other.

From under the hot tent of goose feathers Thérèse peered out at the blazing sky. She stopped and sniffed, as though, like an animal, she were capable of scenting danger on the air. Grand'mère, still holding the photograph in both hands, paused close beside her.

'We must get away from the Meuse,' Thérèse said. 'We will go to Philippeville, where I have a cousin.'

Settling the mattress more comfortably, she began to walk on.

'I understand that you come from somewhere near here, Madame,' said Clothilde, conscious of a desire to make a little pleasant conversation.

'I used to come from somewhere near here,' replied Thérèse in a muffled, expressionless voice. 'But from now on, I come from nowhere.'

They had been walking in silence for some time before they became aware that someone was following them. It was the girl Yvette, rambling carelessly along some short distance in their wake, trailing her fingers through the corn and whistling a tune. Her shoes were broken, the strap of one flapping at every step.

Clothilde tightened her lips and increased her pace slightly. The handle of the sewing machine cut into her hand.

'She is very young, of course,' Thérèse said after a while, 'And she has had an exceptionally poor start in life.'

'That is no concern of mine,' replied Clothilde, staring ahead.

'She needs a friend to guide her. Ideally, an educated person of high moral integrity.'

Clothilde said nothing. The footsteps lagging behind paused for a moment, then continued again. They made a desultory sound.

'I myself,' went on Thérèse from under the goose feathers, 'am a mere peasant. A woman of practicality but no refinement. And much as I would like to help the girl towards a better life, I, alas, have little to offer in the way of learning or gentility.'

'On the contrary,' muttered Clothilde.

Thérèse gave her a sidelong glance then put out her hand to Grand'mère, who was tottering slightly.

'We had better take a short rest,' she said.

'The girl will catch up with us,' replied Clothilde through dust-dry lips.

'No doubt she will catch up with us and overtake us,' said Thérèse, allowing the mattress to slide off her back on to a patch of turf. She wiped her forehead with the palm of her hand. 'She is a good deal younger than we are.'

'But we must remember that she is pregnant.'

'Ah yes,' agreed Thérèse laconically. 'Furthermore, we must remember that she is pregnant with an illegitimate baby.'

Clothilde put down her sewing machine and stood rubbing her aching arm. Something in Madame Aubel's tone disconcerted her slightly.

'All children are alike in the eyes of God,' she ventured uncertainly.

The footsteps behind them faltered, then ceased. There was no more whistling. The girl Yvette stood a few feet away, her face drained by tiredness and hunger. Like a stray cat, she eyed them with a wistfulness that was tempered with wariness.

Thérèse held out her hand. 'When we have had a short rest,' she said, 'we are all going to the house of my cousin.'

Very slowly and without looking at them, the girl moved forward.

CHAPTER TWO

They met the war again on the road to Philippeville.

A long column of motorised wagons passed them, whining along in bottom gear. Unfamiliar with military uniforms and half-blinded by the dust, the four women stood close together and wondered whether they were Belgian, French or German.

'French,' said Yvette hopefully, then a large open limousine rolled past with two army officers lolling in the back. They wore spiked helmets and waxed moustaches and were smoking cigars.

'German,' corrected Thérèse.

And although the war was now two weeks old it was still incredible to see them, to stand homeless and destitute watching the invading army pour its ruthless alien strength along their own familiar roads. A troop of cavalry brought up the rear, jogging knee to knee on sweating horses, and it seemed more incredible still that their faces should bear the sober, faintly bored expression of men who are merely engaged on a routine job.

'How can they? . . . how can they? . . .' whispered Clothilde. Thérèse shrugged, shunted Grand'mère's mattress higher on her shoulders and trudged on, the old woman following at her heels.

They were hungry and very thirsty.

From somewhere across the fields came the spasmodic boom of gunfire and involuntarily they quickened their pace. Hampered by her broken shoes Yvette kicked them off and pattered along in her bare feet. Walking next to Clothilde she slipped her fingers round the handle of the sewing machine.

'Allow me to take a turn, Mademoiselle,' she said. 'It is too heavy for one person.'

Only too aware of her aching muscles Clothilde was about to relinquish her hold when she remembered having heard that pregnant women should not carry heavy burdens.

'Thank you, Mademoiselle,' she replied. 'I can manage.'

'Please,' said Yvette. 'Just for a little way.'

Clothilde stared down at the girl's bare toes twinkling in and out under the hem of her draggled skirt and thought afresh of her sinfulness. She was defiled, debased, and in normal circumstances there would be no question of associating with her. But now . . .

'Mademoiselle,' said Yvette. 'I will carry the sewing machine from here to the next big tree. I assure you it is no trouble.'

'Thank you,' said Clothilde, then added in a low voice, 'But you must do nothing to injure the child.'

'The child will not have an easy life,' replied Yvette. 'The sooner it accustoms itself to that fact, the better.'

She took the sewing machine and Clothilde walked beside her, rubbing the deadness from her arm.

Towards four in the afternoon they came to a small village. Approaching it fearfully they found that most of the houses were roofless and deserted. Without speaking they made their way to the iron pump that remained, apparently intact, in the middle of the street. Setting down the mattress Thérèse worked the handle up and down and after a few moments water gushed out.

'Grand'mère first,' she said.

Cupping her hands the old woman drank, closing her eyes and sucking up the water through her toothless gums.

When she had finished she passed her wet hands over her face then stood looking about her, as if suddenly aware of her surroundings.

'What are we doing here?' she asked.

A good question, thought Thérèse. Aloud, she said, 'We are on our way to Philippeville where I have a cousin who will take care of us.'

It was Clothilde who finally put into words the thought nagging in everyone's mind. 'Supposing the Germans have already reached Philippeville?' she said. 'Supposing Philippeville is also in ruins?'

'In that case,' said Yvette, putting her head under the pump and allowing the water to splash over her, 'we shall just have to find somewhere else.'

'All very well for you,' retorted Clothilde with a bitterness she was unable to control. 'You are young and unused to stability. One place is the same as another, to a person such as yourself. Whereas Madame Aubel and I—'

'I would be very happy to find stability, Mademoiselle,' said Yvette, coming out from under the pump. She began to squeeze the water from her dripping hair. 'Stability is something I have never known.'

Clothilde said nothing more, but held her lace-edged handkerchief under the mouth of the pump and, when it was saturated, folded it into a pad and used it to wash the dust from her face and hands. Refinement was written in every movement, and despite the weight of oppression Thérèse found herself biting back a smile.

'Wait here,' she told her companions, 'and I will see if I can find something for us to eat.'

Sitting in a row on the mattress they watched her walk across the street, sturdy and implacable in her sabots. She disappeared through a gaping hole in one of the houses.

'She is formidable, that one,' observed the girl Yvette, spreading her wet hair over her shoulders to dry. 'And any German would do well to think twice before offending her.'

* * *

The shattered house yielded little that was edible, but a tree left standing in a ruined garden still bore a few apples. Seizing a spar of wood Thérèse swiped at them and they came tumbling down. She gathered them in her skirt.

She was walking down the narrow alleyway that ran behind the gardens when she saw the handcart. Standing outside a broken gateway, it appeared miraculously undamaged and she hastened up to it, tipping the apples into it and then pushing it experimentally. The wheels squeaked, but it was in working order. Delighted by the stroke of good fortune she pushed it to the end of the alleyway, dragging it over stones and across shell holes until she was back in the main street.

'Mesdames—' she cried, 'we have an equipage!'

Equally delighted, Clothilde and Yvette helped to load the sewing machine and the feather mattress into it, and as there was still plenty of room they loaded Grand'mère in as well. Grieved and harassed by the incomprehensible behaviour of a world gone mad she sat in the middle of her striped mattress with an apple held in one hand and the photograph in the other, while she tried yet again to remember the name of the man who had knocked on her door and told her to leave home. All her troubles had stemmed from that moment and when she saw him again she proposed giving him the rough edge of her tongue.

Philippeville was still eleven kilometres away.

Taking turns to push the handcart the three women became aware that the sound of gunfire was increasing; somewhere to the left, above the high belt of trees, the yellow shell-stars were bursting above a fog of acrid smoke. Now and then came the savage stutter of machine guns.

Rounding a bend in the road they came upon a company of German infantry marching slackly at ease, their rifles slung. One of them began to grin at the sight of the women with the handcart, then abruptly spun in his tracks and fell crumpled on the ground. Bullets whined across the road from behind the remains of a barn. Within seconds the Germans were returning fire.

'Run!' shouted Thérèse above the noise. Crouching low between the shafts of the handcart she swept Clothilde and Yvette along with her while Grand'mère clung precariously to her mattress. 'Quick — into the ditch, for God's sake!'

A succession of bullets smacked into the side of the cart and even as they lugged the old woman down and struggled with her on to the side of the road, a stream of goose feathers burst from the mattress and began to eddy wildly round them.

Sobbing with terror Clothilde fell on her knees.

'Get up — get up!' Yvette screamed, tugging at her arm. She began to laugh hysterically, the tears pouring down her cheeks. Feathers flew in their faces, blinding them like flakes of snow while the rifle bullets sang over their head.

Somehow they found themselves in the ditch with their faces pressed against the parched earth. With her arm round Grand'mère, Thérèse shut her eyes and tried to breathe in sanity with the homely scent of soil, but the furious anger rose in her until it seemed that she must go mad.

'Fools — imbeciles — cretins!' she bawled, shaking her fist above her head. We had a good life here until you came . . .'

'In the name of the Holy Mother be silent—' implored Clothilde, dragging at her fist, 'they will hear what you say and kill us all—'

She began to pray, the words spilling out of her convulsively, 'Blessed be the Holy Mother . . . blessed be the Mother of Sorrows . . .'

Huddled against Thérèse, Grand'mère joined in, mumbling in a rapid monotone with her eyes tightly closed. From under her dress she had brought forth a rosary.

Over the top of their bowed heads Thérèse looked at the girl.

'Are you all right?'

'Yes, thank you, Madame.' She managed a trembling smile. 'If only the baby didn't kick so.'

'He will be a fine baby, this one.'

'He?'

'Yes,' Thérèse said grimly. 'It will be a boy. I know it.'

In the road above the ditch the sound of rifle fire grew more sporadic and they heard the thud of heavy boots as the Germans rushed the barn.

Cautiously Thérèse looked over the top of the ditch and after a few moments saw two men in workmen's overalls stumbling out with their hands raised. One of them had blood pouring from a head wound.

Prodded across the road by rifles they stood wearily against a tree as a German N.C.O. strolled up and down in front of them, rolling a cigarette. The man with the head wound was trying unsuccessfully to staunch the flow of blood with his hand.

'What are they going to do?' whispered Yvette, her eyes on a level with those of Thérèse.

'I am not sure,' she lied, her lips barely moving. 'I am not sure.'

Having lifted their dead comrade on to the grass verge and covered him with a groundsheet the Germans stood about in easy little groups. Some of them had removed their soft army caps and were leaning on their rifles; another sat by the roadside and took a lengthy swig from his water bottle.

The N.C.O. waited until he had finished his cigarette and ground the stub of it tidily underfoot before ordering them to fall in. They did so, with the exception of one man who went across to the two Belgians standing by the tree. When he moved away from them, Thérèse and the girl saw that he had bound their hands behind their backs.

Quite casually the soldiers began to line up in single file, raising and lowering their rifles experimentally. The two Belgians stood rigidly to attention.

Yvette swallowed hard and put out her hand to Thérèse.

'Close your eyes,' whispered Thérèse, taking it.

The N.C.O. stepped to one side of the firing party. He nodded, and they raised their rifles. Inappropriately, a bird suddenly began to sing.

'What is happening?' breathed Clothilde, opening her eyes and unclasping her hands. Without looking at her, Thérèse planted her own square hand on Clothilde's head and pushed it down again.

'Pray,' she told her harshly. 'If prayer means anything at all to you, pray now. As for me, I cannot.'

The abrupt crack of rifle fire shattered the tension. When the infantrymen lowered their rifles the bird had stopped singing.

Negligently the N.C.O. walked over to the motionless figures that lay riddled with bullets beneath the tree. He kicked one of them before turning away.

Motionless, the four women in the ditch watched as he walked over to them, his metal-capped boots on a level with their eyes. He stood looking down at them, holding his rifle in both hands. Clothilde gave a tiny sob of terror.

'Go,' he said at length. He jerked his head in the direction of the tree. 'Go, before the same thing happens to you.'

Clumsily they helped one another out of the ditch, and Clothilde was further tormented by the knowledge that her knees were showing.

* * *

They trudged on for some while without speaking. Most of the feathers had been lost from Grand'mère's mattress, although Clothilde's sewing machine and Thérèse's wedding photograph mercifully remained undamaged.

Thirst was beginning to torment them again when they met the first family of refugees coming from the direction of Philippeville.

The man was pushing a bicycle with a sack of potatoes balanced on the saddle and his wife had three small children heaped in a perambulator. Two of them were howling dismally.

'Turn back,' the man said to Thérèse. 'That way the Germans are coming. They are looting and burning and nothing is safe from them. Turn back.'

'Where are you making for, Monsieur?' asked Thérèse, leaning against the side of the cart. The man shrugged.

'Rich people are making for Holland. Many hundreds were able to buy a boat ticket for England before it was too late. But for us—' again he shrugged, 'there are the caves.'

'We have just come from a cave,' Yvette said. 'And they are not pleasant.'

'Pleasant, no,' said the man's wife. She gave the howling children a drink of water from a bottle. 'But safe, yes. We are going to find a cave and there we will stay, until such time as our brave soldiers deliver us.' They continued on their way.

Other people told the same story. With overloaded carts dragged by horses, mules, dogs and bicycles they came straggling down the long road from Philippeville.

'Where are you going to, Mesdames?'

'To Philippeville.'

'That is unwise. The Uhlans are coming. They are setting fire to the houses and poisoning the water in the wells. Those who are not roasted alive will die of typhus.'

Thérèse was pushing the handcart when they came to the narrow lane that turned off the high road. Although the telegraph lines were down, the wayside shrine of the Virgin was still intact; indeed, only recently someone had placed an offering of purple loosestrife at the foot of it.

Without bothering to speak Thérèse changed direction, Yvette and Clothilde following obediently at her heels. The lane was lined on either side by tall ash trees which formed a cool tunnel. They also served to muffle the sound of gunfire.

'This lane,' ventured Yvette when they had gone a little way, 'leads to our village, Madame. To St Louis les Bois.'

'I am aware,' said Thérèse repressively.

'And a little further on there is a small waterfall from which we might drink.'

'I am aware of that also.'

It was true. Every lane and track and footpath that led to St Louis les Bois she could have traversed blindfold. The woods of beech and ash and willow, the lonely streams and the high moorlands that suddenly descended into tiny hidden valleys all held for her the familiarity bred of a lifetime's love.

Yet on the night of Saturday, 15 August, when she had fired the farm, she had vowed never to return until the day when the war was over and they could both rebuild all that had been destroyed.

Both of us, thought Thérèse. Can I still speak of us in such a way?

They found the waterfall and they drank, and when they had finished they took it in turns to go behind a tree, and when Clothilde returned complaining of the stinging nettles Thérèse reminded her not unkindly that war was essentially a brutal affair.

They reached the outskirts of St Louis les Bois as the sun was setting.

Encouraged by the peaceful silence they hurried forward, all three of them shoving the cart in which Grand'mère now lay asleep in the remains of her mattress.

Then they stopped, holding on to the shafts as they stared round at the desolation. The Germans had been, and gone.

The shattered buildings stood black and angular against the pale mauve sky and a twist of smoke, slender as a piece of string, wound its way towards the evening star.

Somewhere down the rough track that led to the Aubel farm a nightingale began its heartrending song.

'We are too late,' Thérèse said.

It was the girl Yvette who grabbed at her elbow, her eager face upturned in the fading light.

'We are not too late, Madame!' she cried. 'If we believe that, there is no reason for us to go on living. Everything is in ruins—' she indicated the desolate street with her torn sleeve, 'but we must rebuild it, Madame. Life is wherever we are . . .'

Weary and depressed, the two elder women nevertheless looked at the shattered street, seeing in the broken buildings a hopefulness, a hint that there might perhaps be some sort of future in the ruins.

Very slowly they began to walk forward again, the iron wheels of the handcart grating harshly over the debris.

'There is the school,' said the girl, indicating a pile of tumbled stone, 'where I never learned anything of importance. And there—' she pointed to the opposite side of the road, 'lie the ruins of my mother's café where all I learned was how to serve beer and smile at men . . .'

'Here is the church,' said Thérèse.

Slowly they walked past it. Denuded of its bell turret it stood with its ancient rafters exposed, picked clean as fishbones. A smell of damp mingled with incense rose from the tumbled stonework. Sorrowfully, Clothilde crossed herself before walking on.

And everywhere was the same. Broken, abandoned, a mute indictment against the senseless savagery of war.

At the far end of the village stood the convent of the Little Sisters of Mercy, a hole blown in its high stone wall. Half-lifting the handcart over the rubble they went inside and stood in the courtyard. Slates from the roof lay round their feet and one end of the building had been badly damaged, yet in the main the convent appeared to have suffered less than anywhere else.

The silence was absolute, but the massive front door stood open as if inviting them to enter. Cautiously they approached it. Thérèse stepped inside.

'Is there anyone within?'

With thumping hearts they waited, listening to the heavy silence. Broken glass littered the floor and lay thick in the upholstered wing-chair that stood by the staircase.

Thérèse called again. There was no answer. Drawing a deep breath she looked at Yvette's bare feet and gently bulging skirt, at Clothilde's face drawn with exhaustion.

'Heaven,' she announced at length, 'is said to help those who help themselves. In the absence of the good Sisters, this is going to be our home.'

* * *

33

And it was miraculous how the tiredness seemed to melt at the prospect of turning the abandoned convent into an anchorage.

The first thing they did was to sweep the glass out of the chair and install Grand'mère in it, tucking her up in her mattress and promising her that from now on life was going to return to normality.

Then they explored the rest of the convent. Most of the furniture in the refectory had been smashed, and in the library devotional books lay tumbled in the dust and dirt. Upstairs, some of the small cell-like rooms also bore signs of wilful despoliation, but the newcomers were still left with the choice of at least six which were habitable, each with its narrow iron bed and plain wooden prie-dieu. There was no sign of the Little Sisters of Mercy, or any hint of the fate that had overtaken them.

They investigated the rambling domestic quarters. Emboldened, Clothilde pulled open a cupboard door and in doing so disturbed a broody hen who had found her way in through a broken window. With an outraged squawk the bird fluttered hastily from her improvised nest, blundering into Clothilde who reeled against the wall, almost insensible with fright.

It was the cry from Thérèse that brought them all running; even Grand'mère left her chair and hurried stiffly towards the sound.

'*Look* . . .' said Thérèse, standing in the pantry doorway. She passed her hand over the lower half of her face to hide the sudden trembling of her lips.

'Holy Mother of God . . .' breathed Yvette.

The food was plain and simple, but there was enough to last them for months. Speckled brown eggs, a crock of golden butter standing cool in a dish of water, a home-cured ham, a sack of potatoes and another one of flour. In an earthenware pot there was yeast.

'Coffee—' cried Thérèse, opening a large tin.

'Salt—' cried Yvette, opening another.

'Lentils — haricot beans — split peas—' called Clothilde, her pale face flushed.

'Honey . . .'

'Dried figs . . .'

'Parsley . . . rosemary . . . chervil . . .'

'And I have great hunger,' said Grand'mère, stretching out both hands.

Laughingly the women began to plan the meal they would have. In the huge kitchen was a scrubbed deal table and on the dresser stood plates and cups and saucers of thick white china, much of it still unbroken. They also found a clean white tablecloth.

'Sticks for the fire—' ordered Thérèse. Clothilde hurried away.

'Water for the coffee—' Seizing an enamel pitcher Yvette went out into the courtyard to find the well.

'Knives and forks . . .'

Pulling open a drawer Thérèse discovered them; homely, horn-handled utensils that Grand'mère snatched up and began to set out round the table.

'Grand'mère,' said Thérèse, suddenly pausing. 'Grand'mère, where is your real home?'

The old woman examined a spoon and then began to polish it on her black apron until it shone. 'Here,' she said, surprised.

A fall of soot had choked the black kitchen range and Thérèse hitched up her skirt before kneeling down to clear it away. Clothilde reappeared with a bundle of dry twigs and they discovered a box of safety matches in the corner where the home-made candles were kept.

The only setback was when the girl returned with an empty pitcher and informed them that the well was blocked by slates from the roof.

'I will go to the village pump,' she said, and paused by the open door. 'But please wait supper for me, Mesdames.' The last rays of sun lit up the laughter in her eyes.

'The young girl should not go barefoot,' observed Clothilde when she had gone. 'It must surely be harmful to the baby.'

'Babies were being born long before their mothers wore shoes,' returned Thérèse, 'but perhaps the good Sisters have left a pair somewhere that will fit her.'

Rolling up her sleeves she measured flour and butter into a bowl and began to make scones. They were too hungry to wait for bread.

'Potato soup,' she said, 'following by omelettes, which in turn will be followed by hot scones spread with butter and honey—'

'And then some coffee,' chipped in Grand'mère. 'Some good black coffee to settle our stomachs.'

Surrounded by all the old familiar articles of domesticity she seemed to be coming alive again, to be emerging from the mist of incomprehension in which she had wandered since leaving home.

The potatoes had been prepared for the soup and the scones were in the oven when they heard the sound of hooves and the grating of iron wheels outside.

Thérèse wiped her floury hands on the kitchen cloth she had tied round her waist, and waited. There was nothing else to do.

The sound of hooves, of grinding wheels, ceased. There came a single decisive thump, as of a man's riding boots hitting cobblestones.

Clothilde drew in a long quivering breath. Thérèse motioned to her to be silent.

The shadow that fell on the kitchen wall was that of a man wearing a spiked helmet. His breeches jutted arrogantly above the knee and his spurs stood out from his heels like castors on a parlour sofa.

'A Uhlan!' whispered Clothilde through white lips.

Watching the wall, Thérèse nodded. The shadow stood motionless for a moment then slid down, telescoping itself towards the dusty floor. Footsteps stamped away over the cobbles towards the open front door. Almost immediately the women in the kitchen heard them enter the hall and crunch over the broken glass. Clothilde began to pray.

With a strange fatalism Thérèse listened to the footsteps crossing the hall, going into the refectory, into the library. Then she heard them coming down the passage towards the kitchen. She squared her shoulders and stood facing the door.

'Good evening,' he said.

Without replying, she inclined her head slightly.

'May I ask what you are doing here?'

Thérèse stared at him with eyes that smouldered a dark, peasant hatred.

'I might demand the same question of you.'

The Uhlan officer stood in the doorway, taking in the kitchen, the three women, the table laid for supper. He was handsome, with very blue eyes set in a tanned skin.

'You are preparing a meal?'

'As you see,' Thérèse replied stolidly.

'You are nuns?'

'By what right do you interrogate us?' she countered.

Clothilde moved forward, impulsively clasping her hands. 'I beg your pardon, Monsieur,' she said, 'but my friends and I mean no harm. We are sheltering from the bombardment until such time as—'

Grand'mère interrupted her. Rocking herself to and fro on the kitchen chair she suddenly said, quite benevolently, 'Take no notice of her, she is weak in the head.'

Boots clattered outside the kitchen door and three soldiers came in. Their tunics were unfastened at the throat, their faces burned red by the sun. One of them held a revolver.

As the officer had done before them, they swept the room with a hard professional stare, automatically checking its possibilities. The officer gave them a brief order. They saluted, then strode across the kitchen and out into the passage. In silence the three women listened to their heavy boots echoing on the uncarpeted stairs. Their eyes returned to the figure of the Uhlan officer.

Very deliberately he unsheathed his sword and walked across to the table, studying the carefully placed knives and forks and spoons, white china plates and mugs. He smiled at the women, then with a graceful, negligent movement of the wrist wiped the table clear.

The china crashed to the floor. The tablecloth wound itself round his sword like a flag of truce. Still smiling, he disengaged it.

'You are a bastard,' Thérèse said, very slowly and distinctly.

The Uhlan bowed his head in smiling acknowledgement, then wheeled abruptly as another shadow fell across the wall.

The girl Yvette stood in the doorway, her long yellow hair curling over her shoulders, her bare feet streaked with dust. Without taking her eyes from the Uhlan she set the enamel pitcher down on the floor and said, 'The village pump is not working. I could find no more than half a jugful.'

* * *

'Good evening, Mademoiselle,' the Uhlan said in his passable French. He bowed slightly. 'I take it that you also live here?'

The girl moistened her lips, glancing uneasily from Thérèse to Clothilde. She looked at the debris on the floor.

'No. Yes. Yes, I do . . .'

He looked her up and down, still smiling. From a room overhead came the crash of furniture.

'A somewhat unsatisfactory life, no doubt, for a beautiful young lady such as yourself.'

Yvette's cheeks flamed scarlet at the compliment. She turned away, tossing her head.

'Our life was quite satisfactory before you came,' Thérèse observed from the other side of the table.

'Be silent,' said the Uhlan, without looking at her. 'I was addressing the young Mademoiselle.'

He continued to stare at Yvette. She shifted nervously, picking up the pitcher of water and then setting it down again. The atmosphere became increasingly tense.

'Life could be far more entertaining, for example,' said the Uhlan, 'in a big city, in the company of an admirer.'

'I do not make friends with my country's enemies,' the girl muttered, scuffing her bare toes.

The Uhlan laughed pleasantly. 'Enemies? Why must we talk of enemies?'

Thérèse opened her mouth to reply. With a curt gesture the Uhlan silenced her. Shrugging her shoulders she bent down and began to pick up the broken china from the floor. Grand'mère left her chair and stooped to help her, while Clothilde remained rigidly upright.

'I am going to Paris with my regiment,' the Uhlan said. 'In one week's time the Imperial German Army will have conquered France and will have liberated the brave Belgian people from the shadow of French domination.' He flicked a speck of dust from his sleeve. 'If by any stroke of good fortune the Mademoiselle would care to accompany me I would make it my personal responsibility to see that she has an extremely pleasant time. And everything she wants.'

'No,' said the girl, still blushing furiously.

'Everything she wants,' he repeated, laughing. He was very handsome indeed when he laughed.

Somewhere in another part of the convent they heard doors banging and then the shattering of glass. Clothilde's fingers began to make rapid little pleats on the front of her blouse.

With a sudden exclamation Thérèse banged down a handful of broken crockery and then ran across to the oven. Smoke poured from it as she opened the door. Grim-lipped she removed the tray of scones then slammed the door shut with her sabot.

'Now, I ask you,' said the Uhlan, smiling deprecatingly at Yvette. 'Is that a fit supper for a beautiful young lady who could be dining on oysters and champagne at Maxim's?'

Still smoking, the blackened scones lay on the empty scrubbed table. The girl bit her lip.

'Come with me,' the Uhlan said, 'and live like a royal lady.' He looked down at her bare feet, her dusty bedraggled skirt and torn blouse.

'Come with me,' he repeated, 'and you shall have everything you want.'

'No,' said Yvette. She, too, stood looking at the burned scones.

'Paris,' said the Uhlan gently. 'Beautiful clothes, servants to wait on you. A setting that would be worthy of a young lady such as yourself.'

A young lady, he said.

The convent kitchen was very bare. Dingy white walls, broken windows, a scrubbed table and a tray of blackened scones. Hunger gripped her even as she stood looking at them, and beneath the heavy folds of her skirt the baby began to stir as if in protest.

The Uhlan smiled again as he watched her, reading with amusement the conflict that tormented her.

'Come with me,' he said once again, 'and I will take care of you properly.'

His uniform fitted his fine body to perfection, and it occurred to her that his epaulettes and his spurs were probably made of solid gold. He was a gentleman, and he thought of her as a lady.

And yet . . . And yet . . .

Mutely pleading for guidance the girl Yvette looked at Grand'mère, but the old woman's eyes had clouded again and she had withdrawn into her own private world. She looked at Thérèse, who answered by shrugging her shoulders. *Do as you please*, her expression read. *The decision is up to you.*

She looked at Clothilde. And winced.

You are a harlot, said the expression in Clothilde's eyes. *You could never be a lady because you have no breeding, no refinement. Even if you strove for a hundred years you would never attain my level of fastidious gentility. You are a slut, a harlot, a common street-walker. To inadvertently touch you is to contaminate myself.*

'Well?' smiled the Uhlan.

'I will come with you,' the girl said in a voice that was barely audible.

The Uhlan swept her a mock bow, then briskly sheathed his sword.

They heard the three soldiers clattering across the hall and down the passage that led to the kitchen. They came in, almost staggering beneath the weight of their plunder. Bedding and curtains and finely embroidered hangings; the one who had brandished a revolver now carried a big silver crucifix under his arm. Clothilde started forward with a cry of horror, then stopped. She found herself staring into Yvette's eyes and the hurt accusation in them struck her like a blow. Overcome by a hopeless despair, she turned away.

The Uhlan officer had walked out of the kitchen and it was with a sinking heart that Thérèse heard his exclamation of triumph. He had discovered the stock of food in the pantry.

With murder in her eyes she stood watching as they filled the white tablecloth with it and then knotted the four corners together. The ham, the butter, which they wrapped in pages torn from a book, the lentils and haricot beans and split peas, all spilling out and running together. The sack of potatoes one of them humped on his back.

They took everything. Even the salt.

'Allow me, Mademoiselle—' the Uhlan said to Yvette, and with a flourish presented her with the basket of eggs.

With a dignity that was carefully ladylike she received them from him, and avoiding the eyes of the other women went out of the door that led on to the courtyard.

There were two horses harnessed to the German baggage wagon, one before the other. The three soldiers piled the plunder in, and when the Uhlan had folded an exquisitely embroidered altar frontal into a cushion for her, the girl placed her bare foot in his linked hands and allowed him to assist her up.

It was the one who had carried off the crucifix who went back to the kitchen.

'Wine,' he said to Thérèse. 'We want the wine, too. Get it.'

'There is no wine,' she said, her face dark with rage.

'Wine—' he repeated, not understanding her. 'Get the wine . . .'

'Get out,' she said. He hit her across the face. She staggered, and fell back against the dresser.

Outside, the wheels of the baggage wagon were beginning to grind, snapping the broken slates that littered the cobbles. The Uhlan was already mounted, his horse tossing its mane.

Before taking his place on the tailboard of the wagon the soldier who had struck Thérèse lit a twist of paper and tossed it inside the main door of the convent as he passed. It landed in the wing-chair and Grand'mère's mattress began to smoulder.

Roused by the pungent smell, Thérèse hurried for the enamel pitcher that was half full of precious water. She doused the burning chair with it.

'And now,' she said bitterly, 'we have nothing.'

'On the contrary,' said Clothilde, managing a desperate little smile, 'we still have my sewing machine and your wedding photograph.'

Thérèse grunted, and went back to the kitchen.

On the other side of the convent wall the baggage wagon began to roll slowly on its way, with the girl Yvette seated on top like a queen on a throne.

She was careful not to look back.

CHAPTER THREE

By the end of August it had become apparent that the German invasion of Belgium was going to succeed.

Towns and villages continued to fall beneath the bombardment from howitzers and heavy siege guns, and civilians who got in the way were brushed aside like tiresome insects.

The French offensive in the Ardennes failed and the waters of the river Meuse and its tributaries ran red with the blood of men and horses.

With three regiments almost totally annihilated the shattered Belgian army withdrew to Antwerp, where the government and the Royal Family had already taken up emergency residence. King Albert himself was serving with the army.

On 20 August, German troops formally occupied Brussels, the capital.

People stared in sullen amazement at the exultant goose-stepping troops who for the first time in history were dressed in field grey, and they learned that on their behalf the Burgomaster of Brussels was to supply the German overlords with the sum of eight million pounds.

Food stocks were requisitioned, curfews were imposed, and schools were ordered to teach Belgian children to speak

German. One morning early in September the first Zeppelin was seen.

But at the convent in St Louis les Bois a determined effort was being made to establish some sort of order out of the surrounding chaos and fear. Plundered almost to its bare bones it needed courage to start again, and on the first morning Thérèse had stood listening to the hollow churning of her empty stomach and wondering what to do first.

For once, providence smiled: the hen that had startled Clothilde on the previous evening strolled unconcernedly into the kitchen. Twenty minutes later it was simmering in the pot.

Then Thérèse discovered the kitchen garden. Sheltered by old lichened outbuildings, it had mercifully escaped German attention, and she stood for a moment with her strong hands clasped delightedly as she contemplated the nuns' neat rows of vegetables. There were cabbages and cauli-flowers, runner beans, artichokes and late potatoes. Vegetable marrows rambled over a compost heap and ripe tomatoes blazed against the wall. Herbs grew in wooden tubs.

The result of all this unexpected bounty was their first adequate meal for many days, and rich chicken gravy was trickling down Grand'mère's chin almost before Clothilde had finished saying grace.

Restored, they set to work. They cleaned out the well, swept up the dirt and washed the kitchen walls and floor. They cleaned what remained of the windows and polished the vast black iron range with a tin of black-lead they found. They fetched in the coal. They drew a supply of water and boiled it for drinking. They picked a bunch of lemon balm and hung it up to make the room smell pleasant.

By late afternoon Thérèse's wedding photograph stood on the newly scrubbed kitchen dresser and Clothilde sat at the table, stitching together the unburned remains of Grand'mère's mattress ticking while the old woman hovered anxiously at her elbow, holding the pins.

Out of the chaos, they had made themselves a home.

Temporarily relieved of the more pressing worries and fears, Clothilde and Thérèse began to contemplate the prospect of a relationship enforced by the bizarre circumstances of war, and sitting in the kitchen they covertly scrutinized one another.

Clothilde became aware for the first time that Thérèse sometimes ate off her knife and was not averse to giving the occasional hearty belch. Strong, resourceful and courageous, she was also, Clothilde was forced to admit, a woman of striking good looks, and given a little rudimentary guidance both as to dress and deportment might well be accepted in all the best drawing rooms of Dinant after the war. But Thérèse evinced no more than a bland indifference towards tales of soirées and genteel ballads sung round a silk-fronted pianoforte. Her one passion in life appeared to be work, and when she wasn't working she slept.

Once Clothilde discovered her taking a bath in a rain barrel and was deeply shocked at the casual way she stepped out of it and stood drying herself while the water ran down her legs and on to the cobblestones. In abrupt contrast to her sunburned arms and calloused hands her body was white and tenderly feminine, and Clothilde thought for the first time of the man in the wedding photograph. Henri Aubel, his name was.

And Thérèse in turn studied Clothilde when she wasn't looking; noting the way her fingers made anxious little pleats in the front of her blouse when she was talking, the way her pale spinster lips folded at the corners and the way she always sat upright with her knees pressed close together. With her little gold pince-nez clipped to her thin nose, there was an air of neat impeccability about her that half amused and half impressed Thérèse. She wondered whether Clothilde knew anything of love, and came to the conclusion that she was above the fundamental urges that preoccupied those less refined in their ways.

Despite their apparent incompatibility, they quite liked one another.

It was Grand'mère who first broached the subject of Yvette.

'The girl,' she said, suddenly looking round her one day. 'The girl should be back by now.'

'The girl has gone,' Thérèse said.

'Gone? Gone where?'

In certain moods the old woman's eyes would became gimlet sharp, her brain would clear of its confusion and she would speak with brisk authority, although she was still unable to tell them anything about herself. Sometimes she said that her name was Eloïse and that she came from Anseremme, but more recently she had been referring to herself as Zéphirin. Whoever she was, she appeared quite content with her new life at the convent and liked to sit on a stool in the courtyard slicing beans or scraping potatoes. Circumstances made it necessary that they should live mainly on a diet of vegetables.

'The girl has gone to make a new life for herself elsewhere,' Thérèse answered.

'She will come to an unfortunate end,' murmured Clothilde, who was sewing.

'If she does,' replied Thérèse, 'it will scarcely be her fault. Her mother ran a brothel and her father is, or was, serving a prison sentence for attempted murder.'

Shaken, Clothilde dropped her sewing in her lap. Her pince-nez trembled. 'Who — who was the victim?'

Thérèse shrugged amiably. 'I have no knowledge. One of his wife's clients, I imagine.'

Clothilde sat with her lips drawn in at the corners.

'Yvette Mazy is not a bad girl,' went on Thérèse, 'merely the victim of a bad world. When she was a very small child she used to sit on the doorstep of the café sometimes as late as eleven and twelve o'clock at night, falling asleep with a doll in her arms. No one ever bothered about her, not even to the extent of telling her when to go to bed. Once she found her way down to the farm and my husband gave her a kitten. I think it was very likely the only thing she had to love.'

46

'Now she has a Uhlan,' said Clothilde.

'Let us be charitable,' replied Thérèse, 'and hope that he will love her in return.'

'Who?' said Grand'mère, rousing herself. 'Who will love who?'

Thérèse stood up with a sigh. 'Come along, my old one,' she said. 'While I dig the potatoes for supper you can pick them up and put them in the basket.'

Clothilde watched them walk out of the kitchen and across the courtyard, which had now been swept clear of debris. They disappeared in the direction of the kitchen garden.

She had been sewing for some while, lost in thought, when a sudden clatter in the courtyard made her jump.

'Thérèse,' she cried aggrievedly. 'What are you doing out there?'

Except for a rhythmical, tinny sound from outside there was deep silence. Her scalp prickled.

'Thérèse?' she called again, then steeled herself to look out of the kitchen door. Thérèse was nowhere to be seen. Neither was Grand'mère. The only moving thing was an iron bucket, rolling slowly to and fro on the uneven cobbles.

Clothilde stood watching it with eyes huge with fright.

It could not have fallen over by itself. And there was no wind to blow it over. The bucket could only have been knocked over by some human agent.

She glanced quickly round the courtyard again and her hand flew to her throat as she saw something white flash momentarily round the edge of a stone buttress.

There was someone behind it, crouching on all fours.

Stepping hastily back into the kitchen her first impulse was to slam the door and bolt it. Then, sickened by her lack of courage, she looked round for something that could be used as a weapon of defence. Taking down a heavy goffering iron from the top of the dresser she turned round again, resolving to die like a true daughter of Belgium.

From the open kitchen door a white goat stood looking at her, its yellow eyes alight with friendly interest.

Very slowly she put down the iron and let out a long quivering breath.

The goat came forward, tilting its rough wedge of beard at her enquiringly. Hastily Clothilde took a step back.

'Mother of God—' exclaimed Thérèse, coming into the kitchen with the potatoes, 'what have we got here?'

Clothilde swallowed hard. 'I believe it is a goat.'

'Where has it come from?'

'I cannot tell. It just appeared.'

'You realize what this could mean?' Thérèse said slowly. 'Yes.'

Thérèse dropped to her knees and passed an exploring hand beneath the goat's belly. She began to smile, and then to laugh, throwing back her head and exposing her fine white teeth.

'What is it?' Clothilde asked, averting her eyes. 'A lady or a gentleman?'

'Go and fetch me a jug,' replied Thérèse, still laughing, 'and you will see.'

* * *

They named the goat Bibi and Thérèse kept her tethered in the little walled orchard that lay beyond the kitchen garden. Like Grand'mère, Bibi was a creature of unknown origin and, like Grand'mère, she accepted her new refuge with equanimity.

Anxious to restock the pantry, Thérèse made a large proportion of Bibi's milk into cheese.

Day by day the work of restoration and improvement continued, Thérèse tending the kitchen garden, harvesting the vegetables as they were ready and then cooking them carefully, so that nothing was wasted. Meat was the greatest problem, and when her work was finished she would set off with a sack over her shoulder, trudging down the rubble-strewn street of St Louis les Bois on the lookout for any stray livestock which, like the hen, might have escaped the bombardment and subsequent pillaging. But there was none, and with each succeeding day the silence of death seemed to thicken about the broken doorways and eyeless windows.

Undeterred, she made a dozen rabbit snares and set them up on the high sandy strip behind the village. She made some bird traps, and one afternoon she caught a basking trout with her bare hands but it yielded no more than a mouthful each. She then sacrificed her petticoat in order to make a fishing net, a decision which Clothilde regarded with folded lips and grave disparagement.

But provident instincts ran very deep within Thérèse, and never before had there been such serious need to take advantage of nature's prodigality. On her knees in the kitchen garden she would scoop up a handful of the warm, finely tilled soil and pour it slowly from hand to hand as she planned the crops that would spring from it next year. The soil was part of her body like the sun and the wind and the rain, and she hoarded the ripening seeds as if each one were a pearl beyond price.

As a reward for walking seven kilometres one day she came across a small general shop that was able to sell her some salt, flour and a little coffee. Next day she returned with the handcart but the shop had received a direct hit and the people were gone.

With the salt she preserved four crocks of runner beans, and she was happy, provided she kept her hands busy and her thoughts from straying towards Henri Aubel and how things used to be.

Clothilde too was hard at work, and like Thérèse she also was driven by an inner fire, an urgency that would allow her no rest.

It had begun on their first day at the convent. Weary after hours of unaccustomed sweeping and scrubbing she had wandered to the other end of the convent building where a shell had ripped open the roof and shattered much of the interior. Squeezing through a gap in the fallen masonry she found herself in the chapel, staring with mounting agitation at the sacrilege all around her; broken statues, pulpit and pews half-buried beneath plaster and slates, fragments of stained glass lying like showers of rubies and sapphires.

She crossed herself and began to walk round, her feet crunching on the broken plaster. In front of the High Altar she stopped with a gasp of horror. The two great candles had been overturned and the Tabernacle lay on the floor, its silk curtain torn and the wafers of the Hosts spilled in the dust and dirt.

Involuntarily she bent to retrieve them, then stopped. As a woman, she was forbidden to touch them. To do so would be a further act of sacrilege.

Twice she stretched out her hand, everything in her crying out against the blasphemy that had been committed, and twice she withdrew it, unable to touch that which was prohibited.

She began to weep, the tears running down her cheeks and falling on to her clasped hands, and her despair was such that it seemed as if she would die of it. She tried to pray, but the words refused to come. On her knees by the desecrated Hosts she could only weep hopelessly and incoherently, beaten down by all the horror that had first begun on 4 August.

Roused by Thérèse's voice calling her she had eventually stumbled to her feet, wiping her eyes and blowing her thin nose on the one handkerchief she possessed. Strangely enough she enjoyed the supper unwittingly provided by the stray hen, and had gone to bed in the little cell-like room with its straw palliasse and one rough blanket in a mood that approached tranquillity. It was as if the storm of passionate weeping had released an unbearable pressure.

The moon shining through her uncurtained window kept her awake, and towards morning she slipped quietly from her bed and found her way downstairs. Strangely unafraid of the shadows and mysterious night-sounds she made her way back to the chapel. It was flooded with silvery light.

Without stumbling she picked her way down the aisle until she reached the High Altar. Making a deep obeisance she crossed herself, then reached out her dry spinster hand and gathered the scattered Hosts and replaced them in the Tabernacle. With bowed head she stood it reverently back in place on the Altar, set the two great candles back in their sconces and swiftly withdrew.

And the next day everything seemed different. The moment she had finished helping Thérèse with more mundane matters she hurried over to the chapel and began the gigantic task of restoration. Much of it was beyond her and she had to sweep round the piles of rubble and blocks of immovable stone. Even so, it was remarkable what one woman could do; clearing up the slates one by one and stacking them neatly against the wall outside, hobbling, bowed-shouldered, with chunks of plaster and sweeping great satisfying swathes in the chinkling glass that littered the floor.

The fragments of statues she collected and carefully stored until such time as she could hope to repair them, and the frontal from the Altar she washed and ironed and replaced, together with a vase of wild poppies and scabious. She polished the candlesticks and the little lamp which but for the lack of oil should be burning day and night by the Tabernacle, and as she worked she thought, with a longing that was mostly but not entirely spiritual, of dear Père Joseph from Dinant.

Somewhere he was alive, and when she had gathered a little more courage with which to face the world outside she would walk back to Dinant and find him. And perhaps one day he would come to the convent to take a service in the chapel.

But courage was the great thing, and sometimes in the middle of her labours she would slip into one of the pews she had cleared of debris and pray humbly that she might be given a little more of the enviable quality that Thérèse already possessed in such abundance.

And as she worked and prayed the blazing summer of 1914 slowly burned itself out.

All over Belgium the corn was harvested wherever there were hands to be spared, but elsewhere it stood neglected, bowing its golden head to the parched earth until the first rainstorms broke it and laid it to waste in the mud and people like Thérèse Aubel cursed aloud at the stupidity of it all.

Then one afternoon in late September the girl Yvette returned.

Thérèse saw her first. Returning from collecting firewood she glanced down the street before turning in at the convent's broken gateway and there was the girl staggering clumsily over the rubble with a live goose in her arms. Her hair hung down and she was still barefoot.

Very slowly Thérèse lowered the bundle of firewood to the ground and stood waiting, her face impassive. Seeing her the girl paused, shifted the goose a little, then came forward again. She was trying to smile.

'You seem to make a habit of following me, Mademoiselle,' Thérèse remarked at length.

'I have come,' the girl began carefully, 'in order to bring this goose for Madame and her friends.'

'Mademoiselle is very thoughtful.'

'On the contrary. I wish to show appreciation of the kindness extended to me.'

'If Mademoiselle had remained with us, doubtless a little more kindness could have been extended,' Thérèse observed dryly.

The girl drew level. Her face was white with pain and exhaustion. Equally exhausted, the goose roused itself and began to nibble feebly at the twine that pinioned its wings and feet.

'It is a fine plump goose at the prime of life, Madame.'

'Might one ask,' ventured Thérèse, 'where the kind Mademoiselle acquired it?'

The girl drew a deep breath, biting her lower lip.

'It is known that I am a harlot,' she said. 'A woman of shameless immodesty and a person of gross impurity. Therefore it may as well be known that I am also a thief.'

Thérèse bent her head to hide the smile.

'The morals of Mademoiselle are no concern of mine,' she replied, 'and in return for the goose I should be happy to offer a bed for the night, that is—' she paused, 'if Mademoiselle has no other bed in mind?'

The girl's face seemed to crumple suddenly. Desperately she strove to maintain the studied politeness that had protected her.

'Madame is very kind,' she managed to say before turning abruptly aside.

'Here,' exclaimed Thérèse, 'for the love of God give me the goose before you drop it!'

Grand'mère was stirring the evening soup when they entered the kitchen.

'See here, my old one,' called Thérèse. 'Our family is complete once more.'

The old woman turned from the stove, and it was remarkable the way her dull eyes lit up with delighted recognition.

'Camille!' she exclaimed, shuffling forward.

'Yvette . . .' corrected Thérèse.

'Camille—' repeated the old woman, kissing the girl on either cheek.

'As you wish,' murmured Thérèse resignedly. Dumping the firewood in the corner she set about untying the goose.

Yvette sank on to a chair. 'But you have made it so *chic!*' she exclaimed, looking round at the spotless walls and floor, the white tablecloth and the shining kitchen range. 'Why, it is just like a home!'

'It is home,' Thérèse said gently, 'until further notice.'

The girl washed her hands and face in a pannikin of rainwater, smoothed her tangled hair and sat down at the extra place laid by Grand'mère. She bent over the bowl of vegetable soup, inhaling the aroma.

'You are hungry, Yvette?' asked Thérèse.

'I could die of it,' she said.

The kitchen door opened and Clothilde came in. Seeing Yvette, she stopped dead.

'Good evening, Mademoiselle,' said the girl and made a tired little effort to stand up.

'Good evening,' replied Clothilde through tight lips. 'I trust you found Paris to your liking?'

'I never reached Paris,' murmured Yvette, without looking at her.

'You astonish me,' said Clothilde.

Grand'mère placed a bowl in front of her, and after a momentary hesitation she took her place at the table. When Grand'mère joined them Clothilde bowed her head and said grace.

They ate in silence until Thérèse asked the girl whether she had heard much news of the war.

'It is very grave,' she replied. 'They say the Germans will be in Antwerp any day now.'

'In *Antwerp*?' repeated Thérèse, astounded. 'But surely they will have to conquer Brussels first?'

Yvette stared at her from across the table. 'Brussels fell on August the twentieth,' she said.

The three older women sat motionless.

'It is not possible,' Clothilde said at last.

'But had you not heard?' asked Yvette, surprised.

'How could we?' Thérèse said bitterly. 'There are no newspapers and we live in a village that might as well be a graveyard. The only stranger I have spoken to has been the woman in the shop on the road to Waulsort. But now even she has gone.'

'Tell us what else has happened,' said Clothilde.

'Louvain was burned down and they shot a lot of civilian men down behind the railway station. Malines cathedral has been destroyed and in Termode there are only one or two houses left standing. They have shot many hundreds of women and children.'

'Do you know what has happened to the people in the caves around Dinant?' asked Thérèse.

Yvette put down her spoon and pushed her bowl of soup away, almost untouched. 'I heard that most of the people in the caves have been deported to Germany for slave labour,' she whispered, 'and they say that there has been a terrible massacre in Dinant itself.'

Clothilde gave a little gasp and then covered her eyes with her hand. She began to pray in a voice that shook convulsively. Only half comprehending, Grand'mère joined in.

'And our army,' Thérèse said, her lips barely moving, 'where is our army?'

'I do not know, Madame,' replied Yvette. Pushing back her chair she stood up. 'Forgive me, but I am not hungry after all.'

She went towards the door. Noticing her slow dragging walk Thérèse left her supper and went with her.

'I will show you where you can sleep,' she said, and took her arm.

The girl was lying outstretched on the straw palliasse in the room next to Clothilde's when she touched Thérèse's hand and said, 'King Albert is with the army, and I have no doubt in my mind that he will take care of Monsieur Aubel.'

'Thank you,' replied Thérèse formally. 'I have no doubt of it, either.'

Downstairs in the kitchen she found Clothilde pacing up and down, her fingers making agitated pleats in the front of her blouse.

'And you let her return here?' she cried when she saw Thérèse. 'After all that has happened, after all she has done?'

'The girl had no part in the massacre,' said Thérèse wearily.

'Perhaps not, but she has — has *lain* with those who have!' Clothilde's voice cracked with anger.

'Be still,' said Thérèse, slumped on to a chair and rubbing her forehead with her fist. 'We have matters of greater importance to consider. I have a feeling, for example, that the baby will be here before morning.'

* * *

Clothilde lay with the single rough blanket pulled up to her chin, staring at the dull grey square of window at the foot of the bed. Her thoughts were bitter.

The girl had returned. Warm from the unspeakable embrace of a German invader she had returned to the convent, and both Thérèse and Grand'mère had welcomed her with open arms.

What about her betrayal of them? What about the baggage wagon piled with loot, the basket of stolen eggs she had held on her lap as they drove off?

Forgive us our trespasses as we forgive them that trespass against us . . . said a voice within Clothilde, but it was impossible. Or at least, very difficult.

She thought of her own chastity and of the chastity of the nun in whose bed she lay. She thought of the beautiful celibacy of poor dear Père Joseph, and it seemed monstrous that this unmarried girl of sixteen should be welcomed into the sacred atmosphere of a convent in order to give birth to an illegitimate child.

Monstrous . . . monstrous . . . thought Clothilde, and turning restlessly on her side watched the lighted oil lamp pass a finger of golden light beneath her door. She heard the creak of footsteps going into the next room.

And that was another thing. The two oil lamps had been filled to the brim with the last of their precious oil because of the girl being brought to childbed, whereas Thérèse had always made it quite clear that oil was far too precious to squander in the sanctuary lamp that should rightly be burning by the High Altar.

Was there no justice?

A soft moaning from the next room made her cover her ears with her hands. With a loudly thumping heart she tried to picture the scene but it was impossible, owing to a lack of knowledge. Having heard a rumour many years ago that children issue forth from that part of the female anatomy normally ignored by people of refinement, she had decided to pursue the subject no further.

Restlessly she uncovered her ears again and sat up, tossing her grey plait of hair behind her shoulders. The door of the girl's room creaked open again and she heard Thérèse call to Grand'mère, then through the open door the girl made a sighing noise as if she were weary beyond all words.

Clothilde slid out of bed, pulled on her skirt and crept downstairs. Making her way to the chapel she slipped into a pew, crossed herself and began to pray earnestly for guidance. When she had finished she sat for a moment looking up at the sky.

The main vestments cupboard had somehow escaped both the shelling and the Uhlan pillaging, and in the early light Clothilde riffled expertly through its contents, knowing by touch the chasubles, stoles, maniples, burses and the great piles of Altar linen. Selecting a soft white cotton surplice she hurried back to the convent with it and bolted like a rabbit up to her room.

By the light of a solitary candle she cut the surplice into pieces, pinned them together and began to sew, sitting on the edge of the bed with the machine on a chair. It was very cramped and uncomfortable but she worked swiftly and unerringly, her gold pince-nez trembling on her nose, and to some extent the soft whirring of the machine helped to soothe the profound agitation within her.

She was biting off the final thread when the baby was born. With the sewing held against her mouth she heard the convulsive gasp as air inflated the lungs before the sharp squalling voice tore the waiting silence.

She closed her eyes.

'Clothilde . . . Clothilde . . . !'

They were calling her, Thérèse's voice warmly excited and Grand'mère's shrill and crackling.

Her legs were shaking but somehow she got to the door, the sewing still clutched in her hands.

'Come in . . . come in and see!' they were calling.

He was lying on the bed by his mother, still attached to her by the cord. He was wet and bloodstained and red and bald, clenching his wizened fingers and yelling with a furious, impotent rage. And between his widely parted legs lay flagrantly exposed to view the other mystery she had always feared and sought to evade. He was all life, all male, and within the space of half a minute he had taught her everything there was to know.

She gave the little nightgown she had made to his mother, but she couldn't speak.

It was Grand'mère, as senior member of the household, who baptised him and his names were Francois, after the saint upon whose day he had been born, and Albert, in honour of the King.

When the brief ceremony was over they all took turns to hold him for a moment before placing him in Yvette's arms, where he snuffled pleasurably at her warm flesh then fell instantly asleep.

'And you too must sleep,' ordered Thérèse, but the girl shifted a little higher on her improvised pillows and smiled radiantly.

'I am too happy to sleep,' she said.

It was the same for all of them, even the old woman, and morning sunlight pouring through the window found Thérèse and Clothilde and Grand'mère sitting on the edge of the bed sipping precious coffee while they made Yvette drink a large bowlful of warm goat's milk.

'I did not go with him,' the girl said, looking at them all very earnestly. 'I intended to because it seemed prudent, but it was really impossible for me.'

'What happened, little one?' asked Thérèse.

'I was foolish to believe he would take me to Paris,' said Yvette. She drained the bowl of milk and then handed it to Clothilde. 'In reality we reached no further than the big house outside Dinant on the road to Namur. It has now been requisitioned as a place for German officers. There was much singing and much drinking. We went to a room on the first floor, and he—'

'Yes?' whispered Clothilde, pleating rapidly.

'He importuned me,' said Yvette modestly. 'I resisted. He tried to force me, so—' she looked around at them all with the smile of an angelic child, 'I removed his revolver from its holster and I shot him.'

Thérèse and Clothilde gasped in unison. Grand'mère passed her speckled hand across her bony forehead and said sternly, 'You shot a man? Whatever for?'

'Because he was a Boche,' Yvette said gleefully. 'I shot him because I am a Belgian woman and a patriot. And because,' she ran her finger over the baby's mossy scalp, 'I thought you would all wish me to.'

'It is an honour that you should think of us at such a time,' Thérèse said soberly, 'but it was a very dangerous thing to do. How is it that you were not caught?'

'No one saw me,' said the girl. 'No one at all, either going in or coming out. For a moment after he had fallen I was very frightened, for there was much blood. But no one came. I think that with all the singing and shouting and crashing of bottles, no one heard the shot. So I gathered my courage, ran quickly downstairs and out through the door. I crept through the shrubbery and I walked away as quickly as possible.'

'Where to?' asked Thérèse, absorbed.

The girl shrugged, and the happiness in her face faded a little. 'I tried Namur, but it was full of Germans and there was a lot of shelling. I saw a woman lying dead in the street. Then I went for a while with several refugee families but they, alas, had many problems of their own. So I stayed by myself. I slept in ditches, sometimes I ate blackberries and drank water. All in all, it was not a good time.'

'Why in the name of God did you not return home?' demanded Thérèse harshly.

The girl looked at her for a long moment. She looked at Clothilde.

'I was afraid you would dismiss me,' she said.

'Well now, what do you think?' Thérèse said to Clothilde. 'After all we have heard, do you not think it wise that we should dismiss her immediately?'

59

'I think,' said Clothilde, looking shyly at the baby, 'that we might do well to wait until he is big enough to protect her.'

And so it was left. Grand'mère hooked an improvised curtain up to the window to shut out the light and Yvette lay down with the baby close against her body and slept.

Later in the day Thérèse left the convent and climbed up on to the high ground behind it to check the rabbit snares. She walked slowly, conscious of a need for solitude.

The air was rich and damp with autumn and she paused to scoop up a handful of soil, sniffing it before crumbling it and letting it slip through her fingers again. She thought about the war news brought by Yvette. For the first time it seriously occurred to her that Belgium would fall to the enemy and she wished with sudden impatience that she had more learning, so that she might comprehend the situation more fully. But political and military strategy both baffled and irritated her, and arriving at the first rabbit snare she consoled herself with the wisdom of attending to one's own affairs and of leaving others to do the same. Having unwittingly assumed responsibility for a family consisting of four ill-assorted women, a new-born baby, a goat and a goose, she had more than enough to keep her occupied.

Her chief worry at the moment was Yvette, and she was secretly astonished that the Germans had not returned to the convent to look for her after the murder. Even supposing that the girl was right in her blithe insistence that no one had seen her arriving at or leaving the house, the three soldiers who had accompanied the officer must have remembered her, and surely her abrupt disappearance must have spoken for itself?

Sombrely Thérèse removed a fat buck rabbit from the snare and then set it up again, a few yards further away.

But on the other hand, perhaps the most hopeful aspect of the whole business lay in Yvette's assertion that all the Germans appeared to be drunk. And perhaps the three soldiers had belonged to a different company and had travelled on elsewhere after the Uhlan officer had arrived at the commandeered house with Yvette. It was difficult to know, for although time seemed to be on their side and with each passing day the likelihood of trouble grew a little less, she was under no illusions as to the penalty for murdering an officer of Kaiser Wilhelm's Imperial Army. Death, not only for Yvette, but in all probability for Clothilde, Grand'mère, the baby and herself. It was not a cheerful thought.

The snares had yielded two rabbits and she turned towards the convent, then changed her mind and wandered towards the edge of the small plateau of land. Silhouetted against the evening sky she stood looking round at the wide sweep of Ardennes country, at the mountains and the deep forests that were flaring into scarlet and gold.

Below her on the other side of the village lay the little stony track shielded by goat willow that led to the farm. Sometimes the longing to return was almost overwhelming, but she remained firm in her decision. The past was past. She had destroyed it with her own hands.

Suddenly overcome by the thought of Henri she sank down on the wet turf and buried her head in her hands. For the first time in many years she wept.

It was the sound of hooves echoing up from the deserted village street that finally roused her. Sniffing and wiping her eyes on her cuff she leaned forward, searching the piles of rubble that had spilled on to the pavements and into the road for the first sign of Uhlans. In imagination she already saw the rays of the dying sun glinting on their lances and helmets as they made their way to the convent and Yvette.

They must have ridden for a great distance, the hooves were so slow. And then she saw them. A man leading a horse and cart piled high with furniture and bedding and children, his wife pushing a perambulator. Behind them came a couple trudging along with a bicycle, then an old man with a dog harnessed to a handcart.

Old men, women and children. She recognised the butcher and his wife, the schoolmaster who had taught her to read and write over twenty-five years ago. There was a cow on a halter, a couple of pigs, a boxful of chickens lashed to the back of a mule.

They came in a slow cavalcade that wound its way with heartbreaking patience between the heaps of shattered stone, and with the two rabbits slung on her shoulder Thérèse Aubel went down to greet them. The people of St Louis les Bois were returning homes.

CHAPTER FOUR

But although a nucleus of villagers had returned, things were not the same. Before the war life had been open, friendly and pleasant; people passing in the street had paused to greet one another, but now they seemed to have little inclination for sociability and went about their business with stony faces and no more than a taciturn nod.

In silence they began the task of reclamation, patching up their houses to form at least temporary shelter from the wind and rain that tore the last leaves from the trees. Without speaking they shovelled the worst of the rubble from the shattered street.

They helped one another and they shared what little they had, but there was none of the easy conviviality that in the old days had lured housewives to their doorsteps and men to the zinc-covered bar of any one of the four cafés. It was too soon after what had happened, and too many of them were haunted by dreams that made them cry out in their sleep. Now the November sun beaming rosily on a powdering of early frost had no power to move them with its beauty, probably because it beamed impartially upon so many broken houses to which the inhabitants would never return.

'And what became of the good Sisters from the convent?' Thérèse asked a man who was nailing a sheet of tin over a gaping window.

'They were given the same choice as the rest of us. Pack up and leave within half an hour or stay and be killed.'

'They took the first choice, I trust?'

'I passed the Reverend Mother leading them along the Namur road. She said they would walk to Brussels to find sanctuary at their sister convent there.'

'It is hard,' Thérèse said.

'It is war,' replied the man with a listless shrug.

'Do you think it likely that the Uhlans will return?' she asked casually.

'Who knows? Doubtless they would return fast enough if they had good reason.'

The man returned to his work and his hammer made a desolate sound in the cold air.

In the convent kitchen Clothilde was sitting at the sewing machine, making a winter coat for Yvette out of a dark grey blanket.

'In the cities,' said Yvette, 'I understand that one wears fur round the hem.'

Having fed Albert she was replacing him in his improvised cradle by the fire, solicitously tucking the covers round him and lingering over his peacefully sleeping features.

'I remember that my dear Maman once had a little moleskin jacket,' replied Clothilde, coming to the end of a seam. 'It had sleeves set high on the shoulders and it fitted very closely at the waist. At the time of which I am speaking, such things were considered extremely à la mode.'

'Madame your mother was a person of distinction,' Yvette said.

'My mother was a person of some consequence in Dinant,' agreed Clothilde, 'and she numbered some of the very best families among her friends.' She shook out the grey blanket then held it up critically, her pince-nez glimmering.

'Come here and try it on,' she added.

Yvette stood in the middle of the kitchen floor wearing the half-made coat. Tacking threads hung from it and the rough material made her itch.

'Stand still,' commanded Clothilde, on her knees. One by one she removed a row of pins from between her front teeth and placed them at strategic points.

'A slight lift at the waist — so — and I think that perhaps the sleeves could be tapered a little more . . .'

'The result will be extremely elegant,' Yvette said.

Clothilde put the last pin in position then stood up and surveyed her handiwork from several paces away.

'No, my dear,' she said. 'It will not be elegant. I think the most we can say is that it will be warm.'

'And I am truly grateful to you for your kindness,' the girl replied very earnestly.

'I must also devise something suitable for Grand'mère,' said Clothilde. 'It is fortunate that we have a few spare blankets. And then there is Thérèse. She also has nothing for the winter.'

'Thérèse never seems to feel the cold,' observed Yvette. 'I believe that she must be a woman of great inner warmth.'

'She has warmth and strength,' replied Clothilde, helping her off with the coat, 'and without her we would all be lost.'

'On the contrary,' said Yvette, 'I venture to think that we would all be lost without each other.'

During the course of the last three months the initial tie of mutual disaster had become strengthened by a healthy respect, each for the other. Despite what sometimes appeared to be temperamental differences of staggering proportions they were able to regard one another's foibles with toleration. If Thérèse considered that Clothilde spent more time working in the chapel than she need have done, she kept her opinion to herself, and if Thérèse's habit of talking with her mouth full discomforted Clothilde, she in turn remained silent about it.

Yvette in particular was very conscious of a family feeling between them, and in spite of the war and their precarious existence in the convent she had never been so happy. In gratitude for her acceptance she had come to regard the older women with something close to reverence, and striving to emulate their mature sense of responsibility found that it came to her with surprising ease. Perhaps it was due to the birth of the baby, or perhaps it had been there all along, stifled by lack of encouragement.

And of course the little Albert himself was at the hub of the family circle. Without ever confusing the identity of his mother, he now lavished smiles on all of them while they in turn loved him not only because of the universal appeal of babies, but because they recognized something strangely symbolic about him; at a time when Belgium's manhood was being laid tragically to waste, his arrival among them seemed like an omen of wonderful significance.

As for Grand'mère, perhaps she was happiest of all. No longer plagued by half-memories of reality she pottered from one simple task to another and in the evenings she would sit in her corner by the kitchen range and tell the other women what they had been like when they were little girls. And because of the prevailing harmony between them, they would pretend to believe every word she said.

The weather grew colder, the nights grew longer and a unanimous decision was taken to fatten Yvette's goose for Christmas.

* * *

Despite their determination to make the best of things, however, there were secret miseries to be endured, and by Clothilde in particular.

With her angular form wrapped in an odd assortment of garments she continued to work in the chapel in between sewing for the family. Every day she swept the broken floors, dusted the pews and polished the brass candlesticks. With the roof above it open to the sky the High Altar was at the mercy of the elements, but lovingly she continued to array it in the frontals and hangings appropriate to the Church calendar, then removing them, rain-soaked and splashed with soot, in order to wash and iron them ready for the next occasion when they would be used. With no priest to conduct services, it made Thérèse think of constantly arraying a young girl for a ball which never took place, but she said nothing.

To begin with, Clothilde had tried to restore order in the chapel merely as a humble act of devotion coupled with a sense of gratitude to the absent nuns for their unwitting hospitality, but recently her thoughts had been turning more and more insistently towards Père Joseph, the curé from Dinant. Steadfastly she refused to believe in the possibility of his death in the massacre Yvette had told them of, yet anxiety as to his whereabouts and his well-being preoccupied her increasingly. She dreamed about him. She found his name constantly recurring in her prayers and during the day his image was always in the forefront of her mind. Once, squeezing through the narrow aperture that led into the chapel, she was positive she saw him standing motionless in the gloom, his long soutane brushing the floor. Fear and a tremulous delight filled her. But it wasn't Père Joseph, it was only the shadow of an old baize curtain.

As the days went by it became increasingly clear what she must do. Despite her shrinking fear of death and the Germans she knew that she must return to Dinant to find out what had happened to him.

It was her duty as a churchwoman and a faithful member of his congregation. And yet . . .

It would mean walking alone and unprotected along the road. Passing Uhlans, with their spiked helmets and cruel faces. Seeing horrors surely not meant for a refined person's eyes . . .

The thought of it kept her from sleeping, yet the compulsion to go gave her no peace. In the end she decided to talk it over with Thérèse, but instead of asking her advice she heard herself saying in the old chill spinster-voice, 'I am thinking of going to Dinant. There may be some news of the friends I have there.'

Thérèse was paring turnips for the evening meal. 'You are going to Dinant? But is that prudent?'

Only too aware that it was far from prudent Clothilde heard herself saying that she was sure it was perfectly safe.

Thérèse stared at her from the other side of the kitchen, her shrewd peasant eyes taking in the faintly twitching lips, the thin dressmaker fingers making nervous little pleats in the front of her blouse.

'Is there anything wrong, Clothilde?' she asked finally.

Clothilde forced herself to meet the searching stare without flinching and suddenly found herself yearning to confide in Thérèse; for even if she was a trifle lacking in gentility she was a woman of warmth and understanding, and to tell her of the wisdom and spiritual beauty of Père Joseph would be to allow herself a moment or two of incalculable happiness. She opened her mouth to speak his name, then closed it tightly as she felt the ignominious blush burn her cheeks and spread its dreadful fire over her face and neck.

'No,' she replied in a tight little voice. 'There is nothing wrong.'

Thérèse returned to her vegetables. 'That is well,' she said. Then added, 'And when do you think of going?'

'Tomorrow,' said Clothilde, who had not actually got as far as planning the day. She took a deep breath and said firmly, 'I will go tomorrow early in the morning, and will return in time for supper.'

Thérèse nodded, and began cutting the turnips into chunks.

'Take care,' she said, 'and be sure not to mention to anyone that Yvette is here. Although one dares to hope that she has escaped the consequences of shooting the Uhlan, one must continue to act with caution.'

A chill ran down Clothilde's spine. 'I will be cautious,' she said, and turned away.

She set off next morning and characteristically was as much harassed by not having a hat to wear as she was about meeting the occupying forces. Although not a vain woman, her appearance was a matter of importance to her, and to face the world outside impeccable in hat and gloves would have lessened her trepidation considerably.

Thérèse accompanied her across the courtyard carrying a plateful of scraps for the goose. Her sabots clattered cheerfully on the cobbles and Clothilde became abruptly choked with the craven desire to beg her to come too. With Thérèse stolid and implacable at her side, she would be brave. Or at least, braver than she was going to be all on her own.

But of course she said nothing, and at the broken gateway Thérèse smiled and wished her good luck before going into the small outhouse where they kept the goose. And Clothilde smiled back before stepping gingerly into the main street of St Louis les Bois.

It was a morning of raw cold, with shreds of wet mist lying in the valleys. There were few people about, but in one of the fields she saw a man ploughing with a pair of oxen. The sight would have gladdened Thérèse, and she made a mental note to tell her about it when she got back.

The road stretched emptily ahead of her and there were no Germans to be seen. If only she had been wearing a hat she would have felt almost cheerful. Her fingers were cold so she tucked them up the sleeves of the coat she had borrowed from Yvette and walked on, thinking of Père Joseph and how wonderful it would be to see him again. Possibly he would have difficulty in recognizing her because of her appearance, but he would understand how things were.

She wished that she had brought him a little offering, perhaps one of the goatmilk cheeses, but it was difficult without first asking Thérèse. And Thérèse, despite last evening's temptation, had no knowledge of Père Joseph and all he meant.

The road ran downhill until it reached the bank of the Meuse, and almost at once she was jerked back to reality. The edge of the river was strewn with the abandoned accoutrements of war. Empty shell cases, rotting fragments of uniform and harness, the remains of a canvas boat. A little further on, the snout of a heavy field gun protruded from the sullen brown water as if it were gasping for air.

She began to walk faster, trying not to look. Then she saw the bridge of Dinant. Its back was broken in two places, the centre of it slumped into the river. And then the houses. At first glance many of them appeared to be as usual, but as she hurried further into the town she could see the grey November light filtering through their empty facades. The Grand Place had been almost obliterated, the church of Notre Dame brutally decapitated.

Stricken, she wandered through the gaunt remains of her home town; although she had fled at the height of the bombardment, the terror she had felt then was nothing compared to the cold misery of the aftermath. It was so quiet. So lifeless. A small child stared at her from a shattered doorway, and two more, playing a mute and solemn game round the wheels of an overturned French howitzer, paused to examine her dispassionately. Their gaze made her feel even more of an intruder than the Germans.

She turned down the rue St-Jacques. Here and there the shell of a house was still standing, its empty windows ringed with fire black, and her heart contracted as a group of German garrison troops turned the corner and came towards her. Timidly she stepped off the narrow pavement and made way for them. They accepted the courtesy as a matter of course, and clumped past without taking any notice of her.

No one took any notice of her. No one spoke, or smiled. The occasional civilian shuffling through the broken streets ignored her completely. With tears pricking her eyes she told herself that it was because she had no hat.

She retraced her steps and made for the little square where her house had once stood, pleasantly guarded by Père Joseph's church. The rubble had been tidied, and she stood staring up at a scrap of bedroom wallpaper that still remained. It was impossible to believe that she had ever slept peacefully there.

There was almost nothing left of the church, or of its presbytery. Like a ghost she wandered round, staring at the mounds of broken stone and seeking to rebuild them in her imagination. It was beyond her powers. Hopelessly she wandered on.

She was passing along the rue Barré when she saw Madame Pascal. With such distinctive red hair it was impossible to mistake her. Madame Pascal had been one of her best clients and had looked like an angel from heaven in the white lace wedding gown it had taken three weeks to make.

Clothilde hastened, her footsteps pattering.

'Madame Pascal—' she cried, and broke into a run.

Madame Pascal paused, and then turned round.

'Mademoiselle Toussant,' she said.

Limply she shook Clothilde's fingers then made as if to turn away again. There was a listless droop to her shoulders, and despite her agitation Clothilde noticed that she was considerably thinner. Her coat needed to be taken in at least two inches.

'Dear Madame Pascal,' she said earnestly. 'How good it is to see you again. Are you well?'

Madame Pascal raised her eyes fleetingly. 'Well enough,' she said.

Clothilde's pleasure withered and died. The words froze on her lips.

'I am well enough,' repeated Madame Pascal as if to herself, and began to walk on again. Desperately Clothilde hurried after her. She took her sleeve.

'Madame Pascal,' she stammered, 'I must know how things go in Dinant. The people I knew — I have been away, and everything has been very difficult . . . I am anxious to know about the people I knew here . . .'

Madame Pascal walked on as if she hadn't heard, then suddenly stopped. They were standing by a garden wall.

'There,' said Madame Pascal, pointing, 'the Germans shot twenty-six civilians. Against the Bourdons' house on the riverbank they murdered seventy-eight, including a baby of three weeks old. In the Place de l'Abbaye there were three separate massacres—' she spoke in a rapid undertone, 'and they have transported more than four hundred people to Germany, including the Burgomaster. My parents were both injured when their house was bombarded and I have had no news of my husband since he joined the cavalry last July. That, Mademoiselle, is how things are with the people in Dinant.'

'Holy Mother . . .' whispered Thérèse. 'Everything that Yvette said is true—' Involuntarily she raised her hand to her mouth, remembering the importance of not mentioning Yvette's name in Dinant.

But Madame Pascal appeared not to have heard. She went on, her voice shaking, 'Everything is terrible. Food is scarce, the Germans have taken everything. They promised us a daily ration of bread but so far they have given us nothing. People are eating boiled potato peelings . . .'

She began to walk on again, too distressed even to say goodbye. For a moment Clothilde stood motionless, watching her go, then with a little gasp ran after her again.

'Madame Pascal—' she said desperately, 'are you able to tell me of the whereabouts of Père Joseph of the Church of St Jacques? I — he was my curé — and I should like to know that he is — is safe and well . . .'

Madame Pascal stopped again. She stared at Clothilde with her lifeless red-brown eyes.

'Wherever you are living now, you apparently hear nothing of the events in Dinant,' she said.

'Père Joseph,' repeated Clothilde rapidly. 'Where is he?'

'He is dead,' replied Madame Pascal. 'He has been dead for a long time. It seems that a Uhlan officer was found shot through the heart in a house requisitioned by the Germans on the road to Namur. The Uhlans came here and arrested twenty hostages. Many of them were children. Père Joseph had opened a shelter for the homeless in the cellar of his house. He heard what had happened and offered his own life to the Germans in exchange for the twenty hostages.'

'They accepted?'

'They agreed to spare the children.'

The world spun on its axis. 'He always loved children,' whispered Clothilde, and closed her eyes.

When she opened them again Madame Pascal had gone.

* * *

At the convent they waited supper for over an hour, and when at last they sat down to eat, the sight of Clothilde's empty place at the table took away their appetites.

Uneasily they sat waiting for the sound of her footsteps, the click of the latch. With the coming of darkness the damp cold had stiffened into a sharp frost and a needling of stars perforated the black sky.

'If only there was a moon,' muttered Thérèse for the third time. 'At least it would have lessened the risk of her losing her way.'

'She is surely staying the night with a friend,' said Yvette. She pushed her bowl of soup away.

'Eat,' Thérèse said sternly.

'I cannot.'

'You are foolish.'

'You also,' said Yvette, looking at Thérèse's own untouched bowl. 'If you will forgive the liberty.'

Restless and irritable with worry, Thérèse insisted soon after that both Grand'mère and Yvette should go to bed.

'I will wait up for her,' she said. 'There is no need for you to do the same.'

Reluctantly they did as they were told and Yvette tucked Grand'mère into the remains of her striped mattress before going into her own room.

'Good night, little Mémé,' she said, kissing the old woman's cheek. 'Try not to worry about her.'

'She is of such a nervous disposition,' fretted Grand'mère. 'When she was a child there were times when I despaired of rearing her . . .'

Dawn was filtering through the kitchen window when Thérèse awoke. Cramped and very cold she lifted her head

73

from her folded arms, listening intently. The convent was silent. Clothilde had not returned.

She stood up, rubbing her stiff legs then thrusting her hands under her armpits to warm them. The range was out, and the cheerlessness of her surroundings did nothing to mitigate the nagging certainty that some disaster had befallen Clothilde.

She began to clear the ashes from the range, then, sickened by a feeling of weary futility, left them. She went to the door, opened it and stepped out into the courtyard. Frost sparkled on the cobbles.

At the broken gateway she stood looking out at the desolate village. There was no one stirring. On the way back to the kitchen she suddenly paused, then began to walk over to the chapel where Clothilde had toiled so lovingly at the work of restoration.

Squeezing through the aperture in the tumbled masonry she stepped inside and moved quietly down the aisle. Frost glittered on the cracked floor and the High Altar with its beautifully laundered linen gleaming in the wan light.

She was very near to Clothilde before she saw her. Near enough to put out her hand and touch her. She was huddled in a corner of a pew, covered by an old baize curtain and she was asleep.

To hide her delighted relief Thérèse said ungraciously, 'In God's name, woman, what are you doing here? You have worried us all out of our wits.'

Clothilde opened her eyes quite slowly. She looked extraordinarily haggard.

'Go away,' she said.

'Thérèse's jaw dropped. 'Clothilde,' she said, 'what in the world ails you?'

'Nothing,' Clothilde said slowly and carefully. 'Please go away.' She drew the baize curtain closer round her and turned her face away. She closed her eyes.

Thérèse went into the pew and sat down beside her.

'Clothilde,' she repeated wonderingly. 'You are ill. You are in trouble. Are you not able to tell me?'

Clothilde remained silent, her face averted. Thérèse sat looking at her, frowning and perplexed. She put out her hand to touch Clothilde's shoulder, hesitated and then withdrew it.

'Go away,' repeated Clothilde.

'Very well,' said Thérèse, at a loss. She stood up, conscious of her cold aching limbs, and then walked away. At the entrance to the chapel she paused, and then walked back again.

'Clothilde,' she said gently. 'Please tell me what ails you.'

Clothilde continued to ignore her.

'Very well,' exclaimed Thérèse, suddenly exasperated, 'if you wish to behave like a wilful child, so be it.'

She walked back to the convent kitchen, her sabots ringing.

They took it in turns to go to the chapel to plead and remonstrate with Clothilde.

Thérèse and Grand'mère she ignored, but to their added bewilderment burst into a torrent of hysterical tears at the sight of Yvette.

'It must be her age,' Thérèse said when they had exhausted all other possible reasons for her incredible behaviour. 'She is in her middle forties, which is known to be a strange and melancholy time for women.'

Clothilde remained in the chapel all that day, but when they got up the next morning they found her in the kitchen, preparing the usual meagre breakfast as if nothing had happened.

Almost, but not quite. For although she answered their tentative remarks it was only with monosyllables, and there was a chill hostility, a strange physical rigidity about her, almost as if something at the heart of her had frozen solid. She never referred to her visit to Dinant, and as time passed it became more and more impossible to ask her about it.

Gradually they began to grow accustomed to the new silent Clothilde, although naturally they continued to discuss the mysterious change in her when she was absent.

'Sometimes,' Yvette said to Thérèse, 'I have a strange feeling that Clothilde's despondency is not unconnected with myself.'

'How so?'

'I know not,' said the girl. 'If I have done anything to anger her I swear it was inadvertently. But sometimes I notice her staring at me almost as if she wished I were dead.'

'Oh, come now,' remonstrated Thérèse, 'that is mere fancy. It is something connected with Dinant, not you.'

'But why did she go to Dinant in the first place?' asked Yvette. 'Knowing all that had happened, it was a strange thing to do.' She sat twisting a long strand of hair round her finger. Suddenly she smiled. 'Perhaps she has a lover there!'

'Who knows?' agreed Thérèse, then inclined her head towards the door. 'Hush, I hear her coming . . .'

With the onset of winter Thérèse redoubled her efforts to make the whole convent as weatherproof as possible but they found themselves living almost exclusively in the kitchen, where they stuffed rags and paper in the cracks of the door and walls, and sealed broken windowpanes with sheets of tin.

This reduced the light to even more miserable proportions, and as their stock of paraffin dwindled to nothing they had to resort to candles. The supply of coal also ran out, but luckily there was ample wood available up on the plateau above the village, and most afternoons Thérèse would set off with a sack over her shoulder, glad to escape from an atmosphere that was becoming increasingly oppressive.

Clothilde, it was now tacitly understood, was suffering from some private crisis of the heart, and although they all sympathised with her obvious suffering, Thérèse in particular secretly wished that she could make more of an effort towards recovery; having to put up with the war was bad enough without the prospect of a silent wraithlike woman to contend with as well.

The days passed, leaden-footed with dank cold outside and a sense of chill forbearance within.

Then came the night of 19 December.

They had gone to bed early in order to save candles and, less ostensibly, because they were bored by one another's company.

Grand'mère lay slumbering in her mattress ticking, Yvette lay asleep with her baby snug against her body and Clothilde lay wrapped in dreams of which no one could guess the nature.

Only Thérèse lay awake, staring beyond the foot of her narrow nun's bed at the cold winter moon floating high above the roofs of the convent outbuildings.

Her sharp ears caught the sound of a familiar creak. Instantly alert she sat up in bed, tossing her thick plait of hair out of the way. Inclining her head towards the window she heard another creak, an unmistakable continuation of the first.

It was the door of the outhouse in which they kept the Christmas goose.

Silently and very swiftly she pushed back the blanket and glided to the window, just in time to see the door of the outhouse swing to. Pulling on the jacket Clothilde had made for her she crept quickly downstairs and across the empty hall.

Outside in the bitter cold of the courtyard she paused for a moment, then drew a deep breath as she saw a movement through the moonlit window of the outhouse.

Someone was in there, stealing the goose.

Motionless, she waited outside the door. The goose gave a sudden harsh squawk and she heard the alarmed beating of its wings. Rage throbbed in her, warming her body and filling it with the urgent need for action. Quietly and smoothly she reached for the hatchet they used for chopping wood. The handle was cold and polished in her hand. Very quietly she opened the door.

After that, everything happened very quickly.

As the goose gave another shriek Thérèse lifted the hatchet with both hands and with a terrible, savage joy brought it crashing down on the shadowed figure that had its back turned to her. The blade struck metal, bounced off and then embedded itself in something soft. Honking dementedly the goose sped round and round the outhouse, its wings beating up the foetid air.

Appalled by the noise Thérèse pursued it and caught it, seizing it roughly by the shoulders and trapping its vociferous beak shut under her arm. It was unhurt, and after a moment or two she succeeded in reducing it to a state of comparative calm.

She turned her attention to the motionless figure on the floor. Stepping past it she pushed the outhouse door open. A stream of cold silver light illuminated the body of a German soldier in a steel helmet lying face down, his limbs spreadeagled. The hatchet lay close beside him and a large dark stain had spread over the back of his tunic. It gleamed stickily.

She stood staring down at him as if she had lost all power of movement, then with a convulsive gasp rushed out of the door, slamming it and bolting it behind her.

She ran back into the convent and down the long dark passage to the kitchen where she flung herself into a chair, drawing her knees up under her chin and hiding her eyes. With her teeth chattering and her body shaking, she was like someone in the grip of high fever.

Gradually the pounding of her heart subsided. After a while she uncoiled herself and crept across the kitchen to get a mug of water. She took it back to the chair to drink it, wiping the cold perspiration from her forehead with her sleeve.

The moonlight filtering through the remaining glass in the window touched her strong square hands; she held them up in front of her, spreading the fingers wide.

I am a murderer, she thought. With these two hands I have taken the life of a human being.

She got out of the chair again and began to pace up and down with her hands thrust under her armpits.

She had killed a German. The right and the wrong of it didn't matter; the immediate thing to decide was her next action. Little by little the methodical, phlegmatic peasant in her resumed control. She began to plan.

No one must know what had happened. And the only way to ensure permanent secrecy was to dispose of the body before morning; to carry it up on to the plateau, or better still, into the forest on the other side of the village. Carry it up there in the handcart.

Thérèse grimaced. Even so, it was a possibility. A corpse might lie there for weeks under a covering of rotting leaves and ferns . . . But as her mind considered and rejected various ways and means, the innermost part of her had already decided on the only possible course. Having killed him, she must dig a grave for him somewhere in the convent garden and bury him immediately. But there must be no sign of a freshly dug grave. The frozen earth must appear smooth and undisturbed . . . She continued to pace up and down.

She wasn't sorry she had killed him. On the contrary, she only wished that she could be given the power to annihilate all the other Prussian bastards who dared to set foot on Belgian soil.

The moon shifted a little, gleaming through a lower pane in the kitchen window. Thérèse roused herself, and with her sabots in her hand slipped out of the convent again and across the courtyard. She fetched a spade and went through the wicket gate that led to the orchard, where gnarled fruit trees threw their convulsed witch-shadows on the silvered grass.

At the far end of the orchard she stopped, and stood measuring with her eye a rectangle six feet by two. She began to dig, severing the frost-stiffened grass and trying to force the spade into the hard earth. It was very difficult.

Impatiently she leaned all her weight on the spade then stamped her sabot on its shoulder. The blade penetrated the soil for about an inch; no more. Cursing under her breath she rammed the spade into the resistant earth, using it like a bludgeon. A thin triangle of frozen turf flew up.

She tried again and again, chipping up bits of the hard-packed earth until at last she succeeded in getting below the frost level. Then she encountered tree roots.

Hacking furiously, she lost her temper. She flung the spade down and kicked it, lashing out with her sabot while tears of angry frustration filled her eyes.

God rot the German. Because of him and his huge stupid war which no one understood, here she was in the early hours of a bitter December morning, trying to dig a grave in which to bury his fool body. It was all his fault. If he hadn't come here she wouldn't have killed him, or had to dig a hole for him in soil so understandably reluctant to receive his unspeakably stinking corpse . . .

Furiously she dashed the tears away and began digging again.

Poor Thérèse Aubel. A quiet, hard-working peaceful peasant woman who wanted nothing more than the warm comfort of her bed. And that was another thing. Due to this rotting Boche and his unspeakable activities she had been deprived not only of her rightful bed, but of its rightful co-occupant. Once she had had a husband called Henri Aubel, but now she was in all probability a widow. A poor homeless, helpless widow living as best she might in a cold convent with a pack of useless women who were of no practical value to her whatever.

Who has the sole responsibility? thought Thérèse, furiously attacking another root. Me. Who worries about food, and the rain coming through the roof? Me. And whom do they all look to when they are frightened, cold, hungry, and about to give birth? Me . . .

The overwhelming sense of grievance ran through her, heating her with fresh fury.

And what if anything should happen to me? Supposing I should die out here, of exposure, of a heart-attack, and they should find my body — would they care? Not they. One is senile, one is concerned only with the welfare of her child, and the other is a poor deranged spinster who, in the midst of the holocaust of war, has the temerity to upset us all with the violence of her menopause . . .

Panting, Thérèse paused for a moment. Aided by the strength of her rage the work was well on the way towards completion.

Then she stiffened, every nerve tingling. Abruptly her anger faded, leaving her helpless and very vulnerable.

A human shadow was advancing silently over the moon-lit grass. She waited until it drew level with her own; until, twin-like, they both fell across the grave she had prepared for the murdered German soldier.

CHAPTER FIVE

'Thérèse,' whispered Clothilde in a shaking voice, 'what are you doing out here at this time of night?'

With her tousled hair and thin body shrouded in a dark shawl she had the appearance of a ruffled, apprehensive bird.

Thérèse dropped the spade and turned to her. She waited until the heavy pounding of her heart had subsided a little.

'I am digging a grave,' she said at length.

Clothilde gasped. In the moonlight her eyes looked enormous.

'For whom?'

'I have killed a German. He was in the outhouse, stealing the goose.'

'Holy Mother of sorrows . . .' whispered Clothilde. She pulled the shawl closer to her throat, glancing round her uneasily. 'Where is he?'

'In the outhouse.'

'And the goose?'

'It is safe.'

They paused, staring at one another, and it occurred to Thérèse that this was the nearest approach to a conversation they had had for several weeks.

'Help me,' Thérèse said simply. 'I am in grievous trouble.'

Taking turns with the spade they finished digging the grave, then crept back through the wicket gate towards the outhouse.

'How did you kill him?' whispered Clothilde, watching fearfully as Thérèse slowly unfastened the bolt on the door.

'With the hatchet.'

'Did he — was it instantaneous?'

I believe so . . .'

They winced in unison as the door creaked on its hinges. Once again, moonlight revealed the dark figure lying face down on the floor. The goose riffled its feathers uneasily.

The two women stared at the body as if mesmerized. At last Thérèse roused herself and said, 'You will have to help me carry him. Take his legs, and mind how you go.'

Obediently, Clothilde stepped inside the outhouse. Steeling herself, she bent down to take the man's legs then recoiled with a muffled cry of horror.

His hand was moving, the fingers slowly flexing against the cold earth floor.

'He is not dead!' she cried.

Without taking her eyes from the man's painfully groping fingers Thérèse said in a voice that shook, 'Cut off a chicken's head and the bird will continue to run until the nerves cease to function.'

'I tell you,' whispered Clothilde again, 'that he is not dead. He is not dead, I tell you.'

Helplessly they looked at one another, searching one another's desperate faces in the fickle moonlight.

'He has lost much blood,' Thérèse said at length, her cold lips barely moving. 'He will be dead by morning.'

Involuntarily their eyes moved to the door and to the heavy iron bolt on it. The sane thing was surely to bolt the door and go away; to leave him for dead, to ignore the truth of the last few seconds and swear to one another that they had been mistaken in thinking that his fingers had moved His pestilential, pilfering Boche fingers, Thérèse thought, suddenly conscious of an overwhelming weariness.

Again, she and Clothilde sought one another's eyes, search-ing silently and deeply for the decision that must be taken.

'Yes,' said Thérèse finally, as if Clothilde had spo-ken. She gave a deep sigh. 'We had better put him in the library. There, with luck, the other two will not discover his whereabouts.'

The German seemed to be unconscious still, and they struggled to lift his inert body off the floor. As they staggered outside with it Thérèse was aware of blood trickling on to her hands.

Somehow they got him into the convent, across the hall and into the library. They crept upstairs to fetch a spare pal-liasse and one of the small straw pillows. Closing the shut-ters, Thérèse lit a candle and stood it on a book, close to the German. The back of his tunic was soaked with blood. She ripped it open, then tore away his shirt. The wound stretched from the fleshy top of his left shoulder and ran diagonally towards his spine. It looked like a jagged, thin-lipped mouth dribbling blood, and Clothilde closed her eyes as she held the bowl of water for Thérèse, who was bathing it, none too gently. When she had finished she made a pad out of some old linen and secured it in place with a long strip torn from a tablecloth.

As an afterthought, she bent down again and removed the man's boots and then, finally, his deeply curved helmet. He had short brown hair with flecks of grey at the temples. His eyes were closed.

They left him lying on his front with his face turned towards a broken statue of the Virgin.

Dawn found Thérèse and Clothilde huddled sleepless and hollow-eyed on Thérèse's bed. The grey silence of winter surrounded them.

'I wish a bird would sing,' Clothilde said, rousing herself.

'For that you will have to wait until spring. And who knows — the war may be over by then.'

'How could it be,' Clothilde said hopelessly, 'with all these Germans everywhere?'

Thérèse got off the bed. 'Take heart, friend,' she said laconically. 'Between us we have already accounted for two of them. And incidentally, if we are to continue the work of extermination on a rotary basis, the next victim is up to you.'

'How *can* you?' exclaimed Clothilde, recoiling. 'How can you joke about such things?'

'Because jokes are all we have left. They have taken away everything else.'

Thérèse unplaited her knot of thick black hair, brushed it, divided it into three strands and began to plait it again. She wound the plait round on top of her head and jabbed the hairpins in place, and once again Clothilde was struck by her matter-of-factness, her enviable ability to take things as they came. By comparison, she felt miserably inadequate.

'Are you never afraid?' she asked in a low voice.

Thérèse lowered her hands from her head. 'Afraid?' she repeated. 'There were moments last night when I almost died of it.'

They paused, looking at one another in the cheerless light, and for a moment the memory of Clothilde's excursion to Dinant touched them with a simultaneous desire to refer to it; brought closer by last night's shared horror it would have been comparatively easy for Thérèse to ask her about it, and for Clothilde, bereaved and desolated, it would have been a marvellous relief to have told her. But they hesitated, and smiling uncertainly at one another felt the moment slip away.

'Considering the sleepless night we have spent,' Thérèse said, turning away, 'I think we both deserve some hot coffee before the other two appear.'

She went downstairs, while Clothilde crept into her own room to perform her toilette.

In the kitchen Thérèse kindled the fire and they sat drinking their coffee.

'Luck is with us in one respect,' she observed. 'The weather has turned so misty that one can scarcely see across the courtyard. With any luck, it may discourage the Germans from searching too diligently for their comrade.'

'You think they will come here?' ventured Clothilde.

Thérèse frowned. 'Who can tell? We must be prepared.'

They sat in silence. During the vigil on Thérèse's bed, shuddering nausea had prevented them from discussing the affair in the outhouse in any detail, almost as if by ignoring it they could undo it. But now with a new day ahead of them came the ability, if not the desire, to face the consequences of what had happened.

At length Clothilde said uneasily, 'I wonder whether he is — is still alive?'

'It would be far simpler if he were dead,' mused Thérèse. 'Then we could simply bury him as arranged.'

'Alive or dead, the situation is terrible.'

'If I had had any sense I would have finished him off, there and then.'

Clothilde shivered, but said nothing.

Thérèse set down her empty cup, rose and went to the kitchen door. When she looked back at Clothilde her face was full of the old, dogged courage. 'It is time to review the situation,' she said. 'Are you coming?'

Very unwillingly, Clothilde went. Crossing the hall they decided to say nothing of what had happened to Yvette or Grand'mère; instinct told them that the fewer people involved, the better.

Outside the library Thérèse took the key from her skirt pocket and slipped it into the lock.

The room was in darkness, and there was no sound. Crossing to the windows Thérèse opened the shutters to the thick tendrils of mist that crept and swayed outside.

The German was alive. Lying on his belly as they had left him, he was breathing stertorously. A quick glance showed them that blood had soaked through the improvised bandaging. Clothilde's thin fingers gripped Thérèse's arm.

With a set face Thérèse walked up to the man and leaned over him. His eyes were half open and spasmodically he raised his close-cropped head then let it fall heavily back on the pillow.

'You are in much pain?' Thérèse asked.

The man grunted. Thérèse straightened up and turned to Clothilde.

'We shall need some more hot water,' she said, 'and some fresh linen.'

White-faced, Clothilde nodded and departed.

When she returned Thérèse had removed all but the final layer of bandage. With a little more gentleness than she had shown the night before, she soaked it away while Clothilde, with eyes averted, held the bowl of water.

The wound gaped at them, fresh blood welling up and spilling over the jagged edges. Thérèse put down the cloth she had been using and wiped her forehead on her arm.

'It is bad,' she said in an undertone. It will never heal left as it is.'

Together they stood looking down on the German, two women in whom the need to kill struggled ever more feebly with the desire to make better.

'It will never heal, left thus,' repeated Thérèse. 'Already he has lost far too much blood.'

There is still a chance. Go out, lock the door, live through today without thinking about him, and he will bleed to death. Then you and Clothilde can bury him. Bury him, and good riddance to his stinking Boche corpse . . .

The man moved his head, closed his eyes for a moment and then reopened them. On the cheek that was visible was a faint stubble of beard. A trickle of blood slipped over the neck of the wound and moved leisurely over his white skin.

Thérèse Aubel drew a deep breath. 'We shall have to sew him up,' she said.

Clothilde, now pale green, raised huge hollow eyes. 'We?'

'By we,' amended Thérèse. 'I really mean you.'

Abruptly galvanized into action she gave Clothilde a brisk shove and said, 'You are the couturier, not I. Go and get your needle and some embroidery silk if you have it. The unspeakable Boche here needs a pleat in his hide.'

Choking, Clothilde fled to her sewing machine, pulled open the little drawer in it and took out her flannel needle-case and a skein of white embroidery silk. She took up her dressmaker's scissors and then, as an afterthought, her thimble.

There was no sound from Yvette or Grand'mère upstairs as she crossed the hall on her way back to the library. Pushing open the door, she was conscious of the weight of sickness in the pit of her stomach. She swallowed convulsively, then walked over to the German.

Thérèse had closed the shutters again and the candle-light seemed to illuminate nothing but the wound.

With a shaking hand she reached for the little gold pince-nez on the fine chain round her neck. She clipped them to her nose, then, sinking on to her knees by the side of the improvised bed, selected a crewel needle and carefully threaded it with a length of white silk.

'Put a knot in the end,' murmured Thérèse with a grim smile.

Helplessly Clothilde dropped her hands in her lap. 'But I have never done anything like this before,' she stammered.

'So here is a fine opportunity for you to begin,' replied Thérèse remorselessly. Wringing out the cloth she wiped away another trickle of blood, then with the palms of her hands pressed the edges of the gaping wound together.

'Commence,' she said.

The man's flesh was cold. Almost as cold as her own. With shaking fingers Clothilde held the lower corner of the wound steady, then with a desperate prayer to the Holy Mother drove the needle through it. The man cried out. Thérèse put her hand over his mouth.

'Get on—' she hissed. 'For the love of Christ, woman, get on with it!'

Somehow Clothilde did as she was told. With her pince-nez glimmering in the candlelight she pressed the needle home, then slowly pulled the reddening silk through the man's quivering skin. She took another stitch. Another and then another. Thérèse removed her hand from his mouth and wiped his forehead with a clean cloth.

The wound grew smaller, shrinking from a wide grimace to a pursed buttonhole. When the last stitch had been taken Clothilde snipped the silk and knotted it. Her fingers were crimson with blood.

Thérèse grinned at her. 'Well done,' she said. 'We'll make a surgeon of you yet.'

They re-bandaged the man, then Clothilde went to warm some milk for him while Thérèse tried to make him a little more comfortable.

'We must be careful, I can hear Yvette talking to the baby,' whispered Clothilde, returning. 'She will be coming downstairs in a minute.'

Thérèse gathered the bloodstained bandages together. 'Give him the milk,' she said, 'while I dispose of these,' Swiftly she withdrew.

Left alone with the German, Clothilde knelt down and held the mug out to him.

'Milk,' she said timidly. 'Please drink,'

The one clouded eye that was visible cleared a little. He made an unsuccessful attempt to lever himself up. Putting the mug on the floor she tried to help him. Clumsily he half-rose to his knees. She offered him the mug, sitting on the side of the makeshift bed, and he began to drink with the uneven gulping noises of a small child.

Her arm was round him, the side of his head resting against her breast. When he had finished drinking he looked at her for the first time and his eyes were full of tears.

* * *

During the day the mist thickened steadily. The wind dropped, and outside the convent the slow drip of moisture was the only sound to break the silence.

Leaving the others to attend to the routine indoor tasks Thérèse groped her way across the courtyard, ostensibly to feed the goose. The blood had dried and become undetectable on the earth floor. She picked up the hatchet and restored it to its accustomed place against the wall outside. From its corner, the goose eyed her suspiciously.

'You had a narrow escape, my friend,' Thérèse observed, giving it the plateful of scraps they could so ill afford. 'But I fear it is merely a short reprieve. In four more days you will be eaten.'

Outside, she glanced towards the orchard and the grave that had been prepared for the German. She decided to leave matters as they were for the present; it was unlikely that anyone would find his way to it in the enveloping mist, and although her medical knowledge was no more than rudimentary, instinct told her that the German might yet need a place of interment. Tired and depressed, it was now a matter of indifference to her whether he lived or died. He must take his chance, and she, his would-be murderer, must do the same.

She returned to the kitchen, where Yvette had finished the baby's washing and was hanging it across the ceiling on a string.

'You had better help me prepare the meal,' Thérèse said.

Yvette did as she was told. They began to clean the vegetables.

'Pare them thinly,' Thérèse said. 'We are going to be very short of food by the spring.'

They worked in silence, filling the black iron pot with carrots and turnips and potatoes and then setting it on the fire to simmer with onions and herbs.

Rolling down her sleeves, Thérèse stared thoughtfully at Yvette.

'Your hands are chapped,' she remarked, 'and now I come to observe it, your face is pale and thin. In some ways, I think that the life here is unsuitable for you.'

Alarm flashed in the girl's eyes. 'I am happy,' she said quickly, 'and I would not wish to be anywhere else.'

'You are too young to be buried away.'

'I am secure.'

Thérèse grunted. Yvette sat down opposite her.

'I am happy here,' she repeated, 'and I would never wish to go elsewhere. But sometimes I do wish, just a little, that something exciting would happen.'

'Exciting?' repeated Thérèse, 'What kind of thing had you in mind?'

'Well,' replied Yvette, linking her chapped hands round her knees, 'I wish we could capture a spy, or ambush some Uhlans, or perhaps rescue a Belgian general. Something brave and dangerous, for life is, you must admit, a little dull.'

Dull, thought Thérèse. With a half-dead German hidden in the library and a hundred others probably combing the area for him . . .

She looked across at Yvette, at her ingenuous young face and at her baby asleep in his wooden box and it occurred to her that she had betrayed their trust.

Supposing the soldier died and his fellow Germans discovered his grave in the orchard? And supposing he didn't die, what would be his reaction to them, once he was well again? Either way the outlook was bleak, and all because she had lost her temper. If only she had stopped to think that the loss of one goose was infinitely preferable to the loss of five lives . . .

'Courage, Thérèse. The war will end and all the dirty Boche will go back home again,' said Yvette.

Thérèse roused herself, forcing a smile. 'I hope you are right,' she replied.

The German didn't die. On the contrary, before two more days had passed he was strong enough to sit up, resting his injured back against a thick padding of pillows and blankets.

In order to keep his presence from Yvette and Grand'mère, Thérèse would divert their attention while Clothilde slipped into the library with a cup of warm goat's milk or a bowl of thin gruel. Twice a day she sponged his hands and face, conscious of the cloth rasping over his cheeks.

'Our sincere apologies, Monsieur Fritz,' said Thérèse, 'but razors are not normally found in a well-conducted convent.'

In spite of her casual tone she eyed him cautiously, trying to read the thoughts which lay behind the invalid pallor and the pleasant, rather homely features, but so far as she could judge he evinced no immediate thirst for reprisal. Perhaps he was unable to remember what had happened in the outhouse. Discussing the matter in whispers she and Clothilde devoutly hoped so, and came to the conclusion that his reactions were probably also hampered by his inability to speak French. For their part, they knew no German.

There was nothing to do but hope for the best.

By Christmas Eve the mists had cleared and a gleam of cold sunlight illuminated the kitchen. Cheered by it, Thérèse went out to slaughter the goose, and when she returned everyone except Clothilde helped her to pluck it and the feathers were saved to replenish Grand'mère's mattress.

Despite the war the spirit of Christmas seized them, and Yvette in particular was filled with a sudden urgent happiness. Tirelessly she worked, sweeping and scrubbing their living quarters and then chopping an extra heap of logs which she stacked in a neat pile by the shining range. Later, she went out and gathered an armful of evergreen, and when she had decorated the kitchen with it her pleasure was so intense that she called to Clothilde and Thérèse to come and share it.

'They are in the chapel,' said Grand'mère, who was sitting by the fire nursing Albert. 'Clothilde has spent all day preparing the chapel for Christmas. Her hands are blue with cold.'

'I suppose it is foolish to prepare the chapel for services when there is no priest to conduct them,' said Yvette, adjusting a tendril of ivy round the photograph of Thérèse and her husband, 'but I understand how she feels. Sometimes it is necessary to be foolish.'

She went down the passage to the hall, on her way to the chapel. Outside the library she stopped. The door was ajar. Surprised, she pushed it open and went in. Thérèse was standing by the window and Clothilde was opposite, a bowl and a spoon in her hand. On the floor between them was a makeshift bed, and in it, sitting up with his back against the wall, was a man.

Yvette said nothing, but her face drained of colour. Thérèse saw her first.

'Yvette,' she said quietly. 'Come here.'

The girl remained motionless. Only her eyes moved. They took in the tired-faced, crop-headed man, the white bandaging under his grey shirt, and the heavy army boots lying side by side. When they reached the deep curved German helmet upturned near the head of the bed she gave a little cry.

'Yvette,' repeated Thérèse, 'come here.'

The girl turned her head very slowly, looking at both of the women in turn.

'You are traitors,' she said finally, then turned and fled. Dismayed, they hurried after her.

Bursting through the kitchen door she tried to slam it in their faces but Thérèse wrenched it open again. Grand'mère, who was still nursing Albert, looked up in surprise.

'Yvette,' said Thérèse sternly, 'for the love of God calm yourself. The Boche is wounded — there was no other alternative—'

'You are harbouring the enemy—' cried Yvette, beside herself. 'I have admired you and love you and tried to emulate you, and now I discover that you are both traitorous—' She burst into noisy tears.

'Please, listen . . .' entreated Clothilde. 'I — that is, we—' She glanced across at Thérèse.

'I refuse to listen — I refuse to listen!' sobbed Yvette, rapidly approaching hysterics.

Thérèse gave her a ringing slap. Abruptly silenced, the girl stood with her hand on her cheek, her eyes still brimming with tears.

'I tried to kill him,' Thérèse said at length. 'And I failed.'

'What happened?' Her voice sounded parched.

'He tried to steal the goose. It was at night. I attacked him with the hatchet but I only succeeded in wounding him.'

'But you did hope to kill him?' As a means of re-establishing her faith in them it seemed extraordinarily important that Thérèse should have intended to take his life.

'His grave still awaits him in the orchard,' Thérèse said wearily.

Fingering her cheek, Yvette said, 'If you wounded him badly, why did you not leave him to die for lack of attention?'

Thérèse stared back at her, her peasant face impassive. 'Try it,' she said curtly.

There was silence, except for Albert gurgling on Grand'mère's lap. Firelight gleamed in the shining kitchen and touched the dark green leaves with which it had been festooned. The goose, trussed ready for the oven, lay in a big oval dish in the centre of the table.

'Christmas is a time of goodwill,' ventured Clothilde, making pleats in her blouse.

'I agree,' said the girl. 'But at no time of the year do I love my enemies.'

She stood facing them, and it suddenly became apparent how much she had changed during the past three months. The ragamuffin girl from the dubious café had found a sense of direction, and suddenly finding it in jeopardy she was confused and deeply upset.

'I do not understand,' she said, turning away from them. 'I just do not understand.'

'As a woman in her middle years,' said Thérèse with a sigh, 'I can only advise you not to try. To comprehend the vagaries of human behaviour, including our own, is beyond most of us.'

'But I wanted to *believe*—' exclaimed Yvette, suddenly turning round, 'in the right and wrong you taught me—'

She stopped abruptly, and in the silence that ensued they heard the sound of hooves outside on the cobbles. Startled, they looked at one another. They heard men's voices, and as they drew nearer Thérèse knew they were speaking in German.

There was no time to speak, or to plan. Helplessly they waited for what was to come, and Thérèse's last coherent thought was that if they saw Grand'mère dozing by the fire with the baby on her lap, there was a faint chance that they at least might be spared . . .

The pounding on the door seemed to shake the convent to its foundations. Grand'mère woke with a gasp. Brusquely Thérèse motioned Clothilde and Yvette behind her, then walked across to the door. She opened it.

Four German soldiers stood outside, their faces livid in the flaring light of a torch. From behind them came the clink of harness.

Thérèse stood looking at them, her lips tightly compressed.

'Food,' shouted one of the soldiers, jerking his head towards the village street. 'The Area Kommandant has graciously permitted a small sack of flour and four kilos of potatoes to each house. You are ordered to collect them immediately.'

She watched them mount their horses and clatter out of the courtyard, their shadows jumping. Closing the door she bolted it and leaned her back against it, and it was some moments before anyone could speak.

* * *

The four women were up early next morning, and whatever emotional undercurrents ran beneath the surface they each made a private resolution not to spoil Christmas Day by referring to them.

Clothilde went out of her way to converse with Yvette, while the girl, still somewhat subdued, did her best not to dwell on the duplicity of the two friends whom she had learned to honour.

While the goose was cooking, they exchanged their pathetic little gifts; Grand'mère had baked some tiny gingerbreads, Clothilde had embroidered a little smock for Albert, while Thérèse presented Yvette with a pair of mitts made from rabbit skins which she had cured herself.

During the course of the morning Clothilde slipped away to the chapel; disturbed by her appearance a blackbird flew up from the Altar, scolding vigorously. His wingbeat disturbed the still air, and when she had finished her devotions she set to work, sweeping and dusting.

And over in the convent kitchen, the roasting of the goose was nearing completion; lovingly basted, it gently sizzled and gave forth its incomparably beautiful aroma, driving the women into a near-ecstasy of anticipation. Flushed by the warmth of the kitchen they spread the table with a clean white cloth and set out the knives and forks, hovering meanwhile over the simmering vegetables to make sure that they would be cooked at precisely the right moment.

With their sleeves rolled down and their hair carefully tidied, Grand'mère and Yvette had taken their place at the table when the kitchen door opened and Clothilde reappeared.

'Hurry yourself, child,' said Grand'mère. All is ready.'

But something about Clothilde's expression made them pause. They stared at her pale features and at her huge eyes, kindled by a strange, shy kind of pleading. As they watched she came slowly into the room and they saw that she was leading the German by the cuff of his grey army shirt.

No one spoke.

He seemed taller, standing up; taller, yet very ordinary. In some respects he might almost have been a Belgian.

Mutely he followed Clothilde to the table, where she pulled out her chair and motioned him to sit down. He did so. He was next to Yvette.

The girl remained motionless, staring into her lap, and they all waited while Clothilde set another place for herself and drew up the last remaining chair. The tension was considerable. Even Grand'mère sat like a figure carved out of wood.

Then Thérèse turned back to the stove, picked up the big oval dish and set it carefully in front of her own place at the table. All eyes were on it. Slowly she picked up the bone-handled carving fork and stood for a moment with it poised above the goose, then abruptly plunged its sharp prongs into the golden, glistening flesh. Rich juices spurted out. Looking up, she met the eyes of the German.

With the carving fork still gripped in her hard possessive fist she stared at him challengingly, defiantly. Then suddenly she grinned. Rather uncertainly, he smiled back. Her grin broadened and she began to laugh, throwing back her head and letting the triumphant sound ring out. The tension eased, and they all began to talk and smile while Thérèse carved the goose and Grand'mère insisted on serving the vegetables. Clothilde said grace, and then the meal began.

It was superb. And when they had finished Yvette took the baby on her lap and trickled a spoonful of the gravy into his gaping-bird mouth, and the German put out his finger and touched him shyly.

'Have you children of your own?' Thérèse asked him in sign language. The German opened his empty hands and shook his head, and there was something curiously forlorn about him. It occurred to them for the first time that he might not be committed to military aggression purely for its own sake; he had tried to steal the goose, but perhaps it was merely to relieve his hunger. And hunger was a thing that everyone understood.

'Who is he?' Grand'mère whispered to Thérèse.

'A friend,' she replied.

During the afternoon the sun disappeared behind a bank of leaden cloud and the wind dropped. Dressed in an odd assortment of jackets and shawls they went over to the chapel, squeezing one by one through the narrow aperture in the broken stonework.

They moved slowly down the aisle and Clothilde gave them all a candle which they lit and placed below the statue of the Virgin which she had so painstakingly put together again. Without speaking they formed a half circle in front of the little crib, and they became part of the extraordinary peacefulness that had fallen over the Western Front.

From Switzerland to the North Sea men were pausing in the business of slaughtering one another, the more venturesome clambering out of their rat-infested trenches to shake hands in No Man's Land. All up and down the line they were exchanging cigarettes, comparing family photos and warming the temporary friendships with nips from each other's flasks.

On 25 December, 1914, the world momentarily regained its sanity, and in the convent chapel at St Louis les Bois the German stood with the four Belgian women and began to sing *Stille Nacht, Heilige Nacht.*

Staring at the High Altar, lovingly dressed in the gold panoply of Christmas, Thérèse was the first to join in.

'All is calm, all is bright . . .' she sang in French, and in a moment they were all singing. Yvette shifted the baby from one arm to the other, and when the German gently took him from her she smiled. They sang all the carols they knew, and it no longer surprised them that they should be familiar to Belgians and Germans alike.

The first snowflake fell, spiralling down through the open roof on to Grand'mère's shawl. Singing, she touched it with her finger and it melted. The second fell on Albert's forehead and the German unbuttoned his field-grey tunic and gathered it protectively round him.

The snow began to settle, dusting the brown pews and hiding the scars on the floor. A candle flame died with a tiny hiss. When they came to the end of the carols they went back to the beginning again, reluctant to break the spell.

Silent Night, Holy Night,
All is calm, all is bright . . .

Singing, they watched the snow falling on the Altar, building up flake by flake until the gold of the cloth was no more than a faint gleam beneath the white.

They stayed until Grand'mère began to shiver. Yvette held out her arms for the baby and she, Thérèse and the old woman quietly left the chapel, their footprints blackening the smooth whiteness of the aisle.

Neither Clothilde nor the German noticed them go. They remained side by side with the snow falling softly on their shoulders. It was growing dark and the gold of the Altar had been completely obliterated when he reached for her hand. She allowed him to take it, and to caress with his thumb the thin spinster fingers that had so reluctantly sewn up the rent in his flesh.

He was the first man ever to take her hand and she didn't even know his name.

CHAPTER SIX

The winter crawled slowly through the cold and wretchedly illuminated houses of Belgium and Northern France.

At the dawn of 1915 there had been a brief spark of optimism that conditions would improve, but as the weeks passed the news was not reassuring. Rumour had it that fifty thousand French had been sacrificed in an advance of five hundred yards in Champagne, while sixty thousand were lost at St Mihiel.

Yet in spite of huge casualty lists the tempo of the war had slowed down, its cumbersome mechanization floundering in the mud of Flanders. Conditions hardened, and hatred solidified.

Nevertheless, fate conceded one or two odd moments of joy, little isolated incidents that sparkled briefly in the surrounding gloom. The Germans were now providing regular if meagre rations for the civilian population and occasionally one might receive a fraction of a kilo more than the allotted portion; firearms being forbidden, an old man in St Louis les Bois shot a deer with an improvised bow and arrow, and the cosseted hen belonging to the Widow LePage laid an egg with a triple yolk. In times of privation, most pleasures are closely allied to the stomach.

In the convent where the four women had made their home, the baby Albert cut his first tooth on 15 February, and two weeks later someone came tapping on the door late at night, mumbled the name of Thérèse Aubel and then thrust an envelope into her hand before melting back into the shadows again.

Filled with misgiving she carried it into the kitchen and sat down at the table, close to the candle.

The envelope was in a bad state. Crumpled and mud-splashed, and with the writing almost indecipherable. It was addressed to her at the farm.

Conscious of the curious gaze of Clothilde and Yvette she cut it open and unfolded the single sheet of paper inside. Her heart began to thump heavily.

My dear Wife, it said in Henri's painstaking script, *I write this to let you know that I am safe and well. There has been much hard fighting but things are now somewhat easier. I hope all is well with you. Did Berthe drop her calf safely? It was due in November. I think of you constantly and pray that we may soon be reunited. I embrace you, my dear wife, Your Henri.*

Abruptly she hid her eyes with her hand.

'Thérèse . . .' began Clothilde uncertainly, 'is it something bad?' She half-rose in her chair.

Thérèse shook her head, then stuck the letter back in its envelope and thrust it down the front of her dress.

'It is a letter from Henri,' she said brusquely.

Yvette sprang up with a shriek of joy. She flung her arms round Thérèse and rocked with her backwards and forwards.

'Oh — *Thérèse!* And is he well? He is well and unwounded and coming home? How did the letter come? Tell us, Thérèse—'

'How can I,' gasped Thérèse, 'while you are doing your best to choke the life out of me . . .'

Restored, she took the letter from the neck of her dress and read it to them. Hungrily savouring every word, they demanded that she should read it again. She did so. After that, it was passed round from one to the other, and

Clothilde clipped her pince-nez on her nose and averred that his handwriting betrayed excellent character.

The letter was the principal topic of conversation for weeks; starved of emotional outlet, the few formal and constrained little words from Thérèse's husband set them all on fire. To Yvette he was the archetypal soldier-lover, and she studied the wedding photograph with renewed attention.

'But in truth, he is not at all notable for his appearance,' protested Thérèse. 'To look at, one would have to admit that he is no more than passing average.'

'Ah, but he has a great spiritual quality,' observed Clothilde, peering over her shoulder. 'One may see it gleaming in the eyes.'

'I regret to say,' said Thérèse firmly, 'that at the time the photograph was taken it was wine gleaming in the eyes, rather than spirituality.'

They laughed, they teased her a little, and beneath their pleasure for her lay a simple and entirely unmalicious envy, for malice was impossible in connection with Thérèse.

Clothilde, like the other two, soon knew the letter by heart, and sometimes as she worked she would find herself whispering it like a prayer, an incantation.

'*I embrace you . . .*' the letter ended, and she would speculate on the nature of love between men and women. For some reason the subject had become a little less distasteful to her.

They had heard no more from the German; the quiet soldier whose naked flesh she had touched had said *Auf wiedersehen* and disappeared out of the convent gateway immediately after Christmas when rain was lashing the walls and wind was howling in the kitchen chimney. Because of the language barrier no one had established where he had come from or where he was going to. Thérèse said that he was probably attached to the garrison bivouacked along the road to Namur and that she didn't give much for his chances when he got back.

'What might they do?' ventured Clothilde.

'Shoot him as a deserter,' said Thérèse laconically.

'But not if he explains what happened,' put in Yvette. 'In which case, do you think it likely that he will give us away?'

'No,' replied Thérèse, and Clothilde wanted to ask what made her so sure. Was it because he would have some personal need for prudence, or because he was a gentleman, and one for whom the betrayal of friends would be an impossibility?

She thought of him often, and after a while the enemy aspect of him became less pronounced, as he began to assume an unattainable dream quality in her mind, as Père Joseph had done before him. Sometimes they even showed signs of blending into one entity, Père Joseph representing spirituality while the German, whose body she had tended, filled in some of the adult physical detail hitherto unobtainable and unrequired. She was happy, and despite the subtle widening of experience her dreams were chaste as those of a little child.

For Thérèse however, the letter had had an unsettling effect, and once the initial thankfulness had worn off she had become torn by fresh longings and hopes and fears, and at night she was tormented by dreams the nature of which was anything but chaste. Her furious impatience with the war revived, but eight months' experience had taught her the futility of hating all Germans blindly and indiscriminately. It was more sensible, she decided, to concentrate on those in command, and once, when Clothilde was painstakingly repairing a little statue of St Anthony, asked whether it would be possible for her to construct a small effigy of Kaiser Wilhelm in order that they might stick pins in it.

Clothilde was very shocked.

'Well,' said Thérèse, tramping restlessly round the kitchen in her old sabots, 'we must do something. We have got to do something . . .'

'It is time I killed another Uhlan,' Yvette said slyly. 'Despite my youth, I appear to be the only one capable of it.'

Thérèse snorted. 'Killing is not difficult.'

'But you bungled yours, my old one.'

'Hold your tongue, girl, and attend to your baby. I hear him crying.'

Laughing, Yvette went to fetch Albert. Thérèse stopped pacing round the kitchen and sat on the edge of the table.

'Seriously,' said Clothilde, regarding the statuette with her head on one side. 'No one can condone killing.'

'I can,' said Thérèse. She jerked her thumb at the old woman who was dozing in her chair by the fire. 'I could kill whoever destroyed Grand'mère's world and made her a homeless refugee.'

'Supposing Fritzy had destroyed it?'

Thérèse shrugged irritably. 'I tried to kill him for stealing a goose, did I not?'

'But you failed, as Yvette pointed out.'

'And he, I would also point out, failed to steal the goose. So where does that leave us?'

They fell silent. 'That is not the same thing, Thérèse,' Clothilde said at last.

'I know, muttered Thérèse. 'I know. Women can kill in theory but rarely in practice.'

She got off the table and fetched her jacket, thrusting her arms into the sleeves and buttoning it rapidly.

'I am going to check the rabbit snares,' she announced.

Outside, the air had turned warm and a thrush was singing ecstatically. The old lilac tree by the convent gateway was almost in leaf. It was early April, and the strain of the long winter was over.

She made her way up on to the sandy plateau that overlooked the village, and found the rabbit snares empty. Since the return of the remaining villagers it had been more difficult to obtain a supply of fresh meat, and sometimes she suspected that her snares were poached by other people.

Empty-handed she wandered to the crumbling edge of the plateau and looked down over the meandering main street of St Louis les Bois. She looked towards the narrow cart track bordered by goat willow that led to the farm which she had deliberately destroyed the day the Germans first bombarded Dinant.

The longing to return to it, to walk back down the rough track that rambled through the meadows until it reached the small stone house sheltered by its barns, was overwhelming. With the coming of spring the tang of warm receptive earth found an echo in her blood, and the longing for Henri was at the heart of her restless irritability.

She began to walk down the steep incline towards the village. Crossing the street she nodded curtly to an old man shuffling along in slippers, then turned down by the side, of Yvette's mother's café. Red cotton curtains torn by the shelling and discoloured by the weather hung from one of the first floor windows that remained. Inside the café the marble tables still lay overturned. The spirit of the place was as dead as Yvette's mother.

She went on until she came to the farm track, and the feeling of spring began again. Primroses spangled the rough grass and rooks soared exultantly overhead, calling to one another in hoarse, jovial voices. They too were infected by the magic.

Suddenly she began to run, stumbling over the rough tussocks in her compulsion to return home, and in the shelter of the high hedge small nesting birds watched her anxiously. Her hair began to slip from its pins and she put up her hands to jab them back in place as she ran. Now the need for home was absolute, and she ran like a woman possessed.

Past the first bend where the two elms stood, the mud was thicker. Impatiently she bunched up her skirt in one hand while she thrust aside a long arm of bramble with the other. The thorns tore into her fingers. Sucking greedily at her sabots the mud finally peeled one of them off, and she floundered on for several paces before she realized that it had gone. Her much-darned black stocking was encased in a glistening brown plaster.

She slowed down, panting for breath, and then she noticed the big smoothly fashioned iron wheel that seemed to hang motionless from the sky. She stood on one foot staring at it confusedly, then her eyes traced the long rusting muzzle that lay half-buried in the ditch, festooned with blackberry and convolvulus. It was the remains of a French 75, and across the track, barring her way home, lay the skeleton of a gunner, still dressed in rotting shreds of uniform.

Stunned, she stared down at it and the bleached skull stared back at her, the shining white teeth parted in what looked like a spasm of helpless laughter. Bird droppings lay in one of the empty eye sockets.

She covered her face with her square peasant hands that were covered in blood from the brambles, and she cried bitterly, hopelessly, standing on one foot in the mud of 1915 Belgium. There was no home, no spring; the war had swallowed it all.

She turned back towards the convent, and seeing her face none of them dared to ask where she had been.

* * *

Thérèse was not the only one to be affected by the poignancy of spring, and as the days lengthened and the leaves unfolded the girl Yvette took to going for long walks with her baby propped up in the old handcart.

At six months old Albert was a round-faced, round-eyed person with a light covering of hair the same colour as his mother's. Ensconced in the handcart he viewed the outside world with considerable interest, and when he tired of watching the trees and the birds he would contemplate his mother's face as she trudged along between the small wooden shafts.

She told him about the war, and said that if he wanted to be a famous soldier when he grew up he must work hard and be brave and clever and then he would be like General Leman, who had commanded the defence of Liège.

'And then Maman will be proud of you,' she said. 'And so will Thérèse and Clothilde and Grand'mère.'

The opinions of the three other women were of great importance to her, and whenever she found herself thinking about the future when they would have to leave the convent and go their separate ways she would always push the thought from her mind, telling herself that there was no point in meeting trouble half-way.

At the age of seventeen, day-to-day security was still sufficient.

She was meandering through the woods that stretched away towards Dinant one afternoon when the sudden snapping of a twig made her jump. She froze, and immediately remembered that Thérèse had warned her not to go too far from human habitation as the garrison troops from along the Namur road were not to be trusted, especially when they were drunk.

Trying to appear unconcerned she looked round, searching the gold-speckled shade under the trees, and then she saw him. A lean copper-headed boy in tattered jacket and trousers, leaning against the smooth bole of a tree as if he would fall down without its support.

At the same instant he saw her, standing on the beaten footpath and gripping the shafts of the little handcart in which sat a solemn-eyed baby.

'Grosse Tête . . .' said the girl.

The boy passed his tongue over his dry lips then inclined his head in acknowledgement.

After all that had happened recently it seemed a long while ago to Yvette since she had been at school, sitting next to the supercilious little boy who scorned friendship with the village children. His name was Jean-Baptiste, but because he was unusually clever they nicknamed him *Grosse Tête*.

'Grosse Tête . . . Grosse Tête . . .' they used to chant after him, half derisively and half enviously.

He lived in a hut in the woods with his father, a pale taciturn man who painted strange tortured pictures and offered them for sale in Dinant on market day. Few people bought them, and at the end of the day the man would gather them up again, pile them on to the cracked saddle of his old bicycle and push them home to the hut hidden deep in the trees.

107

Earning so little money people sometimes wondered how he managed to feed himself and the boy Jean-Baptiste, who was apparently his son. There was no sign of a woman.

At irregular intervals the boy would appear at the school in St Louis les Bois, furtively sliding his under-nourished body along the polished form and listening with extraordinary attention to the teacher's words. He seldom spoke unless he was asked a question, and although he was sometimes absent for weeks at a time he always managed to come top in the end of term exams, covering the paper with an urgent and unchildlike scrawl. Once in an arithmetic test Yvette attempted to copy from him, and the force with which he jabbed his thin stick elbow into her ribs drove all the breath from her body. Angered, she kicked him sharply on the ankle and he retaliated by stabbing his pen nib into the back of her hand. The pain made her cry, and they were both sent outside the room in disgrace.

'I hate you,' she said, mopping her eyes. 'You stink.'

He summed up her appearance and her character in one brief and filthy epithet before turning away to read the noticeboard.

He was thin and dirty and ill-mannered, with a wild mop of red hair and boots with soles that gaped in a crocodile grin, and standing in the wood looking at him she suddenly remembered that old Grosse Tête had been awarded a special scholarship to study at Louvain University. The schoolmaster, Monsieur Groult, had been very excited about it because no one from St Louis les Bois had ever done such a thing before; but of course, that was last summer. Before the war, and before the Germans came.

'What is the matter?' the girl asked, frowning. 'Are you ill?'

He sagged against the tree, his head hanging.

'It is possible,' he muttered, then, pulling himself up with a great effort, added, 'How far am I from home?'

'From the hut?'

He nodded.

'I am not sure. I believe it lies somewhere beyond the next clearing where the shrine stands.'

He didn't answer, but leaned against the tree with his eyes closed. Suddenly concerned, she pushed the handcart over the soft sandy loam towards him.

'Grosse Tête,' she said, 'what has happened to you? Where have you come from?'

He opened his eyes and looked at her and their lifelessness frightened her.

'Germany,' he said.

It took some time to find the hut because, like everyone else from the village, she had no more than a vague idea of its exact whereabouts, while the boy himself seemed too exhausted to remember the way.

The second time he stumbled she made him sit on the edge of the handcart while she pushed it, his broken boots trailing through the leaves. Albert regarded him impassively.

The place stood in a bramble thicket, impenetrable on three sides. Yvette approached it warily, unsure of the reception she would receive if the man were there.

But the hut was empty. Giving way against her weight the door opened with a groan and the soft tearing of spiders' webs. Growing used to the gloom she saw the two rough bunks down either side, the iron stove gingered with rust and the table still covered with faded newspaper. Against the far wall stood a pile of canvases knitted together by cobwebs and in a cardboard box was a pile of books. Mice had nibbled the only candle.

'Welcome home,' murmured Grosse Tête. He stumbled over the threshold and collapsed on to one of the bunks. A small cloud of dust rose up from the moth-eaten blanket and hovered in the stale air. He lay on his back, contemplating Yvette. He was very thin, the pale skin stretched tightly over his bones.

'My father and I were deported to Germany,' he said. 'About two hundred of us were taken from the cave near Mont Fat. We walked to Liège. There we were herded into cattle trucks. My father had been wounded by a shell splinter and he died on the second day. We were given half a loaf each and some water. When we reached Germany we were given a bowl of soup. We were put in prison at a place near Cologne. It was very cold and the old man next to me died in his sleep. They took the youngest and strongest and put us to work in a munitions factory. I had to load shell cases on to goods trains in the sidings. At night we were marched back to the prison. I escaped.'

Outside in the handcart, Albert began to cry. Quickly the girl ducked through the low doorway and brought him in. She sat down on the edge of the bunk with him and stared at Grosse Tête over the top of his head.

'Yours?'

She nodded.

'To whom are you married?'

'I am married to no one.'

A faint smile flickered over his face. 'That is bad.'

'On the contrary,' said Yvette. 'It is good.'

'How so?'

'Men are stupid.'

'Is that not the beginnings of a man you hold in your arms?'

The girl bit her lip. 'That is different,' she said. 'He is my son.'

Ah,' said the boy, closing his eyes. 'Then of course it is different.'

She sat looking at his pinched white face, then blushed when he suddenly opened his eyes again. She stood up, holding Albert against her shoulder.

'You must have some food,' she said. 'And you need nursing.'

'Food, yes,' he replied. 'But nursing, no thank you.'

'You are ill. You cannot remain alone.'

'I can,' he said, and closed his eyes again. She stood in the doorway, irresolute. Albert was heavy in her arms.

'You are stupid,' she said, 'and I will return with food.'

He didn't answer. He had fallen asleep.

Thérèse was in the kitchen garden planting a second crop of peas when she got back to the convent. Seeing Yvette, she sat back on her heels.

'The broad beans are up,' she said, and held out her arms for Albert.

'Magnificent,' said the girl. 'I wish I could grow things the way you do.'

'You have just grown a very fine baby,' replied Thérèse, playing with him. 'Truly, he is second to none.'

'Thérèse,' said the girl. 'Can we spare a little food for a boy I was at school with?'

'Has he no food of his own?'

'No. He has nothing.'

Thérèse regarded Yvette through narrowed eyes.

'Who is this boy?'

'His name is Jean-Baptiste, but everyone calls him Grosse Tête. His father was very strange and lived in a hut in the woods and painted pictures. They were both deported to Germany but the father died and Grosse Tête escaped. He is weak and ill.'

'I remember the man,' Thérèse said slowly. 'He was a recluse and painted pictures of Hell. And I believe I remember the child. Had he not red hair?'

'Yes, Thérèse. His hair is red.'

'And where is he now?'

'In the hut.'

Thérèse jounced Albert absent-mindedly. 'There is some milk and some bread and there are two eggs. But if he has escaped all the way from Germany he must surely be weak and in need of nursing.'

'He is,' replied the girl. 'But he is also very stupid. He wishes to remain alone.'

Thérèse shrugged. 'That is his affair. But wait — is he not the boy who won the scholarship to Louvain University?'

'Yes,'

'In which case, he cannot surely be stupid.'

'He is clever at books,' the girl replied. 'But he is stupid at everything else.'

'I understand,' Thérèse said equably.

Leaving Albert with Clothilde and Grand'mère, Yvette set off again carrying a small enamel can filled with hot bread and-milk which she had sprinkled with a little of their precious sugar ration. The door of the hut was still open and he lay sprawled on the bunk in the same position in which she had left him. He was so deeply lost in sleep that she thought for a moment he had died.

Faintly exasperated she set down the can of bread-and milk with a clatter and stood looking round her, hands on hips. The place was horrible. Dirty, dusty, smelly and untidy. With the toe of her shoe she stirred the bit of rag-rug that lay between the two bunk beds and released a cloud of dust. She kicked the rug out of the door and a handful of black beetles fled panic-stricken towards the four corners of the hut.

'Not only are you stupid,' she said to the sleeping boy, 'but you are extremely unclean into the bargain.'

Rolling up her sleeves she set to work, grimacing at the spiders and the beetles and shuddering over the whiskery morsel of food stuck fast to a tin plate. The food cupboard was an orange box nailed to the wall.

Hurling everything out into the dancing sunlight, she went in search of water. When she returned he was still asleep and the bread-and-milk was almost cold.

'Wake up—' she ordered, slapping his cheek.

There was no response. She reached for the worn tin spoon she had just washed, dipped it in the bread-and-milk and passed it slowly in front of his nose.

A slit of eye glimmered momentarily. His cracked lips parted slightly. She slipped the spoon in between them, raising his head with the flat of her hand.

'More,' she commanded, still very stern. 'Open your mouth and eat the good food you are given.'

He swallowed, still asleep. When the bread-and-milk was all gone she allowed his senseless head to fall back on the bunk. Half-jestingly, she crossed his hands on his breast.

She continued to work on the hut, and when she left there were wild laburnum flowers in a mug on the table.

* * *

Incredibly, he slept for five days and five nights.

For the first two days he remained where he had fallen, spreadeagled across the hard bunk in an abandonment of exhaustion. Twice a day Yvette trickled warm milk into his mouth and he swallowed it, quite unaware that he was doing so.

On the third day he shifted his position, and when she arrived he was lying on his side with his bony knees drawn up close to his chin. It was as if he had passed from temporary death into a state where the first groping instinct for self-preservation was beginning to reassert itself. He looked like a fox cub in a corner, a foetus curled snugly in the womb.

'Grosse Tête,' said the girl. 'Wake up. I have brought you an egg beaten in goat's milk . . .'

He smiled as if he were having a marvellous dream, but he didn't wake up.

Not until the evening of the fifth day did he become aware of her. As she approached with the spoon he rolled on to his back and opened his eyes, and they were as fresh and blue as if they had been laundered.

'Mademoiselle Yvette Mazy,' he said. 'And how do you find yourself, this fine day?'

'I find myself very well, thank you, Monsieur Grosse Tête. And you also?'

He nodded, then slowly raised his lean forefinger and touched her cheek.

'At school you were very ugly.'

Affronted, she drew back. 'If I remember correctly, you stank.'

'But you are pretty now. Very pretty . . .'

'Unfortunately,' said the girl, 'you still stink.'

His eyes closed and he drifted into sleep. Presently he said, 'Do something for me . . .'

'Give you a bath?'

'No, thank you.' He smiled with his eyes closed. 'Call me Jean-Baptiste.'

'Jean-Baptiste.'

'And never mind the bath.'

'I could not bring myself to touch you with a pitchfork.'

But when she unwrapped the tattered rags he had worn inside his boots she cried out with pity at the sight of his blistered, suppurating feet.

'Oh, why did I not think to tend them before?' she exclaimed, distressed. She bathed them in spring water then hurried back through the woods to the convent to consult Thérèse, who gave her some boracic from the nuns' little pharmacy cupboard, and some strips of clean linen to bind them with.

'I am overwhelmed by your solicitude, Mademoiselle,' he said. 'What have I done to deserve it?'

She began to wind the bandage carefully round the first foot. 'My name is Yvette,' she said. 'And it is understood that you have won a scholarship to Louvain University. You must be made fit to avail yourself of it in due course.'

He withdrew his foot from her lap so sharply that she almost lost her balance.

'University—' he said bitterly, 'that is the last thing I have in mind. From now on, I propose to devote my life to slaughter, not study.'

She sat on the floor, staring up at him.

'You are a scholar,' she said quietly. 'God made it so.'

'God?' he cried, tense with anger, 'who talks of God? Is there a God who can allow Belgium to be laid in the dust, and a God who saw fit to create Boche hordes to desecrate our soil?'

'Someone must have created them,' she said mildly. The hostility in his expression reminded her of the contemptuous poverty-stricken child who had sat next to her at school. She was amused by him, and a little afraid. To hide it, she reached out for his foot and planted it firmly in her lap again.

114

'Keep still,' she said, 'or else how can I bandage it?'

'I can bandage my own foot,' he said sulkily. 'I have no need of a nitwit woman to do it.'

Exasperated by his ingratitude she flipped the ends of the bandage together and pushed his foot away.

'Very well,' she said. 'Do so. Look after yourself entirely and see how quickly you can return to the level of a pig in a sty—'

'Get out!' he shouted. 'Get out and never come back!'

She went, snatching up Albert and the remains of the boracic and slamming the door behind her.

* * *

'In any case,' he said. 'Louvain has been burned down.'

'I know. But I was trying to say that you will go there to study when it has been rebuilt. When we have won the war.'

'Won the war . . .'

'Of course. Men knock things down, and then they build them up again.'

He grunted. Slowly regaining his strength he was sleeping less, and lying hour after hour on the bunk with only bitter thoughts for company made him increasingly irritable. When she arrived with a little meal for him it was a relief to have someone to snap at.

'Forgive me,' he muttered once. 'Perhaps my temper will improve when I am in the army.'

She said nothing.

'In the army,' he repeated. 'The day after tomorrow I am going. I shall make for the Ypres area.'

'You are not well enough to go. You must wait.'

'I am well. See, I am going for a walk now.'

'Lie down . . .' she said, but he swung his legs over the side of the bunk and stood up. He staggered drunkenly then fell, sprawling like a day-old kitten.

Back on the bunk he turned his face away, but not before she had seen the tears of anger and weakness.

115

'I will go home now,' she said quietly.

'Stay,' he said in a muffled voice. 'I am full of a terrible hatred, but not for you.'

She sat down on the side of the bunk with her hands pressed between her knees.

'I wish you could meet Thérèse,' she said. 'She gets full of hatred too.'

'For whom?' He sounded as if he had a heavy cold, and after a momentary hesitation she offered him a handkerchief made neatly on the sewing machine by Clothilde.

'Oh — the Boche. She and her husband lived at a farm on the other side of the village and Thérèse fired the haystacks and burned the house and the farm buildings rather than let the Germans have them. She never speaks of it, and never visits the place. She is strong and brave and truly exceptional.'

He turned over on his back and she was careful to ignore the tearstains on his face.

'Do you still live at the café?'

'Ha—' the girl said. 'You have not seen the village, of course. It was devastated in the bombardment, and both the café and my mother were—' she grimaced.

'Like me, you are an orphan,' he observed.

'I suppose so,' she said distantly. 'My father may well be dead, for all I know.'

They sat regarding one another cautiously.

'You are very strange,' he said at length.

'And you also,' replied the girl, and it was as if they were looking at one another for the first time.

'Jean-Baptiste,' she said, 'stop playing with my son and attend to what I am saying. I have laundered your shirt and patched your trousers and they are ready for you to put on. I have been unable to find a suitable pair of boots, but as your feet are still far from healed you will no doubt manage with this pair of nun's pattens which I have brought from the convent.'

The boy, who was lying on the bunk with Albert sitting on his chest, glanced across at her and said, 'Would it cause

116

you too much social embarrassment if I changed my mind about meeting your lady friends at the convent?'

She stopped, his clean clothes held in her arms.

'Of course not,' she said after a second's hesitation. 'Please yourself. What you do is no concern of mine.'

She laid the garments aside and began tidying the things on the table with hands that shook slightly.

'I am not accustomed to meeting people,' he said finally. 'I have no knowledge of the right things to say and do.'

'But you have no need of it,' she said, leaning her arms on the table and looking at him earnestly. 'Not with them.'

'They mean a great deal to you?'

'They are my family.'

'Family . . . family . . .' he repeated, shifting restlessly. 'One should have no need of families. One should be capable of standing alone.'

'Are you?'

'But of course.'

'Oh, Jean-Baptiste—' she said.

'What ails you?' he asked sharply.

'I am confused,' she said, rubbing her forehead. 'You think and feel with the same simplicity that I had until last August, and since then I have been discovering that life is not simple at all. And strangely, I have felt so much wiser since I have discovered how little I know.'

'You have frequently called me stupid,' he said. 'I realise now that you meant it.'

'But you cannot *really* be stupid,' she cried, deeply perplexed, 'when you have won a scholarship!'

They sat looking at one another while Albert rolled off the boy's chest and lay on his back, sucking his fingers.

'You are wrong,' Jean-Baptiste said at last. 'Life is quite simple. It is good or it is bad. It is just or it is unjust. Cruel or kind, and mostly—' he added, 'it is cruel.'

'And all Germans are cruel?'

'The only good German is a dead one,' he said.

'And what about me?' she demanded. 'What am I?'

117

'Oh — you,' he said with a grin that annoyed her, 'you are an idiot. But a very pretty one, and one that I suddenly want to kiss.'

He took her hand. She snatched it away, anger flaring.

'Kiss me, Yvette.'

'Kiss you?' she cried, 'I would sooner kiss a pig. I would sooner kiss our goat. At least, she is some use in the world — she gives good milk—'

Reaching across him she swept Albert up in her arms. Disconcerted by his mother's emotion, Albert began to cry. To add to the noise the boy lay back on the bunk, roaring with laughter.

'How dare you laugh at me?' she choked, beside herself with rage. 'How dare you make immoral suggestions to me?'

The boy's laughter increased, Helplessly he stretched out his hand and unexpectedly caught her arm. He held it tightly.

'Yvette . . .' he said. 'Oh beautiful, wise Yvette, have pity on me . . .'

She fought him off, but it was difficult with the howling baby in her arms. He pulled her closer.

'Let *go* of me!' she shouted, and burst into a paroxysm of furious tears. Infected by her wild emotion Albert's howls also increased.

'Let go of me — I loathe and abominate you! You are like all the rest of them . . . but understand once and for all, you stupid, under-nourished evil-smelling pig, that I am not a light woman . . .' She struggled violently, then the rag-rug slipped under her feet and she fell heavily, the roaring baby squashed between them, 'I am no light woman who may be dallied with for a few dirty sous . . . I am not my mother's daughter . . .'

The boy's laughter died. His nostrils became filled with the scent of her long fair hair and her huge hot tears fell on his face like rain. Somewhere between them the baby was fighting a furious battle for freedom.

'Yvette,' the boy said.

'I am not a light woman . . .'

'Oh, my God,' he said, groaning the words against her wet face, 'Oh my God, I love you so . . .'

CHAPTER SEVEN

'You must put on your clean apron, my old one,' Thérèse
said to Grand'mère, 'because the girl Yvette is bringing her
friend to see us.'

'The girl has a friend?' demanded Grand'mère. Why
have I not been told?'

'She has only just—' begun Clothilde, then glanced at
Thérèse. 'It is a friend she had at school, and just recently
they have met again. His name is Jean-Baptiste.'

'Jean-Baptiste,' nodded the old woman. 'It is a good
name.'

'And he is a good boy, by all accounts,' added Thérèse.

Grand'mère nodded again, and composed her ancient
features into an expression of sagacity. A few months ago
it seemed as if she had triumphantly survived the horror of
the German invasion, and that a settled life at the convent
had stabilized the distraught see-sawing of her memory, but
during the past week there had been a gradual return of the
old bewilderment and she would stare at the other women
and wonder who they were. Sometimes it was obvious who
they were, but impossible to recollect their names.

And while the exercise of a little ingenuity generally ena-
bled her to conceal her lapses of memory from them, it was

becoming more difficult to hide the strange lassitude that was creeping over her body like a paralysis. Accustomed to hard work she found weariness no novelty, but this deep clogging sense of fatigue was different from anything she had known before.

Pride forbade her to speak of it, but sometimes it seemed as if the woman Thérèse suspected how things were.

'Keep to your bed for an hour longer, old one,' she would say, going into Grand'mère's room with her meagre breakfast ration set out on a wooden tray. The world will continue to turn as usual, and if the war should suddenly end one of us will certainly remember to tell you . . .'

And so the old woman would lie there after a peck at the food and a sip or two of warm milk, her veined and speckled hands lying at rest on the blanket while her clouded mind drifted somewhere between sleeping and waking.

But on the day the girl Yvette took the son of the recluse artist to the convent she was sitting in the kitchen chair wearing her new black apron and the little lace cap that Clothilde had crocheted for her. Thérèse had managed to assemble the ingredients for a pigeon pie for supper and the smell of baking stirred pleasurable memories in her; somewhere a long time ago there had been another kitchen, a family of small children, and herself at the hub of it all.

'Who did you say is coming?' she asked, rousing herself. 'Is it someone I know?'

'Yvette is bringing a young man to meet us,' Thérèse said patiently.

'Is it arranged that they will marry?'

'I know not,' replied Thérèse, opening the oven door and inspecting the pie. 'That is a matter for Yvette to decide.'

'If he is acceptable I shall advise her to marry him,' the old woman said, suddenly brisk. 'It is time we had a marriage in the family. All you girls need husbands. Especially you.'

'Thank you, but I already have one.'

'Then where is he?' demanded Grand'mère, peering round the kitchen. 'Where is he?'

Thérèse shoved the oven door shut with her sabot. 'I only wish to God I knew,' she said.

* * *

In the forests of the Ardennes the trees were in full leaf and the voice of the cuckoo, drunk with self-esteem, echoed and re-echoed through the gold-flecked shade.

'One could not contemplate living anywhere else but here,' Yvette said as they followed the footpath towards St Louis les Bois.

She was pushing the handcart in which the baby sat while the boy Jean-Baptiste hobbled at her side. He was wearing his freshly laundered shirt and darned trousers, and he had attempted to slick his wild red hair down with water. His feet were still very tender.

'I will be happy enough in the army,' he said. 'Living in a trench.'

Already she had learned to side-step the challenge in many of his statements. 'And after the war?'

'After the war, who knows? I may be dead, and you may be married to a fat profiteer.'

'I will still be here,' she said.

'And will you think of me?'

'Occasionally,' she said, tossing her long hair back. 'If I have nothing better to occupy me.'

They walked on in silence, utterly happy.

When they reached the convent Thérèse was crossing the courtyard with Bibi the goat on its chain. Seeing them, she stood waiting.

'Thérèse,' said Yvette, trundling the handcart to a standstill, 'may I present my friend Jean-Baptiste? Jean-Baptiste, this is Madame Aubel.'

They shook hands very formally and the boy looked like a young animal poised for flight. Thérèse, to whom social formality was almost equally painful, stared down at the wooden pattens he was wearing and said, 'And how are your unfortunate feet, of which we have heard much?'

'My feet are greatly improved, I thank you,' replied Jean-Baptiste, then after a strangled silence had the presence of mind to compliment Thérèse on the fine goat she had.

'A war refugee,' she replied laconically, 'like the rest of us.'

The kitchen door opened and Clothilde appeared with Grand'mère holding her arm, and the sight of them moved the girl to a sudden sparkling conviction that all would go well at this important initial meeting.

'Jean-Baptiste,' she said. 'Allow me to present the rest of my family.'

Introductions accomplished and the ice broken, everyone began to make conversation; Thérèse led the way to the kitchen garden in order that he might view the peas and beans and the early potatoes in full flower, then Yvette showed him some of Clothilde's exquisite embroidery and they all took turns in describing to him the chaos in the convent when they first arrived.

And the boy behaved nobly. Perhaps it was because of Yvette, but possibly he may have sensed that they liked and accepted him because they too loved her; whatever the reason, he dropped his guard little by little and became almost friendly, smiling gravely at them and responding courteously to Grand'mère's lapses of memory.

Several times she addressed him as Gustave, then peering hard at him demanded to know whether or not he was her grandson.

'I think not,' he replied. 'But I wish I were.'

And Yvette flashed him a look of love and warm complicity and he felt glad that she would be safe among such worthy women while he was away fighting in the trenches. After supper he took Albert on his knee with a proprietorial air and in answer to their eager questioning gave them the bare outline of his escape from Germany.

The light was beginning to fade and the earth was releasing its rich evening scent when they heard the hollow ringing of hooves in the courtyard. Sitting over the remains of supper, they looked at one another sharply. Through the open door came the creak of a saddle then the thump of boots on the cobblestones. Very slowly Thérèse stood up.

He seemed to block the doorway with his field-grey bulk, and his face, dusty from travelling, was creased in an anticipatory smile.

'I am happy to see you all again,' he said in guttural, halting French.

'Our German,' whispered Clothilde, ashen-faced.

* * *

The boy pushed back his chair and it fell with a crash. He dumped Albert unceremoniously on his mother's lap without taking his eyes from the German soldier.

'Jean-Baptiste—' began Yvette.

Without hearing her he launched himself in the direction of the soldier, his fingers hooked like savage claws. His red hair stood wildly on end.

The German took the impact of his hurtling body with a grunt, snapping his hands round the boy's wrists like a pair of handcuffs. Holding him off, he studied him with honest perplexity.

'Who are you?' he asked.

The women began to move and talk all at once with the exception of Clothilde, who stood making agitated pleats in the front of her blouse. Her eyes were huge and dark and spilling with emotions she was unable to conceal.

'Jean-Baptiste—' Yvette repeated, al lack of ceremony dumped the baby on Grand'mère's lap. 'Jean-Baptiste, this is our German — he is a friend of ours and he is different from the others!'

The boy struggled in the German's grasp, closing his eyes as he felt the newly-built strength ebbing from him.

'Boche—' he shouted in a high raging voice. 'Stinking Hun — bastard German!'

Out of the ensuing uproar the only voice to make itself heard was that of Thérèse.

'Jean-Baptiste,' she said, 'you are a guest in this house. The German is also a guest. And until you are in full possession of the facts I would be grateful if you would kindly refrain from brawling in the presence of women.'

Defeated, and with his strength gone, the boy drooped from the German's upraised hands as if he were crucified.

Solicitously the older man placed him on a chair by the fire where he sat huddled, looking small and frail and sick with disillusion. Yvette went over and quietly knelt beside him.

'The women you hold in such esteem are traitors,' he said, without looking at her.

'I thought that once,' she whispered urgently, 'but it is not as simple as that—'

'Simple — simple—' he sneered, 'is that all you have to say?'

'For the moment,' she told him.

'And now that order has been restored,' continued Thérèse, 'perhaps we can find the means of making a little extra coffee.'

'Coffee,' said the German, 'Ah, so . . .' Saluting delightedly he went out to the courtyard, and came back with a small grey sack which he placed on the table while he untied it and with the air of a conjurer produced a bottle of brandy, some coffee and sugar and a considerable length of German sausage. Digging deeper into the sack he drew out a little wooden horse for Albert, and last of all a melodeon inlaid with mother-of-pearl from which he coaxed the first lilting bars of a waltz.

'My friends,' he said in his execrable French, 'I come to return a little of your hospitality.'

And there was nothing they could do but accept it.

As there were no glasses in the convent they drank brandy from the familiar white china mugs, and relaxing in its genial warmth they had to admit that it tasted none the worse for that. The tension eased, and Thérèse asked the German in slow schoolchild French how his injured shoulder fared. In answer he stripped off his tunic, hauled his shirt tails from his trousers and exposed to them the white scar line and the stitch holes that winked like little pearls in his pale flesh.

'Clothilde did that,' Yvette whispered to Jean-Baptiste. He shrugged scornfully.

'Thérèse almost killed him with the hatchet, but when she and Clothilde found out she hadn't, they had to make him better even though they hated him — like I did you — and Clothilde sewed him up and we discovered that he is just an ordinary nice man who cannot help being a Boche,' Yvette continued rapidly.

'The only good Boche,' the boy hissed, 'is a dead one.' But to Yvette, his tone lacked conviction. She rubbed her face against his sleeve, like a cat.

'And what happens to you now?' Thérèse was asking the German.

He spread his large kindly hands. 'I have been attached to garrison troops,' he said. 'Very safe and very boring. But now the word has come that our sector go west. I go to the Western Front, with my comrades. It will not be boring, and I think it will not be safe, either.'

He laughed, but the sound fell like a stone in the silence. Clothilde turned aside.

'The trenches,' said Thérèse, taking a sip of brandy. 'They are not pleasant, from all one hears.'

'Ah so,' the German said philosophically. Picking up the melodeon again he slipped his hands through the straps and began to play, the slow nostalgic tune filling the women with an indescribable yearning.

'One day,' Yvette said with a sigh, 'everything will be calm and sensible again.'

'But not—' Jean-Baptiste suddenly cried, 'until I have killed such swamp rats as the man who sits opposite me!'

Apart from Clothilde's sharp intake of breath there was silence.

'Me?' asked the German above the music he was playing.

'You,' said Jean-Baptiste, 'and all your kin. Tonight I am going to Ypres to join the Allies fighting there.'

The German contemplated him gravely and without rancour.

'It will not be possible for you,' he said at length. 'Our forces are there in such number that one Belgian civilian would immediately be taken for a—' he hunted patiently for the word, 'for a spy. You would be shot.'

'I am going,' the boy said coldly. 'I have escaped from Germany and I know how these things are managed.'

Still playing the caressive little tune the German said gently, 'Stay at home. There is much to do here. Stay at home with your girl and the baby.'

The boy started up. 'You think I am a coward?'

The German shook his head. 'To be a coward in such times as these requires courage. More courage than I have, alas.'

Jean-Baptiste sat silent, filled with a resentful misery. 'I am going, nevertheless,' he said finally.

The German laid aside the melodeon and reached for the brandy bottle. He tipped a little more into the boy's mug then splashed some into his own. He raised it to Jean-Baptiste.

'A man must do as he thinks best,' he said with a sigh. 'I drink to your success.'

The boy raised his own mug. 'I will be successful,' he said, and drank.

* * *

The sudden appearance of the German they had nicknamed Fritzy affected Clothilde profoundly, and because of it she strove very hard to maintain a demeanour suitable to that of a respected Dinant dressmaker encountering a chance acquaintance. So she gave him a prim smile — but when they shook hands in greeting and her cold spinster fingers lay for a second within his own, her heart pounded in her throat.

As for the German, he treated her with the same gentle and rather wistful courtesy that he showed to the others, but while Thérèse was helping Grand'mère to bed and Yvette was preparing Albert for sleep, she found him at her side as she stepped through the kitchen door into the courtyard. A young moon was floating free of the lilac tree and white moths were fluttering. The German's horse glanced at him, chinking its bit as he passed.

Without speaking, they found themselves walking in the direction of the chapel. They went in, squeezing through the narrow aperture in the collapsed doorway. Silently they walked to the statue of the Holy Mother and the German bent to light a candle.

After a moment he turned to Clothilde, searching her thin face in the small pool of light.

'How are you?' he asked in his awkward halting French.

'I am well,' she replied, without looking at him.

'I have thought of you many times.'

Her heart began its pounding again. 'And I of you.'

Putting his hand in his tunic pocket he drew out a tiny box and gave it to her. She bent over it, holding it towards the candlelight.

'Please open it,' he said.

She did so, and inside the box lay a little enamel brooch edged with marguerites. In the centre of it was an inscription and she bent her head closer to read the words.

To my Dearest Friend, it said, and as she stood incapable of speech he took it out of the box and clumsily pinned it at the neck of her blouse. She put her hand on it and kept it there, then turned and fled into the shadows.

Thérèse and the boy Jean-Baptiste were alone in the kitchen when they returned.

'When do you go to the Western Front, Fritzy?' asked Thérèse.

'Tonight. My leave expires tonight.'

Yvette slipped into the kitchen. The German looked at her, then looked at the boy. 'And you?' he asked.

'Now.'

The German sighed and his leather belt creaked. 'You had better come with me.'

'I have no need of your help.'

The German sighed again. 'You do. Alone, it will be impossible. But together we can perhaps think of a reason to explain your—' he paused, searching for words, 'your diso-bedience of the curfew.'

'I have no need to hide behind a Boche uniform.'

The German spread his hands humorously. 'Look,' he said, 'you want to kill me. I only try to help you.'

'He cannot go tonight,' began Yvette, panic-stricken. 'He is not strong enough. Tell him, Thérèse—'

'I cannot,' Thérèse said stolidly. 'What the boy does must be his own decision.'

'I am going tonight,' the boy said very coldly. 'And I do not travel with the enemy.'

'You are indeed a man of iron,' the German said resignedly.

'I am going to kill you,' Jean-Baptiste said slowly, 'for all the harm you have done.'

An hour later they were both gone, the horse and the two men melting into the heavy shadows. Yvette stood lis-tening to the desultory sound of hooves fading on the other side of the village, then flung herself against Thérèse in a passion of weeping.

'I know well,' she murmured, stroking the girl's hair. 'They never understand how hard it is for us to be left behind.'

* * *

The summer advanced, tormenting the three younger women with its languid dreaming beauty. Thérèse spent much of her time up in the kitchen garden, weeding between the rows of vegetables and thinking about last summer when she and Henri Aubel were still ignorant of the fact that time was running out.

If only we had known, she thought, trowelling the warm earth, we would have savoured it more. We would have spent less time in sleeping . . .

And Clothilde, her equilibrium profoundly disturbed by the unexpected return of the German, shut herself away in the chapel while she pondered her feelings and prayed earnestly for guidance. It was fitting that Thérèse should be deeply concerned about her husband's welfare and it was equally understandable that the girl Yvette should agonize over the boy she had known at school, but observed through the cold eye of reality Clothilde Toussant was a spinster who had committed the ridiculous indiscretion of becoming emotionally involved at the age of forty-five. And with a German; a man with whom she had been unable to exchange more than a few halting words and who, by virtue of his birth, was her enemy. She was a traitor as well as a fool and she replaced the brooch she had received from him in its little box and kept it hidden under her pillow. But every night she slept with it in her hand and she no longer dreamed of the saintly Père Joseph from Dinant.

As for Yvette, most afternoons she spent trundling Albert through the woods to where Jean-Baptiste had lived with his father. She swept and dusted the hut with the same punctiliousness with which Clothilde tended the chapel, and sometimes while Albert crawled happily among the ferns outside she would sit on the bunk, reverently turning the mildewed pages of his books and trying to come closer to the side of him that had won a scholarship to Louvain. The hut was full of his presence and his mercurial changes of mood, just as the pillow still bore the imprint of his head. To cheer herself, she made up her mind that he would have won the war and returned home in time for Albert's first birthday.

Thus preoccupied, Thérèse, Clothilde and Yvette failed to observe the first warning signs of Grand'mère's sickness, and it came as a shock to them when they found that she was no longer capable of leaving her bed unaided.

Under the calico nightdress made from a convent sheet her body had become little more than a loosely tied bundle of twigs, and as her physical dissolution progressed she appeared to be slipping further and further beyond the confines of everyday awareness. She showed no interest in food, and it was difficult to persuade her to swallow more than a teaspoonful at a time.

They took it in turns to sit with her, holding her worn speckled hand while she hovered somewhere between waking and sleeping, and one day towards mid-morning they detected a subtle change in her.

'We must fetch a priest,' Clothilde whispered urgently. She buttoned her cuffs and smoothed her hair. 'I will go to Dinant.'

'It is a long way,' Thérèse said, 'and I think you will have to hurry.'

But Clothilde was already on her way, her thin figure picking its way rapidly through the shattered village.

Inside the convent Yvette and Thérèse sat beside Grand'mère's narrow bed. Once, she roused herself and asked sharply why the children were so silent.

'They are asleep, old one,' Thérèse said. 'They are tired with their play and have fallen asleep.'

'Sleep,' said the old woman, sinking back. 'Sleep is good.'

Silence filled the room.

'It is strange to be a woman,' Yvette whispered, contemplating the intricate network of wrinkles on the old woman's face. 'To work and to love and to die.' She touched the wide gold wedding ring on the little claw hand. 'Who was he, the man who placed it on her finger?'

Thérèse shook her head. 'That, we are never likely to know.'

It was three o'clock when Clothilde returned with the priest, a rubicund man in a dusty soutane. Yvette met them at the door with a lighted candle, genuflected, and led the way to Grand'mère's room, and immediately the presence of death became tangible.

The three women knelt as the priest administered Extreme Unction, touching the old woman's motionless features with the holy oil while he prayed for her soul in a low monotone that blended with the droning of bees outside the window.

She died with no more than a sigh. Filled with a profound sorrow Thérèse stood up and slipped out of the door as the priest began to recite the *De Profundis*.

Out of the depths I have cried to Thee, O Lord . . .

Lord hear my voice . . . came the weeping response from Yvette and Clothilde.

She walked quietly downstairs and out through the silent kitchen to the courtyard. Without noticing the direction she was taking she wandered down the broken street of St Louis les Bois and her preoccupation was such that she brushed against the old schoolmaster without noticing him.

'Good day, Madame Aubel,' said a woman filling a bucket with water at the pump. 'It is a fine day, is it not?'

'It is a fine day indeed,' Thérèse replied absently.

Golden sunshine covered the stricken houses and pitted cobblestones, and a fat old woman sat outside her door simmering in the heat and listening with sleepy delight to the trilling of her canary. The war had rolled past her and she was content. Thérèse nodded a greeting, then her thoughts returned to the other old woman who lay on the nun's narrow bed at the convent.

The death of one nameless female refugee in the vast European conflagration was hardly likely to cause international concern — she doubted whether the Recording Angel himself would have time for more than a perfunctory note on his cuff — but to her, and to Clothilde and Yvette, the passing of Grand'mère was a cause not only of sadness, but also of fear. For the past eleven months the four of them had survived the storm, riding quietly at anchor in the deserted convent, and the loss of the old woman meant the loss of a cornerstone. Things would no longer be the same. And sameness, in time of uncertainty, was something to cling to.

Deep in thought, Thérèse turned the corner and walked on. Crickets chirruped in the long grass and a rabbit bounded out of the hedge almost at her feet.

She wondered about the funeral arrangements; no one, so far as she knew, had died in St Louis les Bois since its furtive reoccupation by the inhabitants, but interment in the churchyard would be impossible as it lay obliterated by a cascade of rubble. In any case, Grand'mère would have wished to be buried in her own village, with the rest of her family. When death called it was only fitting that one should lie in close proximity to family and friends, but because of the war this was too much to ask.

'The war . . . the war . . .' she muttered savagely, then stopped dead with a shock of surprise. She was in the lane that led to the farm and at her feet lay the laughing skull of the French gunner.

And suddenly, the vow she had made never to return seemed childish and needlessly dramatic and she looked back on the woman who had made it with weary scorn.

Stepping over the remains of the gunner she walked on, noting how the grass had thickened in the wheel tracks and the hedges bulged. She turned the last corner and there it was. Desolate and deserted, the blackened windowless house staring blindly at the ruined farm buildings.

Impassively she stood taking it all in, then began to walk towards the farmyard. In the hard sun-dried earth there were still the faint impressions of cows' hoofmarks and by the well was the old scoop she had used for the chicken meal.

But everything else had gone. Staring in through the gaping doorway of the house she saw that it had burned to an empty shell. Only a few charred timbers remained of the upper floor. Despite the hot weather the place smelt of damp and decay.

She walked over to the shippen. The roof was open to the sky. Leaning against the doorway she folded her arms and contemplated the huge white bones of the cows. Flavie, Berthe, Lolotte, Mirabelle, Nanette. The high swelling arches of their ribs made them look like fallen cathedrals.

She didn't notice the man until he moved away from the smoke-blackened wall opposite. He was wearing shapeless uniform trousers, a civilian jacket and a black cap that shaded his eyes. As he moved, the left sleeve of his jacket swung emptily. It seemed a long time before the irrational suspicion that it might be Henri became a certainty.

He spoke her name. She said yes. He stepped carefully over the ruins of Mirabelle, then halted. With equal care she stepped over the remains of Lolotte, her long skirt brushing the bleached bones.

He asked her how she was. Very well, she told him, and you? Not at all bad, he said.

There was only Flavie between them.

'Henri,' she said very steadily, 'if you have come back only to say goodbye again, I will not be able to endure it.'

'I am home for good,' he said.

She flung herself at him, leaping the smooth skeleton of Flavie, and she almost devoured him with her arms, her hands, her hungry mouth. They tried to speak but the words were obliterated by kisses and the tears streamed out of her eyes and she cursed violently because she couldn't see him properly, and then they both laughed like mad people and the fire grew between them and they were lying under the open roof with the hot, healing sun pouring down on them.

'Your arm,' she said afterwards, when they lay at peace. 'Oh, your poor arm.'

'It is only at the elbow,' he said. 'At the shoulder it would have been grave.'

'Tell me how it happened.'

'No,' he said. 'Not yet.'

She began to cry again, but only gently, and her strong square hand traced his arm from the shoulder to where it ended. 'I must see it,' she said. 'Take off your coat.'

'Not now.'

'Yes, please,' she said. 'Now.'

He moved away from her and sat up, peeling off the civilian jacket with a quick, expert movement of his right hand.

'There,' he said.

The part of his arm that remained looked the same as it had always done, pale and strong as whipcord. The stump of it was rounded and pink, the skin shiny as a baby's.

'Watch,' he said, not without pride, and picking up a stick held it in his right hand then with a sharp blow of his stump broke it in two. 'I can use it for a hatchet.'

'A hatchet,' she repeated, and winced.

He sat with his shirt sleeve rolled up, the pink stump gleaming from under it.

'Does it upset you, Thérèse?'

'No,' she said, forcing herself to stare at it. 'I am fortunate to have ninety-five per cent of you returned to me.'

'A German patrol brought me in from a shell crater. There were six of us, the others were French. Two died. The German base hospital was very efficient, in my case.'

'When did it happen?'

'Early in March.'

'I had your letter on the last day of February, and I was so happy.'

He smiled. 'Poor Thérèse . . .'

Tears still sparkled in her eyes. She dashed them away and said, 'The others were so envious of me, having a letter.'

'The others?'

'The other women. I have a new family now.'

'Who are they?'

'Fellow refugees. We live in the convent in the village.'

'Might there be room for a repatriated Belgian infantryman?'

She ran her hand down his arm and without flinching cupped the stump of his elbow in it.

'There will be room,' she said.

They made love again, this time tenderly and without haste and when it was finished she moved apart from him and lay looking up at the sky.

'It was I who killed them all,' she said. 'The cows.'

'Because of the Germans coming?'

'Yes. I killed the chickens and then I set fire to it all. I poured paraffin over everything so there would be nothing left when they arrived.'

'You were brave,' he said, solicitously watching her profile. 'Now tell me about the other women at the convent.'

'One died today,' she said, and the tears began to roll down her cheeks again. 'She was old and lost and I loved her and now there is the problem of her funeral . . .'

'I will help you,' he said.

'There is also Yvette Mazy from the café. She has a baby named Albert, and then there is Clothilde Toussant from Dinant, and she is a dressmaker and very prim, or at least she was until — until . . .'

'A lot has happened?' he said quietly. She nodded, wiping her eyes on her sleeve.

'Come,' he said, helping her to her feet. 'We will go and find them.'

He put the old civilian jacket on again, and the cap, and they walked out into the farmyard.

'How long had you been here?' she asked presently.

'About an hour before you came.'

It was her turn to be solicitous. 'Was it a very bad shock, Henri?'

'It was to begin with,' he replied. 'I was sure you were dead.'

They lingered in the golden sunlight by the well, and in the long cool shadows made by the walls of the house. They discovered a patch of self-sown nasturtiums flaring defiant red and yellow among the weeds under the parlour window, and it seemed as if there was still hope that one day things would be different.

'We will build it all again,' Thérèse said with a final sniff.

'They used gas at Ypres,' he said.

'Gas?' She halted.

'Poison gas. Fumes that kill people. The Germans used it in the trenches for the first time last April.'

'Poison gas,' she said slowly. 'How *abominable*.'

'It is,' he said. 'And the war will go on for a long, long time yet, Thérèse.'

'But it cannot!' she cried, suddenly agitated, 'people cannot go on for much longer—'

'They can,' he said. 'I have seen them.'

They began to walk across the farmyard again, towards the fields. They held hands for the first time since before they were married.

'You think the war may not be over this year?'

'I think,' he said, 'that it will not be over for another two years at least. Perhaps even three.'

'But three years — that would be 1918!'

'I hope I am wrong,' he said.

They walked in silence, their clothes brushing through the long grass.

'The fields are full of tares,' he said. 'There is much work for us to do.'

She moved closer to him, reaching behind his waist for the remains of his left arm. 'Tomorrow we will begin,' she said.

PART TWO

CHAPTER EIGHT

During the October of that year the Allied Powers declared war on Bulgaria. Greece became involved. The Austro-Germans beat the Serbs to their knees and early in 1916 the German Supreme Commander transferred almost half a million men to the Western Front. On 21 February began the Battle of Verdun, perhaps the most hideous and protracted battle of all time. It lasted for five months, and although the British alone lost close on four hundred thousand men, no one appeared capable of calling it a day, The war went on. And Belgium remained occupied.

The idea of living at the Convent of the Little Sisters of Mercy had filled Henri Aubel with initial unease, but within a short space of time he had grown accustomed to the huge broken rooms and haunted atmosphere. He had even reconciled himself to the chaste narrow beds, preferring to make love to Thérèse in what remained of their own home. To work in the fields planting the few precious seeds saved from the convent garden and to make love in the shadow of the blackened walls helped in some measure to sustain the spirit of the old days when things had been different.

But although Henri often counselled Thérèse to have patience with the war during the early summer of 1916, he found it increasingly difficult to follow his own advice.

The only information available to the civilian population was contained in the official newspapers published by the Germans, and sickened by the pompous propaganda he had long ago ceased reading them. No one knew what was happening. Only rumours could germinate in the vacuity left after the suppression of freedom, and he had soon learned to discount wild tales of sudden victory along with whispers about reprisal and mass executions. Not knowing what to believe, it seemed wisest to believe nothing. And to believe nothing, Henri Aubel sometimes thought, was akin to being dead.

He found himself talking to Clothilde about it, sitting in the convent kitchen watching her sew. May sunlight twinkled in the gold pince-nez clipped to her thin nose, and although he sometimes teased her about her primness and love of refinement, he had grown fond of her.

'Sometimes,' he said, 'I wish that I were back in the trenches.'

'That is selfish talk. Think of Thérèse.'

'I do think of her,' he replied. 'I think of her growing thin and weary and losing heart. I want to help in hastening the end of the war.'

'You have given your help,' she said, and glanced fleetingly at his empty sleeve. 'And God willed it that you could do no more.'

He got up from the chair and walked restlessly round the big scrubbed table.

'I can do more. Much more.'

'In what way?' She bit off a thread.

'I know not. I—' He sat down again, massaging the back of his neck. 'I can do nothing without knowing how things stand with us. We hear the rumble of guns on the Western Front, we live with the sound day after day, but we have no knowledge of what is happening. No knowledge, nothing.'

'We have our faith,' Clothilde said quietly. She threaded her needle with white cotton.

'Your faith means much to you,' he replied, not unkindly. 'But for myself, I would prefer something of a more tangible nature.'

'Tangible—' repeated Thérèse, coming in through the door. 'Here is something good and tangible—' and she dumped Albert on the end of the kitchen table. She stood back, rubbing her arm and smiling. 'I swear he must weigh more than his mother!'

Now seventeen months old, Albert was a cheerful child dressed in a frock made by Clothilde from an old curtain. He was holding a bunch of bluebells which he abruptly offered to her, and she accepted them with a smile that illuminated her chill spinster features with a touch of beauty.

'I hear someone speaking of me,' said Yvette, coming in behind Thérèse. 'And they say that listeners always hear ill of themselves.'

'We were saying that you are thin,' answered Thérèse. 'Far, far thinner than your son.'

'Oh, I am well enough,' said Yvette, pushing back her hair. 'See, Thérèse, I have brought us a cabbage big as a bridal bouquet.'

'But you *are* thin,' repeated Thérèse, scrutinizing her. She walked over to the girl and touched her throat with her stubby peasant fingers. 'Your salt cellars are showing.'

'So are yours,' replied Yvette a little defensively. 'And so, were we permitted to see them, are Clothilde's.' She laughed. 'Have you not read the latest fashion decree that elegant Belgian women must all be thin as a nail?'

Thérèse grunted. 'Before the war, I for one was plump as a laying hen . . .' She turned to Henri for confirmation and saw from his expression that his thoughts were far away.

'Poor Henri is tired,' Yvette exclaimed suddenly. 'We irritate him with our chatter.'

'Sit in the armchair and rest, husband,' suggested Thérèse.

Aware of the three pairs of eyes watching him concernedly, Henri leaned his head against the wall and said, 'I am not tired. And your chatter does not irritate me.'

'He is hungry,' observed Clothilde. 'The dinner today was an exceptionally lean one.'

Yvette hurried over to the bread crock and took out the remains of a loaf. It was dark grey in colour.

'There is also a little margarine,' she said encouragingly, 'I could make Henri a sandwich.'

'Thank you, I am not hungry,' he said, closing his eyes.

'Neither are we . . .' chorused the three women with a promptitude that filled him with a sudden impotent rage.

After his return from the Western Front he had found the ministrations of his feminine companions far from unpleasant, to begin with he had been harmlessly flattered by their innocent attentions and had accepted with good-humoured gratitude their insistence that his should be the largest portion of food, the most comfortable chair, the place nearest the fire.

But now the role of hero, of warrior returned from the dead, was beginning to sicken him, and he found himself becoming increasingly impatient with their eagerness to cosset him as if he were one of a rare and delicate species instead of an ordinary Ardennais farmer.

Once he said as much to Thérèse, blurting out the words while they were undressing at bedtime. She had turned to him, standing in her patched petticoat with her thick black hair tumbling from its pins.

'But it is true,' she had said sadly. 'And if this war continues, ordinary men like you will be rare as the Dodo.'

He knew it was true, but as the months went by the knowledge of it did less and less to help ease his frustrated impatience with the meaningless life that circumstances were forcing him to lead.

'Eat, husband . . .' Thérèse was now saying coaxingly. 'There is plenty for all of us.'

He opened his eyes and looked at her. And his rage melted. He looked round at them all; at his wife, at the spinster

Clothilde and at the girl Yvette who stood so close to her little son. And it was no use.

He drew himself up to full height in his lovingly washed and patched trousers and traditional workman's blouse and said, 'I am not hungry. And furthermore, I have decided to go to Brussels to find news of the war. I go tomorrow, and I go alone.'

* * *

In a way it was far easier than he might have anticipated, for there was a surprising lack of tears and recriminations and tender pleas to take care of himself.

Clothilde and Yvette accepted his decision with a resignation that touched him more deeply than any display of emotion, and Thérèse's eyes were stonily dry as she said goodbye to him at the gateway of the convent early next morning.

'Take care,' was all she said. 'Find out how the war progresses, but take good care.'

'I will be back within a week,' he said, and taking the little packet of food she had prepared, kissed her cheek and walked away down the street.

He had walked no more than a dozen paces before he became aware of her wooden sabots clacking after him, and for an instant he found himself re-living the summer day in 1914 when he had walked away from her to join the Belgian Infantry. On that occasion too, she had run after him; and it had been to throw her arms round him for a last embrace.

But this time she didn't embrace him. She merely stood there in the early morning light and said, 'While you are seeking news of the war, try your best to seek news also of poor Jean-Baptiste. He is very young, he has bright red hair, and Yvette loves him to distraction.'

'I will try,' he said.

'His name is Jean-Baptiste Dion.'

'Dion,' he repeated obediently.

'When he was a boy of sixteen he won a scholarship to Louvain University, but the Boche burned it down.'

'I know. You have often told me of the boy and his circumstances.'

'Yvette loves him.'

'That I also know.'

They stood for a moment in the wan light, only too aware of the futility of searching for news of Jean-Baptiste. Perhaps he had been lucky in his attempt to join the Allies. Perhaps he had not.

'Ah well,' Henri said at length. 'I must go.'

She stood back against the broken wall and raised her hand.

'Come back to me,' she said.

Aware that it was forbidden to travel for any distance without a permit he decided that it would be imprudent to use the main road. Instead, he kept to the lanes as much as possible, making his way past ruined farms and grass-grown shell craters until, towards evening, he came to the outskirts of Namur.

Here, he hesitated. With two-thirds of the journey to Brussels still before him it would be foolish to risk interrogation by the Boche; on the other hand, Namur itself was a town of considerable importance — the largest he knew — and it seemed likely that he might gather news there. People in Namur would know how the war fared; they might in fact be able to furnish him with so much information that the journey to Brussels itself would no longer be necessary.

A walk of more than thirty kilometres had left him tired and a little depressed, and with Thérèse's package of food already eaten, he was also becoming hungry again.

The lane he found himself in had already left the open fields behind and was winding its way between groups of warehouses separated by neglected apple orchards. There was no one about. He decided to continue a little further.

The twilight thickened, but the very tiredness in him seemed to bring with it a new sense of dogged endurance. To his mind it seemed clearly ridiculous that the Boche should find anything of particular importance in the movements of one Henri Aubel, peasant farmer from the Ardennes. No, curse them, he would go into Namur where he would find a café, and with luck a glass of cold Belgian beer.

The lane faltered among a tangle of slum alleyways, then squared its shoulders and marched towards the centre of the town. Henri Aubel marched with it.

The houses were shuttered and dark. There were few people about, and as he walked past the silent mass of St Aubain's Cathedral his footsteps echoed emptily. With hunger rumbling he fixed his thoughts on the café he had visited once before, on an excursion with Thérèse. A snug little café where the food was cheap and the beer cool and sparkling . . .

A hoarse voice shouted at him from the gloom and his tired eyes took in the steel glint of a bayonet.

He came to a halt, his heart sinking. The German sentry shouted something he didn't understand. He stood quite still, and waited. The steel glinted a little nearer to his face.

'Identity card,' the German said in impatient, guttural French. 'Show me your identity card.'

Relieved, Henri groped inside his blouse with his one hand and brought out the requested document. In glimmering lamplight the German sentry examined it.

'You come from a place near Dinant. Show me your permit to travel.'

So this was it. Show me the permit you haven't got.

For a split second he considered making a run for it, but the weight of tiredness in his legs convinced him that it would be a waste of time.

'I have no permit,' he said very quietly.

'No permit?' The German examined his identity card again, then placed it carefully in his tunic pocket.

'To travel without a permit is forbidden,' he said. He jerked his head. 'Come.'

With a face devoid of expression Henri Aubel began to walk, and guided by a series of meaningful prods in the back traversed a couple more silent and shuttered streets until they came to a *préfecture*.

The walls both inside and out seemed to be papered with official notices. The sentry threw open a door that led into a small dingy office and shoved Henri inside. A grey-haired man in civilian clothes sat writing at a desk. He looked thin and tired.

'Comes from Dinant,' the sentry said in his bad French and threw Henri's identity card down on the desk. 'Travelling without a permit.'

He stamped out. The man at the desk laid his pen aside and contemplated Henri.

'Why have you no permit?' His French was perfect.

Henri shrugged, and said nothing.

'Are you not aware that it is an offence to travel without one? That you could be deported, or imprisoned for five years?'

'I am—' began Henri, then stopped. It occurred to him that there were times when honesty was not necessarily the best policy. 'No,' he said woodenly. 'I am not aware.'

'How so?' The man regarded him intently.

'I am recently discharged from the army. I have no knowledge of the new civilian rules and regulations.' He allowed a note of superiority to enter his voice, and saw that it was not lost upon his companion.

'You were in the Belgian Army?'

'Where else?'

'Insolence,' said the civilian, 'will avail you nothing. When did you receive your discharge?'

'Last week.' The lie came easily.

In the silence which followed, Henri studied the notice on the opposite wall. *It is forbidden upon pain of death to* ... He read no further.

The man at the desk picked up his identity card, glanced at it briefly and said, 'The date of issue is July 1915. Yet you were demobilized from the army only last week?'

Henri said nothing.

'Where were you going?'

'To Brussels.'

'For what reason?'

'I have an aged aunt who lives there.'

'And?'

'I am concerned about her welfare.'

'It is expressly forbidden,' continued the man in the same flat, tired voice, 'to travel from one area to another without first obtaining official permission so to do. The regulations are made by the German High Command purely for your own safety, and for the safety of all the Belgian population under its care. Failure to comply with these regulations can have extremely serious consequences, and although we are naturally reluctant to—'

'*We?*' repeated Henri slowly. 'You are a Belgian. You have a local accent.'

The man said nothing. His expression betrayed no sign of emotion.

'A Belgian,' repeated Henri in growing amazement. 'And you are working for the Boche—' He took a step forward.

'Be prudent, my friend,' the man said coldly. 'Remember that you have only one arm.' Pulling a printed form towards him he dipped his pen in the inkwell and began to write.

Sickened by the calculated insult Henri stepped back again. Even so, it was hard to remain silent, and with the man composedly filling in the form for his detention there was nothing more to lose. Stammering and stumbling over the words, he said, 'You are vermin, and should be crushed underfoot. You are a traitor and a cheat, a murderer of innocent women and children. You are a collaborator, a kiss-my-arse—'

'In times like these,' the man said without pausing in his writing, 'it is advisable to blow with the wind.'

He blotted what he had written, scanned it through, then pinged the bell on his desk. The German sentry clumped in.

'I am satisfied that this man had a travel permit and lost it,' he said, and sighed. 'There is no greater fool on earth than a Belgian peasant.'

He held out the completed form to Henri, who took it numbly, together with his identity card. He seemed power-less to move.

'Well, what are you waiting for?' demanded the Belgian irritably. 'A carriage and pair?'

Aided by a powerful shove from the sentry Henri stum-bled from the room and down the steps into the cool night air. Never before had it smelt so beautiful.

* * *

With his identity card and the permit to travel to Brussels safely in his pocket, Henri Aubel walked swiftly away from the *préfecture* and down the next couple of streets without worrying about the direction he was taking.

To be free was sufficient, and after his extraordinary experience he felt as if he had been under fire as a civilian for the first time. The horrors of the trenches were one thing, but the insidious fears of the man in the street were not to be under-estimated, and he realized ruefully that he had not acquitted himself very well. The detestable civilian had made a fool of him within the space of three minutes; made a fool of him, and then told a deliberate lie in his favour. Why? The answer was a mystery.

At the end of the second street he paused, and once again became conscious of his tiredness. He had been walking since early morning and his legs were leaden. He was also very hungry.

Crossing over the cobbled street he walked slowly through a little alleyway lined with small shops. They appeared to be lifeless. He looked in through the windows of a bootmaker, a watch-repairer and a second-hand shop. When he came to a café he rattled the door handle, but it was locked. The chairs were stacked on the tables.

He wandered on, and it was as if all Namur were either asleep or dead.

He came to a broad avenue lined with plane trees. One or two carts passed him and an electric tram whined away in the distance. He sat down on a bench by the side of a horse trough.

But tomorrow, he thought, I will go to Brussels. Everything will be simple tomorrow. I will find a café and have a good breakfast, and now that I have a travel permit I will go some of the way by train if the fare is not too expensive. And in Brussels everything will be easier . . .

Tucking his one hand deep in his blouse pocket he slumped in the corner of the bench and went resolutely to sleep.

He woke at dawn, cold, stiff and wet with dew. The stump of his left arm ached as it had not done since the first weeks after amputation. He stood up and began to walk about, stamping his feet and listening to the desultory sound of his farm boots on the empty pavement. There were no Germans to be seen.

A horse and cart loomed out of the silvery light, slowed down and came to a halt by the trough. The driver, a shrouded figure with a sack protecting his head and shoulders, got down from his seat and led the horse to drink, patting its nose encouragingly.

Henri Aubel wished him good morning.

The man muttered a reply without looking at him.

'I think it will be a fine day,' Henri said.

'For some, I daresay,' replied the drover. The horse laid its lips against the surface of the water and began to drink.

Longing for the first café to open so that he might do the same, Henri sat down on the bench again. The light was strengthening, turning from silver to an opalescent pink.

'Can you give me the correct direction for Brussels?' he asked.

For the first time the drover turned to look at him and Henri saw that he was old, with a seamed face and white hair framed by the sack.

'I shall take the road to Brussels in due course,' he said. 'So you would do well to follow me.'

'Thank you,' said Henri.

The old man went round to the tail of the cart and unhooked a nosebag which he fastened to the horse's bridle. The horse tossed its head, then began to munch. The old man then climbed stiffly on to the hub of the front wheel, and rummaging among the straw he had been sitting on found a canvas bag. Descending with it he seated himself on the bench next to Henri, opened it and began to unroll a length of sausage. He brought out a bottle of beer and a lump of rye bread.

With his eyes fixed firmly on the road in front, Henri said, 'I hear that Brussels is a very fine city.'

'Was,' said the old man laconically, and hacked off a lump of sausage with his clasp knife. He began to eat at the same unhurried pace as the horse.

'I have never been there before.'

'It was a good enough place until *they* came—' The old man jerked his knife meaningly, then fed a large chunk of bread into his mouth. Henri's stomach rumbled enviously.

'How goes the war?' he asked presently. 'Do you hear much news?'

The old man regarded him cautiously from under his sack. His eyes narrowed. 'Who are you? Why do you ask?'

'I ask because I come from the country, where we hear nothing. I am a farmer.'

The old man's eyes travelled over him and came to rest on the empty sleeve.

'I was at Ypres.'

The old man stopped chewing. Without taking his eyes from Henri he broke off a piece of the rye bread and cut off a hunk of sausage. 'Here,' he said. 'Eat, my son.'

The daylight was strengthening, and when they had finished eating the old man removed the sack from his head and tossed it in the back of the cart. He unclipped the horse's nosebag, adjusted the harness, then jerked his thumb at the straw-covered seat.

'Up,' he said to Henri, and sitting side by side they trundled slowly out of Namur and along the road that led to Brussels.

* * *

The sun was high when Yvette loaded her son into the old handcart and pushed him out of the convent courtyard in the direction of the woods. They were going to collect sticks for the fire.

The rubble had been cleared from the village street and attempts made to repair the shell-shattered houses. Two boys, not yet of military age, were chipping stone ready for rebuilding and old Monsieur Groult the schoolmaster was up a ladder mending a window. He waved to Yvette as she passed.

'When you are big,' she told Albert, 'Monsieur Groult will teach you how to read and write and how to calculate.'

She walked on, and the woods that stretched between St Louis les Bois and Ciney were golden with sunlight and ringing with birdsong.

When she reached the hut she lifted Albert out of the handcart before opening the door. Inside, the floor was scrubbed and the one window shone. A jam jar full of blue-bells stood close beside a pile of books.

Yvette sat down on one of the bunk beds and looked round, her hands pressed between her knees.

'Jean-Baptiste,' she said to the empty air, 'Jean-Baptiste, where are you?'

She had heard nothing from him since the night he left the convent with the German soldier, but the place was still alive with his presence.

She picked up one of his books, and with a frown of concentration spelled out the word E-u-c-l-i-d, then with a sigh polished it on her long skirt before replacing it with the others.

Relocking the hut, she wondered whether Henri had reached Brussels; he was a quiet man, yet the convent seemed curiously hushed without him.

Albert staggered towards her with his arms outstretched and she picked him up, hugging him to her. Pleased, he pressed his mouth against her cheek in what passed for a kiss. Sinking down among the young ferns she buried her face in his midriff. He squawked with delight and they played together, happy and mindless as two young animals.

'Albert,' she said at length, sitting up and pinning back her yellow hair, 'you and I are supposed to be gathering firewood . . .'

* * *

The sight of Brussels filled Henri Aubel with astonishment. Although he had seen photographs of it he was totally unprepared for its size and splendour. He walked through the Grand Place and marvelled at the Hôtel de Ville, then climbed the hill to the Parc Royal where he stood entranced by the statues and fountains.

The Germans were much in evidence, and he noticed the way in which civilians pointedly ignored their presence and went about their business with a brisk animation that he imagined to be typical of big city dwellers. But for all their bustle, the Bruxellois were shabby and thin and their eyes were haunted. There was also a terrible absence of men between the ages of eighteen and forty.

He found a café and ordered a meal. The woman brought him a bowl of soup and a slice of the usual dark bread. He ate hungrily, and when he had finished sat back in his chair and surveyed the room.

A group of elderly matrons were sipping ersatz coffee at a table in the window and over by the cash desk two girls in striped blouses and long dark skirts giggled together. Old men sat playing dominoes, and a smart woman with a little dog on her lap inclined her head in mocking acknowledgement when he stared at her. Discomforted, he averted his gaze.

At the next table to his own sat a middle-aged man in a dark suit and a high starched collar. He was reading a book. Covertly Henri took in the details of his well-tended hands, the gold watch chain looped across his waistcoat, and wondered about his place in the present scheme of things. What did he, possibly a merchant or a banker, think of the Boche? How had the change of circumstances affected his way of life, and above all, what knowledge had he of the war's progress?

Four Uhlan officers came in, their spurs clinking, and seated themselves next to the two girls, who stopped giggling and quietly removed themselves to another table. The calculated insult filled Henri with a sudden surge of joy and he glanced at the man with the book. Their eyes met briefly, then the man closed his book, paid his bill and walked out. Impulsively Henri followed him. He caught up with him at a flower-seller's stall.

'Forgive me, Monsieur . . .'

'What do you want?' The man sounded annoyed, and Henri became conscious of his workman's clothes, his countrified appearance.

'I would like to talk with you,' he began uncertainly. 'If you have the time . . .'

The man walked away from him, his face set.

'I only wished to speak with you of the courageous young girls in the café—'

The man quickened his pace. 'I saw no young girls,' he muttered.

Defeated, Henri dropped back. Soon the man was lost in the crowd.

And that was how things were all the time. In a vast city teeming with people it seemed extraordinary that no one should wish to speak with him, to exchange a few harmless words about the weather, even. He helped an old lady to cross the road, he smiled sympathetically at a nursemaid trying to deal with a howling child and he murmured good day to a variety of elderly men, none of whom betrayed the slightest desire to strike up an acquaintance with him.

By the late afternoon of his first day in Brussels he was hot and footsore and deeply depressed. To travel to Brussels to gain news of the war had been naive in the extreme, but what more, he asked himself bitterly, could one expect from a fool peasant farmer from the Ardennes. The tired civilian in the *préfecture* at Namur had summed up his capabilities only too well.

He was still walking aimlessly along the boulevards when he became aware that the traffic had halted and that passers-by were collecting on the edge of the pavement in small silent groups. He joined one of them, and staring in the direction of the rue Royale saw an endless vista of spiked helmets bobbing to the sharp clatter of hooves on cobblestones. The Hussars rode past, knee to knee in a dense cavalcade of jingling harness and pungent horseflesh. Behind it chugged a huge staff car with hood rolled back and German pennant fluttering, and the sullen murmur that rose from the Bruxellois distracted Henri's attention from the solitary figure sitting pompously upright in the back seat.

Behind the car came motorcycles, then more cavalry, and he had to wait for the noise to die down a little before asking the man next to him to identify the lone figure in the motor car.

'Him?' The man spat neatly between Henri's boots and said, 'That was von Bissing, His Excellency the German Governor General of Belgium.'

Henri closed his eyes and wished that he had a gun, and two hands with which to use it. He was about to turn away when the man touched his empty sleeve.

'The war?'

Henri nodded.

'My two sons died in the defence of Liège.'

'We never thought,' Henri said bitterly, 'that the Liège forts would surrender. We all believed them impregnable.'

'My sons,' said the man, 'could give no more than their lives.'

'Forgive me.'

His companion smiled, and it occurred to Henri that this was the first time anyone had smiled at him since he left Dinant.

The crowds dispersed and the two of them fell into step. At the end of the street they stood looking at one another uncertainly. Weary of trying to make contact with the Bruxellois through their barrier of suspicion and mistrust, Henri suddenly said urgently, 'Look. I have come to Brussels from Dinant because I want to know about the war. I want to know what is happening. Where are the Allied armies now? Where is General Leman? Will the Americans help us?'

The expression of fear that he had seen so many times in the past three days flittered in the man's eyes. He glanced over his shoulder.

'Don't go,' Henri said, gripping the man's jacket.

'It is dangerous to speak of such things—'

A madness seemed to overtake Henri. 'I want to know,' he said, spitting the words between clenched teeth, 'I want to know about the progress of the war that has swallowed my country, laid waste my land and caused my woman much suffering. I want to know of the progress it makes, and I want to know when I shall see the stinking Boche leaving the village where I was born—'

'In the name of heaven hold your tongue—'

Henri gripped his jacket even harder. 'I will not be silent,' he hissed, 'until I have found the information I seek.'

'I know nothing . . .'

'Then lead me to someone who does!'

To Henri's surprise the man appeared to hesitate. He stood blinking rapidly for a moment, then said, 'Very well. Number sixteen rue Floris which is on the far side of the Jardin Botanique—'

'Jardin Botanique,' repeated Henri rapidly.

'And ask Papa Vilain for two pairs of black bootlaces.' With a quick movement the man wrenched his jacket free and disappeared into the crowd.

* * *

Thérèse Aubel walked along the lane that led from the farm to the convent with her head bent and her hands clasped behind her back. She was lost in thought.

When the war is over we will start the new herd with two cows and two calves. We will have a sow and fifty chickens. Horses will be scarce and expensive, but somehow . . .

She turned into the street of St Louis les Bois and was roused from her dreams by someone calling good afternoon to her. It was Monsieur Groult, the schoolmaster.

She paused by his gate, smiling at the hammer in his hand.

'I see you have changed your profession, Monsieur,' she said. 'You have exchanged the chalk for a hammer and become an excellent carpenter in the process.'

'I have learned to mend a window frame,' the old man said, 'and I have repaired some of the furniture. But I fear that the number of bent nails and the soreness of my thumb indicate a sad ineptitude.'

'War teaches one strange skills,' Thérèse replied with a humorous grin. 'Perhaps it is not altogether a bad thing.'

Monsieur Groult laid down his hammer and rubbed his injured thumb on the front of his faded shirt.

'How is Henri?' he asked. 'I have not seen him about for the past few days.'

'Henri is well, and much occupied,' replied Thérèse, and her grin faded. The old man inspected his thumb.

'More than one person of my acquaintance is finding it prudent to remain out of sight.'

'Indeed?'

'The twin sons of the Widow LePage, for example. Two months ago they celebrated their eighteenth birthday, although on second thoughts perhaps *celebrated* is hardly the correct term. For on the day they were eighteen it was their duty to report to the *préfecture* in Dinant and become German conscripts. Consequently they remain hidden in the house and only venture forth at night.'

'It is damnable,' muttered Thérèse.

'And it happens everywhere. The young boys of St Louis les Bois are not alone.'

'I wish we could do something,' Thérèse said.

'We can do nothing,' replied Monsieur Groult, and picking up his hammer walked away into his house.

* * *

The rue Floris proved to be a short and narrow street guarded at either end by a stone archway. The old gabled houses had strings of washing hanging from the upper windows and the place was deserted except for a tall, remarkably thin man turning the handle of a small street organ. The music he made was soft and melancholy and seemed to linger in the stillness.

Number sixteen was a boot repairer's shop and dust lay thickly over the wrinkled shoes that stood in the window. The place seemed deserted.

Henri hesitated, then turned the door handle and went inside. A bell pealed above his head and he looked round him, trying to penetrate the deep gloom of the place. There was a smell of leather and glue.

A round yellow light came towards him and he heard the soft padding of slippers on a stone floor. He stood still, and the person with the oil lamp placed it on the shop counter, adjusted the wick and asked him what he wanted.

'Monsieur Vilain?'

'That is my name.'

Henri hesitated for a moment, then said, 'I wish to purchase two pairs of black bootlaces.'

Monsieur Vilain picked up the lamp. He held it high above his head and Henri found himself face to face with an old man whose benign and chubby face was framed by curling white hair and a beard of startling whiteness. He then lowered the lamp a little and inspected his visitor's feet.

Replacing the lamp on the counter, Monsieur Vilain shuffled across to a cupboard and took from it a cardboard box which he placed in the pool of light by the lamp. He opened it, and began to rummage carefully among pairs of laces. Outside, the melancholy little tune on the street organ ceased.

'I think Monsieur is a stranger in this part of Brussels,' the old man remarked, still rummaging. 'Perhaps someone recommended him to my shop?'

'A man who shared my feelings when Monsieur von Bissing drove past,' Henri said abruptly. 'I do not know his name.'

The old man laid the bootlaces on the counter and stared at Henri unwinkingly.

'I came here,' Henri said, 'because I want to know how things are going with the Allies. I want to know our chances of winning the war, and above all I want to know the truth.'

'Where do you come from?'

'A small village near Dinant.'

'I see you are a *mutilé*, Monsieur.'

'I lost my arm on the Western Front.'

For a last searching moment the old man stared at him, then clapping the lid back on the cardboard box said, 'My wife has just made a jug of coffee. There will be sufficient for three.'

He led the way down the dark stone passage and Henri found himself in a large kitchen with an iron range flanked by two tapestry chairs drawn up on a threadbare rug. Religious pictures decorated the walls, and among the general clutter on the table he noticed a quantity of brown foolscap envelopes. The atmosphere in the place was curiously stifling.

A woman turned round from the iron range as they entered. She was tall and well built, with thick hair draped round a heavy face. She appeared considerably younger than the old man; about fifty, Henri decided.

'Marthe,' said the old man, setting down the lamp. 'We have a new friend to share our coffee.'

The woman stared hard at Henri before accepting his proffered hand. She murmured good evening before going over to the cupboard for another cup and saucer. The old man invited Henri to seat himself and he did so, taking the hard-backed chair by the table. The woman poured three cups of coffee.

'There is no sugar,' she said.

They sipped the bitter ersatz mixture, then Papa Vilain put down his cup and said to Henri, 'So you want to know about the war, eh? Well, you have an honest face and you have given a limb for your country, so I will tell you the unpalatable truth. The situation is as the Germans claim.'

Henri sat motionless. 'We are losing?'

'We are not winning. The Germans have undoubtedly crushed the Serbian armies in the Balkans, and appear to have dealt successfully with the Russians. Proof of this lies in the fact that Falkenhayn has been pouring fresh troops on to the Western Front.' He sighed. 'The losses on both sides at Verdun appear to be beyond belief, yet after three months the outcome is still unsure.'

'I have heard of a place called Verdun.'

'I fancy that the name will never be forgotten,' the old man said heavily.

They sat in silence, the woman with her hands folded on her apron. Then Papa Vilain roused himself and went over to the fire. Peering inside the coffee pot he announced that there was still enough for half a cup each. He poured it out.

'Come,' he said to Henri, 'there is no point in becoming despondent when there is work to be done. When do you return to Dinant?'

'I shall begin the journey tonight. There is no reason to stay longer in Brussels.'

The old man smiled. 'It would be far wiser to go tomorrow when you have rested and when we have talked together. My good Marthe can provide you with a bed, but first, let me show you something.'

He picked up one of the brown foolscap envelopes from the table, tore it open and removed from it a small, neatly folded newspaper.

'There you are, my friend,' he said. 'Take it home to Dinant and tell your friends that despite military setbacks, our hearts are still full of hope.'

Henri unfolded the paper and found himself looking at a large photograph of King Albert, and at a message of affectionate greetings from him to all his subjects. Blinking rapidly, he read the name of the paper. *La Libre Belgique, Bulletin de Propagande Patriotique.*

Without reading any further he re-folded it and held it close against his blouse.

'Where did it come from?'

Papa Vilain smiled happily. 'My dear friend, have you never heard of the Resistance Movement?'

It was almost dawn before they went to bed, and when Henri bade Marthe Vilain good night he was too bemused to notice the look of sullen hatred in her eyes.

He reached home on the day his permit to travel expired and stood inside the kitchen door of the convent, looking at them all.

Clothilde was busy at the sewing machine with her little gold pince-nez trembling earnestly on her nose, while Yvette, with her long hair pinned up on top of her head, was bathing Albert in a big earthenware bowl at the other end of the table.

He felt affection for them, and he felt love for the woman who stood over by the fire, stirring the evening soup. She was wearing a patched shirt-blouse with its sleeves rolled up, a long calico skirt with an uneven hem that showed black woollen stockings and the old familiar sabots that were so much a part of her. She was a peasant of the Ardennes soil, a creature nurtured by the sun, wind and rain, and to his way of thinking she was inexpressibly beautiful.

'Thérèse,' he said.

She spun round, then dropped the spoon in the soup with a splash and it was bitterly wrong that he had only one arm with which to encompass her.

Then they all saw him, Albert rising up in the bath and sending a shower of water over Clothilde's sewing. Clothilde jumped to her feet so eagerly that she ran a pin in her hand and Yvette flew towards him with a shriek of joy and scattered sops of bathwater that glittered in his hair like little diamonds. The soup boiled over. And they all laughed with relief and happiness and dragged him by his one hand over to the armchair and made him sit down while they loosened his boots and unfastened his collar and smoothed his hair.

And while he struggled to maintain an air of calm pre-eminence, he looked back in wonderment on his fretful impatience with their solicitude.

During supper he told them of his adventures, and because they were so starved of news they insisted that he should begin at the very beginning and proceed chronologically to the end. Clothilde turned pale when he described the interlude in the *préfecture* in Namur, and they all expressed a sense of outrage that a Belgian should earn his living by working in an office at the beck and call of the Boche.

'What did he look like, this pen-and-paper scum?' demanded Thérèse.

'Thin, like the rest of us,' Henri said, 'with a pale face and grey hair. And he seemed more weary than any man I know.'

'Would you recognize him again?' asked Yvette.

Henri broke off a piece of rye bread and began to chew it thoughtfully. 'There is no doubt of it,' he said.

He told them of his journey to Brussels with the old drover, and Yvette was eager to know how the women of Brussels were dressed. Hunting through his recollections Henri thought of the two girls in the café and told her that they were very pretty and chic, then noticing her wistful expression added that they had none of the natural comeliness of country girls.

They continued to ply him with questions, and Thérèse had lit the lamp in the centre of the table when he reached inside his blouse and drew out the copy of *La Libre Belgique*. The three women crowded close, and Clothilde reached for her pince-nez.

'You asked me about many things,' he said, 'but here is the thing of importance. Here is the voice of free Belgium.'

Wonderingly they examined it, reading snatches here and there and turning and re-turning the flimsy pages.

'The people who publish this newspaper are heroes,' Clothilde said reverently, 'and may the Blessed Virgin protect them.'

He told them then about Papa Vilain, and all that he had learned from him about the secret network of patriots who were operating throughout Belgium. Working in isolated groups ensured that no one knew too much, and everyone — including Papa Vilain — worked in ignorance of those who were in command. And the nature of the work was the discreet sabotage of railways and factories, an unrelenting policy of dumb insolence towards the conquerors and the publication and distribution of *La Libre*.

There was another important publication, and he told them about *Mot du Soldat*, the organization founded by a Madame Pol Boel which carried letters between Belgian soldiers and their families.

'Was that how I received yours?' Thérèse asked.

'I gather so.'

They fell silent, remembering.

'So perhaps Jean-Baptiste . . . ?' Yvette began.

'There is a chance,' he told her gently.

They went to bed with their minds filled with hope because of the new world Henri had brought back with him, and the moon was low in the sky when the silence was shattered by the harsh clatter of hooves and the sound of shouting. Jerked from sleep, they lay straining their ears.

Quietness fell, and they relaxed. Then a new sound tore the silence: rigid with fear they heard the demented screaming of a woman followed by a fusillade of rifle shots.

CHAPTER NINE

They heard the news early next morning.

The twin sons of the Widow LePage, who had elected to remain in hiding rather than become German conscripts, had been dragged from their beds by armed military police and shot, standing side by side against the garden gate. Their mother had been a witness.

Stunned, the people of St Louis les Bois stood outside their houses, then gathered in silent groups to read the official notice pasted on the gate now pitted by bullet holes and splashed with blood. The notice said that having remained patient with Belgian reluctance to co-operate, the German High Command had decided that it was now time to make an example of the more flagrant acts of civil disobedience. It went on to say that the execution of the LePage boys could well be the first of many; the decision lay in the hands of the civilian population.

Now alone in the world, the Widow LePage stormed and sobbed behind closed shutters and the bodies of the two boys were buried without ceremony in a corner of the graveyard that even now was still littered with chunks of the shell-shattered church. Two German N.C.O.s stood guard over the proceedings and displayed ominous signs of impatience when the weeping became excessive.

But overnight the nakedness of the double grave became defiantly covered with flowers and green leaves and with pictures of the Virgin. Slipping out of the convent, Clothilde Toussant also placed a bunch of white violets there and prayed in the long trampled grass for the peace of their souls.

The murder of the LePage boys brought people from other villages to pay their respects; they came in small illicit processions, and farmers arrived from the remote moorlands with little gifts of vegetables or a few eggs for the bereaved mother. People trudged up the narrow road from Dinant, and despite orders to the contrary a priest conducted a Mass for the victims.

Standing bareheaded in the roofless church of St Louis les Bois Henri Aubel looked round at the embittered faces, the work-thickened hands clasped in prayer, and came to a sudden decision.

To help circulate *La Libre Belgique* was not enough. Somehow, with the aid that Papa Vilain had promised, he would produce an underground newssheet expressly for the people of his own area, and listening to the low resolute murmur of voices in unison, there was only one possible name for it. *La Voix des Ardennes.*

He told Thérèse about it that evening, mentally bracing himself for the many awkward questions that would undoubtedly arise because of the sheer impracticality of the idea. But to his surprise and gratification she was warmly enthusiastic, and instead of pointing out his woeful lack of penmanship made the sensible suggestion that Schoolmaster Groult would be the very person to help them.

'Can we trust him?'

'With our lives,' she said.

They broke the news to Clothilde and Yvette, and in the lingering summer twilight *La Voix des Ardennes* became so real that it was almost possible to turn its pages.

'Ours too, will have a photograph of the King,' said Yvette. 'And it will also bear advice for women about how to remain chic despite shortages.'

'It will also carry news of the war,' Henri said mildly. 'Provided Papa Vilain keeps in touch with us as he promised.'

'How will he do that?'

He shrugged. 'We must wait and see.'

Next day Henri cautiously approached Monsieur Groult.

'It is time that something should be done,' the old man said. He stared across the street to the widow LePage's tightly shuttered house. 'Somehow we have got to find a little hope and share it out among our neighbours.'

There were endless problems to face before they could even begin to plan, but no one in St Louis les Bois appeared to notice the frequency with which Monsieur Groult strolled towards the convent where the Aubels lived with the two other women.

'There is no possibility of our employing printers,' the old man said. 'Apart from the secrecy, there can be very few firms in existence. The Boche will have seen to that.'

'So we must write each copy by hand?' asked Thérèse.

'There is a middle course. One that would involve the use of a typewriter to make stencils which could then be run off on a gelatine duplicator.'

They stared at him, in their monumental ignorance of such things.

'I can print neatly with a pen and ink,' muttered Yvette. The old man turned to her affectionately.

'My child,' he said, 'at school you acquitted yourself nobly. You learned everything that you were taught, and it is not your fault that you were taught so little.'

'Do you remember a boy called Jean-Baptiste, Monsieur?' she asked, with her head bent low.

'I remember him well. Why do you ask?'

'No especial reason,' she said.

'Jean-Baptiste,' repeated the old man. 'He would have been an exceptionally fine scholar.'

'Will be,' said Thérèse, looking at him significantly. 'Will be, Monsieur, not would have been.'

'You do right to correct me,' he said. 'In wartime, the difference between the past and future tense has a terrible significance.'

A melancholy silence fell, then Henri said, 'A typewriter. And where do we begin searching for such a thing?'

'We begin searching in my attic,' Monsieur Groult said, 'where among the broken slates and the accumulation of a lifetime's rubbish I believe we may find one.'

So it was arranged, and when Clothilde came in Henri grinned at her and said that her nimble fingers were to forsake the profession of dressmaker for that of typist.

She accepted the idea calmly, and setting out the bone-handled soup spoons Thérèse looked back on the old Clothilde of August 1914 and marvelled at the difference. Still reserved, still impeccably ladylike, there was a quiet strength in her now and it seemed to go hand-in-hand with the rare sweetness of her smile.

A week passed, and Yvette was alone in the kitchen when she looked up and saw a man hovering in the doorway. He was tall and unbelievably thin. His dusty black coat and trousers hung limply on him and he constantly shifted his weight from one foot to the other as if he were doing a macabre sort of dance.

Amazed, and rather afraid, Yvette asked him what he wanted. The man smiled at her from behind a ragged moustache and asked for a man called Henri Aubel. Immediately she thought of *La Voix des Ardennes*, and her fear increased.

'Monsieur Aubel the farmer?' she asked. 'He is working in his fields.'

The man smiled again, then jumped convulsively from one foot to the other.

'Perhaps I could help you?' went on Yvette, determined to keep danger at bay until Henri returned.

'Perhaps I could help you,' repeated the man in a curious sing-song that had nothing particularly offensive about it.

'I don't know. Perhaps you could, and perhaps you couldn't.'

His loosely jointed limbs shook themselves in a brief tap-dance on the stone doorstep.

Yvette stood up, leaned her hands on the table and began to say with suitable dignity that he could come in and wait if he chose, then to her great relief saw Henri and Thérèse appear in the doorway behind the stranger.

'This man,' she said, 'says he wants to see you, Henri.'

Henri frowned. He and Thérèse had been weeding the cultivated strips in their fields and were both at their dustiest. They were also very tired. He stared hard at the stranger, taking in the angular black-clad limbs, the rough drooping moustache and the large sad eyes shadowed by a peaked cap. Memory stirred.

'Monsieur Henri Aubel?'

Henri nodded, while he searched for a clue to the man's identity. He had seen him before somewhere; but fleetingly, as if in a dream. Then suddenly it came to him. He had been playing the street organ outside Papa Vilain's house in Brussels.

* * *

'I have come with a message,' the man said to Henri, and drew an envelope from inside his ill-fitting jacket. The same type of brown foolscap envelope, Henri noted, that had lain in dozens on Papa Vilain's kitchen table.

He took it in his one hand, staring narrowly at the man who bobbed from one foot to the other. 'Who are you? What have you to do with me?'

'The people for whom I work call me Greco,' the man replied, as if that explained everything.

'And for whom do you work?'

'It varies. From now on I will sometimes be working for you.'

Holding the envelope between his knees Henri tore it open and read the letter it contained. It was from Papa Vilain and said very briefly that arrangements had been made for him to travel to Namur to meet some people who might be of assistance to him.

'When?' Henri looked up from the letter.

'The meeting is tomorrow night,' the man Greco said.

'And how do I get there?'

'I have a conveyance,' Greco said. 'And a set of forged papers.'

Thérèse stepped forward, took the letter from Henri, read it and then went across to the stove. She dropped it in the flames and watched it burn.

'Burn everything,' said Greco, nodding vigorously. 'Burn everything that can tell tales, and one day we will burn the Boche himself!'

'If those are your true sentiments,' Henri said, 'then we are willing to share our evening soup with you.'

He came over the threshold, bobbing and bowing like a nervous marionette, and when Clothilde came in from the chapel they introduced him to her. She shook his hand and smiled composedly.

It was decided that they should leave for Namur next morning and Greco accepted their offer of a straw pallet in an absent nun's cell. He slept in his clothes.

'I sleep anywhere, like a cat,' he told them.

After supper it occurred to Henri to enquire about the nature of the conveyance that was to take him to Namur. He had no recollection of seeing anything in the courtyard.

'I will show you,' Greco said, springing to his feet, and they followed him out of the kitchen door.

Parked discreetly behind an embrasure stood a bicycle with a two-wheeled, home-made handcart attached to the rear of it. Inside the handcart and taking up most of the room was a large box which Greco lifted out and unfolded on to four rickety legs, and instantly Henri recognized the little street organ he had heard playing outside Papa Vilain's shop.

'Play it — Oh, play it!' cried Yvette, clasping her hands. Scarecrow thin in the shadow of the war-stricken convent

Greco did so, and the haunting melancholy of the sound reduced them all to silence.

'And I,' said Henri, forcing a joke when it had ended, 'am permitted to use the small space in the cart that is not required by the organ?'

'That is so,' agreed Greco, smiling. 'With the knees folded under the chin, so, there will be no grave problem.'

Thérèse threw back her head and began to laugh.

'Perhaps you would care to go in my place?' Henri suggested.

Then Greco gave him his forged travel permit and identity card and they were back in the old twilight world of loneliness and fear.

Auguste Bourget was the new name. And his profession was that of street musician.

'I feel that we are entering a new and terrible epoch,' Thérèse whispered later that night. 'It is brave and wonderful to fight the enemy, but it also fills me with great foreboding.'

He pressed close to her in the darkness, stroking her long thick hair with his one hand. And he could think of nothing to say that would reassure her.

He left for Namur, sitting in the little cart with his back resting against the organ while he watched the bony haunches and thin piston legs of Greco, who was riding the bicycle. They stopped once and ate some bread and goat's cheese that Thérèse had given them, and the summer wind of 1916 came down warm and fragrant from the Ardennes hills and it could almost have been peacetime.

Henri asked Greco where he came from, and Greco smiled his timid, hesitant smile and said he didn't know, but someone had given him to understand that his father had been a Greek sailor.

'It is of no consequence.'

At Wepien they were stopped by a German military patrol, and it seemed to Henri that the soldier took an inordinately long time to examine his forged papers. Eventually they were allowed to proceed, but on the outskirts of Namur they were stopped again. This time it was more serious.

They were searched, and the organ was taken out and carefully scrutinized while Greco danced agitatedly round it, wringing his hands.

'You are street musicians?'

'As you see from our papers.'

'Why do you not work for a living?'

'Because you have taken away our work,' said Greco, surprised by the German's obtuseness.

'We are searching for smuggled food.'

'And neither have we food,' Henri said. 'Thanks to you.' The German raised his hand and struck him across the mouth. Henri staggered, but maintained his balance.

'Respect your betters,' the soldier advised him, 'or you will live to regret it.'

He rode off with his two companions. Tenderly Greco examined the organ, and as if conscious of his concern it gave a long wheezing sigh.

They reached Namur at dusk, the little cart containing Henri and the street organ bumping painfully over the cobbles while Greco cycled unerringly through an area of tall dilapidated houses.

A few yards from a small café he halted, and while Henri stood rubbing his cramped muscles began to unload the organ. He set it up on its spindly legs, fitted the handle in place and began to play. Anxious to conform, Henri removed his cap and held it out to passers-by. They collected a few centimes and a little girl who danced in front of them holding out her ragged skirt. Something about her reminded Henri of Yvette, and he recalled with sudden affection having given her a farm kitten when she was about the same age as this child.

Greco edged his way down the street, smiling and nodding while Henri followed with cap extended. Then an upstairs window opened and a man in shirtsleeves leaned his arms on the stonework.

'You make a sweet sound . . .'

'Thank you, Monsieur,' Greco said, smiling and bobbing convulsively.

'What is the name of the tune?'

'It is an old Flemish folk song, Monsieur, called *Do Not Forget*.'

The man smiled and dropped a key down to them. Henri picked it up.

'Come and join us for a glass of beer,' called the man at the window. 'And bring your friend with you.'

The stone stairs were gloomy and smelt of mildew. On the first landing Henri paused, trying to stifle a feeling of uneasiness. From over the iron balustrade above him the thin white face of Greco looked down, his eyes very dark and his ragged moustache twitching. He beckoned, and despite acute misgivings there was nothing to do but follow.

The man from the window met them at the entrance to his apartment. He was short and thickset, like an ex-pugilist. He welcomed them, shaking Greco by the hand and patting Henri amiably on his empty sleeve. The apartment, like the stairway, smelt of mildew.

The man led the way into a room and Henri was conscious of a number of people seated round a table with a torn baize top. The atmosphere was heavy with tobacco smoke and he blinked. Then stood quite still.

Seated at the head of the table was the tired, greyhaired Belgian who had issued him with a travel permit to Brussels. The Belgian whom he had called a murderer and a collaborator.

'Good evening, Auguste Bourget,' the man said. 'I have been looking forward to meeting you again.'

* * *

Thérèse wandered restlessly through the cool bare rooms of the convent until she came to the library. She opened the door and went in.

Clothilde was sitting at the table, her pince-nez clipped to her thin nose while her fingers pecked hesitantly at the keys of Monsieur Groult's old typewriter.

'Well, well,' grinned Thérèse, 'we now have a secretary in place of a seamstress!'

'I am exceedingly incompetent,' Clothilde said, frowning at what she had written. 'But I am at least a little faster than I was to begin with.'

'By this time next week you will be going like a galloping horse.'

'Unless Monsieur Groult is able to find a duplicator,' Clothilde replied dryly, 'I imagine I shall have to.'

She typed to the end of the page, then said, 'Yvette has drawn a very fine picture of the Belgian flag for the first issue of *La Voix*, but is hesitant about showing it to Henri for fear it is not good enough.'

Thérèse seated herself on the edge of the table.

'How the war has changed us all,' she mused. 'Do you remember Yvette when you first met her? A tawdry, defiant little strumpet with a bastard baby under her skirt? And regard her now; gentle, sweet-smelling, and filled with a humility for which one could weep.'

'You have changed too,' Clothilde said. 'You are less impatient, less prone to fits of rage.'

They sat silent for a moment.

'And you, my dear Clo',' Thérèse said suddenly, 'have changed most of all.'

'In what way?' asked Clothilde without looking at her.

'You have learned courage. Sometimes I suspect that you have more courage than the rest of us put together.'

'And who knows,' replied Clothilde with a smile. 'Perhaps the day will come when I will need more courage than the rest of you.'

She inserted a fresh piece of paper in the machine and began painstakingly to type.

Henri returned alone next day, Greco having left him in Dinant in order to pursue another mission entrusted to him by the men they had met in Namur. Greco, it had now become apparent, was a courier who formed a vital link between one little group of Resistance workers and the next.

'I had a strange premonition of disaster,' Thérèse, said when she saw Henri. 'Thank God I was wrong.'

He lowered the sack he was carrying on to the floor and began to untie it.

'So had I,' he said. 'Particularly at one point.'

He told her of the man from the *préfecture*, who was known as D. and who appeared to be the leader of the Namur group.

'But he works for the Germans.'

'By day, yes. But what happens in the evenings is another matter.'

'How can we be sure of him?'

Without replying Henri pulled a big parcel from the sack and laid it on the table. It was wrapped in newspapers. Slowly he removed them and Thérèse gasped.

'Yes,' Henri said. 'A duplicator, and he was the man who gave it to me.'

Still doubtful, she said, 'Ah yes. But no doubt he will want his price.'

With his one hand Henri unfastened the duplicator and opened the lid. It was in excellent condition.

'He wants his price indeed,' he said delightedly. 'He wants the first twenty copies of the first issue of *La Voix des Ardennes*!'

'But suppose you had been caught carrying the thing? It was a terrible risk.'

'We must be prepared to take risks from now on.'

'I suppose you are right.' She braced herself. 'And I must tell you that the first issue will have on its front page a magnificent drawing of the Belgian flag by our Yvette.'

'Our Yvette is an artist?' he asked, surprised.

'Second to none,' Thérèse replied firmly.

And the new life started. Like an object gathering momentum it began slowly and hesitantly, but within a few months was working with surprising smoothness. Monsieur Groult assumed editorial charge of *La Voix* while Clothilde typed his words and Yvette sometimes illustrated them with a little drawing, and the result was transformed on the gelatine duplicator into foolscap sheets of pale mauve print. They began with fifty copies, folding them into envelopes and slipping them through the doors of the occupied houses after dark. From the outset it was essential that they should tell no one of their connection with the paper, and Yvette in particular derived much amusement from pondering the mystery of its origin with various neighbours encountered on her walks with Albert.

Although they had planned to issue *La Voix* fortnightly, by the time August came the paper was appearing weekly and the number of copies had doubled. The man known as D. continued his support not only by helping to widen the distribution but by providing much of the raw material needed. Already, the cupboard in the library was stacked with sufficient foolscap to last them for several months.

As a product it was poor; the print was faint, the paper thin and grey, and the amateurish little drawings etched with a darning needle were in painful contrast to Monsieur Groult's rolling rhetoric. But its effect on the scattered population of the Ardennes area was instantaneous, and crumpled copies of it passed from hand to hand and were read greedily, and for those who had never mastered the art of reading there was a wonderful satisfaction in merely holding *La Voix des Ardennes* in their hands. For they were holding the faith and courage of ordinary people, and the proof that, however tenuous the link might *be*, they were no longer alone.

The war entered its third year and for Belgium, deprived of its manpower, there was little harvest to reap.

The shell-cratered fields lay empty under the blazing sun and peasants dug up their potatoes and hid them away as if they were nuggets of gold. For by now, potatoes formed the main diet of the entire country and it was a crime punishable by death to hoard them. A woman found carrying a bag of potatoes disguised as a baby-in-arms was discovered on a tram, and shot, while the rest of the passengers looked on. This happened in Anseremme, and *La Voix* instructed its readers to hold a regional day of mourning for the woman who had paid with her life for the crime of taking a little extra food to her grandparents.

At the convent in St Louis les Bois little Albert celebrated his second birthday.

On that day Greco also appeared on one of his brief clandestine visits and, unfolding the street organ from its box, produced from the secret compartment in its base a little gingerbread man with currant eyes and a scrap of blue ribbon for a necktie.

'There is one more thing I have brought from Namur,' he said, 'and that is a request for help.'

Henri looked at him sharply. 'How so?'

'I know little,' Greco said mournfully, 'and prudence tells me that the less I know the better. But D. wishes me to ask whether you would be prepared to shelter one or two guests for a night.'

'Here?'

Greco nodded.

'When?'

'When they arrive.'

Thérèse narrowed her eyes. 'And who, or what exactly, will these guests be?'

Greco gathered his scarecrow limbs together, smiled at her and said, 'I regret I am unable to say. But rumour has it that they are people making their way to the Dutch border for private reasons of their own. And if they could wait here until the guide arrives to escort them safely past the German patrols, they would be exceedingly grateful.'

Henri frowned at his boots, then said slowly, 'The penalty for hiding escapees is death.'

'I understand that running a Resistance newspaper carries the same retribution,' Thérèse said laconically.

Henri looked hard at her, then shrugged.

'Very well,' he said. 'We can only die once, no matter how many crimes we commit.'

'Wait,' Thérèse said suddenly. 'What of Clothilde? She also has a say in the matter.'

Clothilde, who had taken no part in the conversation, looked up from the little smock she was embroidering for Albert. 'I am willing to take my share of responsibility,' she said.

Greco departed soon afterwards with the latest copies of *La Voix* hidden in the organ. Thérèse and Henri watched him from the gateway, his angular legs pedalling away with the little cart rattling along behind.

'He is a strange one,' Thérèse said. 'Where does he come from? Where is he going to?'

'I have no idea where he comes from,' Henri said. 'But he is going in the same direction as the rest of us, and that is sufficient for me.'

CHAPTER TEN

The guests arrived at the convent on a moonless night in October, when a cold wind was driving the wet leaves from the trees.

Cautiously Henri opened the door and scrutinized their faces by the light of a hurricane lamp.

'Who are you?'

'We are friends of D. We were told to remain here until the guide comes to fetch us.'

They slipped through the door and stood close together, staring apprehensively at Henri and at the three women who sat by the table.

Thérèse was the first to break the silence.

'Merciful heaven,' she said. 'They are children!'

The one who had spoken to Henri drew himself up. 'If I may correct you, Madame, we are eighteen years old and we are adults.'

And staring into their fresh young faces was like staring at the LePage twins.

'So you are on your way to Holland,' Henri said. 'It is a dangerous journey.'

'It is preferable to the one to Germany,' said the boy.

'And you are wet and cold,' exclaimed Thérèse, going over to them. 'Take off your coats and come by the fire . . .'

It was strange to have newcomers in the convent, and conversation remained polite but guarded. When they had drained the jug of ersatz coffee, Henri led the way to the attic which had been prepared. The four young Belgians wrapped themselves in the thin grey blankets and laid themselves down on the straw palliasses to sleep.

Downstairs in the kitchen he found Thérèse surveying the steaming coats and mud-sodden boots arranged in front of the stove.

'We ought to hide them,' she said. 'In case.'

'Leave them,' he replied. 'I shall sit up and wait for the guide. He is expected to arrive at about five o'clock.'

'As you will.'

He went over to her and touched her shoulder. 'You are not afraid of the risk, are you?'

'Afraid?' She took his one hand between both her own. 'I am aware of the risk, but when I remember the LePage boys I am not afraid of it.'

'You are a good woman,' he said.

It was still dark when the guide woke him by tapping cautiously on the kitchen window. Startled out of a fitful sleep, he opened the door a chink.

'I come from D.'

Staring at him in the dim light of the hurricane lamp Henri recognized a man from whom he had bought a pair of geese some years ago. A man who had a fine poultry farm near Marche.

Impulsively they clasped hands.

'I find you in a curious setting, Monsieur,' said the man, glancing round the high convent walls.

Henri grinned. 'We are living in curious times and a man must seek shelter where he can. How are things with you?'

The man loosened his dark coat and pushed his workman's cap to the back of his head. He had a cheerful pockmarked face.

'My livestock was slaughtered by the Boche when they passed on their way to Rochefort. I have nothing but a broken house and four fields full of shell holes. So I must content myself with doing a few jobs here and there, some of them of an unorthodox nature.'

'Such as guiding boys of conscription age across Belgium to the Dutch border?'

'I do not take them all the way. At a certain spot they are handed over to someone else, so there is quite a number of us involved.' The man winked. 'Including you, Monsieur Aubel.'

'Including me,' repeated Henri. 'And while I am engaged in such activities, my name is Auguste Bourget.'

'I too have a new name,' said the guide. 'For the duration of hostilities I am known simply as Bertrand.'

'And now you have called for the four boys?'

'That is so,' said Bertrand. 'And if you have no objection, I prefer to think of them as *parcels.*'

* * *

The autumn of 1916 slid wet, foggy and cold into winter.

In Brussels the queues lengthened before the soup kitchens and the Americans distributed a consignment of blankets which people cut up to make into clothes. Tuberculosis increased, and hospitals were ordered not to admit civilians as both beds and medical supplies were to be reserved exclusively for German military personnel.

But despite the wretchedness at home and the apparently hopeless deadlock that existed between the armies on the Western Front, the Belgian Resistance Movement continued to grow, silently extending its tentacles throughout the nine provinces and undermining the German administration. Munitions trains unaccountably exploded. Copies of illegal newspapers mysteriously appeared on the desks of high-ranking staff officers, while letters from Belgian soldiers found their way in an equally mysterious fashion into the hands of those to whom they had been addressed. The *Mot du Soldat* organization was still flourishing.

Somehow the flame of hope was kept alight, and at the convent in St Louis les Bois it was no longer a matter of waiting passively and after the departure of the first four young Belgians and a warning from D. that more were likely to arrive, Henri decided that additional security measures were to be taken.

As a first step, he changed the hiding-place from an attic room of reasonable proportions to a small unused space in the thickness of the wall. It had no window, and he made access to it from the back of a cupboard, concealing his handiwork with a miscellany of bedding and old curtains.

Thérèse was aghast when she peered through the small tightly-fitting doorway into the blackness beyond.

'But it is hell!' she exclaimed.

'It is safe,' he replied. Nevertheless, he relented when the women insisted on furnishing the hiding-place with mattresses and a candle and an old pack of playing cards that Yvette had found in the ruins of the café.

Henri then turned his attention to the equipment used for the production of *La Voix*. Until recently they had been fairly casual in their approach, often leaving paper and ink and even the duplicator itself on the library table from one day to another. But now, prudence made him insist that the newspaper was to be produced in the cellar that ran beneath the kitchen. Although it was a dank and cheerless place, it had the great advantage of a well-concealed exit giving on to the courtyard.

Clothilde, by now a reasonable typist, sat clicking away at the stencil copies of Monsieur Groult's patriotic outpourings while Yvette in an ink-stained pinafore ran them off on the little hand duplicator. As the cold increased, their breath hung on the air in white clouds, but they went about the work without complaint and the circulation of *La Voix* continued to increase.

One evening in late November Greco arrived with the rumour that the Germans had begun the systematic deportation of every able-bodied Belgian male between the ages of eighteen and seventy, and that whole towns in Eastern Flanders had already been deprived of such manpower that remained to them.

'And what happens to the wives and children left behind?' demanded Thérèse.

Greco shrugged mournfully. 'They must manage as best they can.'

A depressed silence fell, then Yvette came into the kitchen, an old shawl pinned tightly round her. She gave a pile of foolscap envelopes to Greco with hands that were blue with cold.

'The cellar is chill as death,' she said. 'And your expressions are similar.'

They told her the news of the deportations.

'Holy Mother, soon there will be no men left—' She glanced at Henri, then looked away again, biting her lip.

'Except the occasional useless *mutilé*,' he grinned.

Little Albert ran across to her. 'I am a man,' he said.

She stood looking down at him and he seized her hand in both his own, squeezing it and trying to warm it against his chest.

'You are indeed a man,' she said, picking him up. 'And furthermore, it is high time that you were asleep in bed.'

He went with her without protest, glad to have her undivided attention for a while. The cellar where she worked was territory unknown to him and he sometimes grew fractious at her long periods of absence.

'I want Maman.'

'Maman has gone to catch a rabbit,' Thérèse would answer as she cooked and scoured pots in the kitchen.

While Yvette put her son to bed Greco stowed the new copies of *La Voix* in his bicycle trailer and prepared to depart on the long ride to Namur. Henri went out to the courtyard with him.

'You risk your life,' he said, thinking of the German patrols.

Greco smiled his melancholy smile. 'It is a life that matters to no one but myself,' he replied.

Henri watched him go, and stood picturing his black scarecrow figure flitting from house to house as he slipped the envelopes containing *La Voix* through letterboxes and under front doors, and then cycling on with the remaining fifty copies of the paper concealed in the secret compartment fitted in the base of the street organ.

Three more Belgians of conscription age arrived at the convent during the ensuing week and were hidden in the new space provided for them. On the second evening of their stay Clothilde carried a jug of cabbage soup to the cupboard and after removing the objects that concealed the entrance, crept inside their hiding-place. They were sitting huddled together inside a nest of blankets, their young faces illuminated by the golden haze of candlelight.

'I fear it is a poor supper,' she said, proffering the jug.

The one who sat in the middle smiled at her and said, 'You are giving us shelter, Mademoiselle Toussant. That is enough.'

'You know my name?' she said, startled.

'I come from Dinant, Mademoiselle. And once when I ran an errand for you, you gave me a chocolate mouse.' He took the jug from her. 'But when I ate it all in one mouthful you tapped me on the head with your thimble and told me that I should learn to make my pleasures last.'

With a hand that trembled slightly Clothilde clipped her pince-nez to her nose and peered closely at the boy.

I remember you,' she said slowly. 'You are Louis Lemonnier, and your mother was . . .' She faltered.

'My mother was the housekeeper of Père Joseph,' said the boy. 'She died when the Germans shelled the presbytery.'

She averted her face from the candlelight, and from the three pairs of eyes that regarded her steadily.

'And afterwards the Germans shot Père Joseph because he offered his life in exchange for the twenty hostages they took in Dinant.'

With her face still in shadow, she said, 'They refused to release all the hostages, but in return for his life they spared the children.'

'I was one of them,' he said.

* * *

By the second week in December they learned that the rumours of mass deportations were true.

Burgomasters of chosen towns and villages were ordered to produce the name of every man living within the area, and they were then summoned to appear before the German authorities with identity card, spare clothing and sufficient food for twenty-four hours. The majority of them were marched to the railway stations, pushed into trucks and taken away.

It happened at St-Ghislain, at Quiévrain and also at Ninove, and on 13 December it happened at Marche, only fifteen kilometres from Dinant. One of the men ordered to report to the railway station was the guide known as Bertrand. Silently his wife and children stood in the drizzling rain and watched him go.

Shortly afterwards Henri went to Namur in response to an urgent request from D. He found him in the same dilapidated house, at the top of the same stone staircase.

Surprisingly, he greeted Henri in a manner that was almost jocular.

'My dear friend,' he said, clapping him on the shoulder. 'Things are now resolving themselves. There are strong rumours that the Boche are negotiating for peace.'

'We heard the same rumour last Christmas,' Henri observed.

'Sometimes rumours come true.'

'But Belgium is on her knees.'

'So is Germany,' said D. 'They commandeer our men because they have so few left of their own. In Germany, both industry and agriculture are at a standstill, the country has been bled white by the war. People are starving and their morale is pitiful. Believe me when I tell you that the end is in sight.'

'How do you know this?'

'Our organisation is larger than you think.'

Henri sat in silence with his cap on his knee. The room was damply cold and rain ran down the window like tears.

Suddenly D. leaned across the table and began to speak in a low voice, '*Believe—*' he said urgently. 'Only *believe* in German defeat, and by some miracle it will happen. What I have just told you is a pack of lies, but believe them — hold tight to them, love them, cherish them, and in return your belief will give you courage and renewed strength.'

He drew a deep breath. 'In truth, the news is terrible. They have taken three of our guides, including Bertrand, and we have had to change the escape route into Holland. And now, one of our most reliable contacts has been caught with four boys hidden in her house. We await the outcome of her arrest with considerable anxiety.'

'She may talk?'

D. nodded.

'How much does she know?'

'No more than concerns her. But the Boche are aware of our organization. It is merely a question of time.'

'For many weeks,' Henri said slowly, 'I have had a premonition that things will go badly with us.'

'German patrols are being increased,' said D., 'and the secret police are active. In fact, they have been here.'

Henri drew in his breath sharply. 'How did they come to suspect you?'

'I am not sure. But sometimes I wonder about the integrity of those within the network.'

'Me, for instance?'

'If there is a leakage,' replied D., 'I have reason to believe that it is in Brussels, and in the circumstances it would be prudent to cease our activities for a while. But recent developments make that impossible.' He leaned forward again.

185

'Our work is now more vital than ever. Your work, in particular. Despite the difficulty and the danger you must be prepared to shelter more escapees. Perhaps many more.'

'It is not easy.'

D. sighed. 'I know. And I have more to ask of you. We are desperately short of guides.'

Henri sat staring down at the homely cloth cap on his knee.

'We need reliable guides between Dinant and the Louvain area. Without organized help the majority of those who are determined to make their way to Holland will be caught.'

'Yes.'

'And shot.'

'Yes.'

The cold damp room and the bitter tears of a Belgian winter trickling down the windows. The forlorn cry of a tram crossing the rue de l'Ange.

'I will return to St Louis and await your instructions.'

'I am grateful for your courage and your loyalty.'

'The first time we met,' Henri said from the door, 'you saved my life.'

'Despite your calling me a kiss-my-arse,' murmured D. with a small pained smile.

Henri returned to the convent, walking swiftly and unerringly through the winter dark with his one hand tucked deep in his jacket pocket and his mind busy with many problems.

Two hours after his arrival the first contingent of new escapees arrived. Cold and unshaven, the men of all ages who had become hunted outcasts in their own country stood in the convent kitchen, and only one of them appeared to have retained a sufficient hold on normality to be able to slip an arm round Yvette's waist when she offered him a warm drink, and to suggest that she might extend her generosity by warming his refugee bed for him. Laughing, she declined.

With three young conscripts already hidden in the secret space behind the cupboard there was only room for two more. The remaining five had to be accommodated elsewhere, and there was nothing for it but to put them in the attic that Henri had only recently condemned as too risky.

A new guide came to collect them on the following night, escorting the seven men and three boys down the dark street of St Louis les Bois on the next stage of their journey. Watching them go, Henri worried about the attention that eleven men would inevitably attract, however unobtrusive their movements.

Two days later four more men arrived, all from the area of St-Hubert and all of them chilled to the bone with the freezing rain. On Christmas Day Henri received instructions from D. via Greco that he was required to escort his current guests to an address on the outskirts of Louvain. Forged papers were provided, and the women at the convent did their best to supply a little food for the journey.

'At least,' said Yvette, pausing tear-streaked over a pile of sliced onions, 'we are too preoccupied with the problems of others to worry about our own.'

Thérèse agreed. Rising each morning before dawn they worked together to fill the big cauldron with thin vegetable soup which was by now their main means of sustenance, for with so many extra mouths to feed even the stock of home-grown vegetables was dwindling.

Coffee beans had been non-existent for many months but they had learned to make a passable beverage from hawthorn berries, while a woman living nearby had evolved a method of making substitute soap from wood ash and ivy leaves. Nothing in the entirety of Belgium was wasted. Fields and hedgerows were scoured for food and fuel while boots and clothes had never before been mended so assiduously.

'Even the good God Himself,' said Thérèse, 'could not mend and re-mend a pair of honest Ardennais sabots with more ingenuity than the shoemaker of St Louis les Bois.'

'When the war is over I shall have a pair of lady's shoes made out of real crocodile skin,' Yvette said, 'and a pair of fine silk stockings coloured pink. What for you, Clo'?'

'I have a premonition that after the war clothes will be of little use to me,' she said.

Yvette turned to look at her, and suddenly shivered.

Despite the long months of bitter cold and the extra work they had taken on, Clothilde still found time to care for the convent chapel. With her angular form wrapped round in a blanket and with mittens on her chilblained fingers she wiped the rain-blinded eyes of the Virgin and swept snow from the High Altar. Wild birds tamed by hunger and cold crouched in the shelter of the wall, watching her, and despite the shortage of food she generally had a few titbits in her pocket.

The chapel was a melancholy, mildewed place now, but she refused to relinquish the self-imposed task of caring for it until its rightful owners returned. On the contrary, when the wind screamed through the broken windows and icy March rain tarnished the newly polished Altar brass she was conscious of a strange exaltation and she looked back on the old shivering, finicking Clothilde with wonderment.

The spring of 1917 moved into summer, and with Henri frequently away from home Thérèse worked hard striving to surpass last year's vegetable crop. She was returning from the farm one sunlit afternoon when the Widow LePage stopped her, and indicating a man who stood a few feet away, said, 'Madame Aubel — I believe this person must be looking for you.'

Thérèse glanced briefly at the man then shook her head. 'I do not know him,' she said.

The Widow LePage came a little closer, lowering her voice. 'Perhaps not. But with all the visitors who call on you, might it not be possible to forget a face, just once in a while?'

Thérèse frowned. 'I fail to comprehend, Madame.'

The widow's smile was knowing. 'It is difficult to keep a secret in a small village,' she said, 'and it is rumoured that Monsieur and Madame Aubel have at one time and another kept a great many secrets hidden in the convent.'

Thérèse stared at her impassively.

'Secrets,' whispered her companion, 'that come and go during the hours of darkness.'

'Good afternoon, Madame LePage,' said Thérèse, and walked away with her heart thumping. The widow stood watching her.

So it had come at last. The evidence that people were talking. It was hardly surprising of course, and having discussed the possibility with Clothilde and Yvette, she and Henri had long ago decided that whatever the circumstances they would deny having any connection with either the escape route to Holland or with *La Voix des Ardennes*. Not only for their own safety, but for the safety of St Louis les Bois.

She went back to the convent, and in the drowsy summer silence became aware that someone was following her, the footsteps dragging softly through the dry dust. She walked on, keeping to the same nonchalant pace while she thought rapidly. From her one quick glance at the man she had gained an impression of more than average height and build, and she was positive that she had never seen him before. If she had, she would have remembered him.

Why was he looking for the convent? Who was he? Escapees sent by D. were carefully briefed, never travelled singly and always arrived under cover of darkness.

The footsteps were still shuffling behind her when she turned in at the convent gateway, and when she reached the kitchen door she went inside, closed it and leaned heavily against it.

Clothilde looked up from her sewing.

'What ails you, Thérèse?'

'Nothing. At least . . .' She came into the kitchen and sat on the edge of the table. 'There is a strange man outside. He followed me.' She decided to say nothing of the conversation with the Widow LePage. With Henri away in Namur there was no sense in causing unnecessary anxiety.

'Who was he?' Clothilde's eyes glimmered behind her pince-nez.

'I have never seen him before.'

'What did he want?'

'I know not.' She passed her square peasant hands over her black hair, smoothing it back from her forehead.

Clothilde opened the mouth to speak, then sat motionless. Their eyes met as they heard the soft footsteps shuffling over the cobblestones outside. Someone knocked on the door.

Thérèse stood up. The knock was repeated. She hesitated, glanced at Clothilde, then walked over to the door and opened it.

The man stood on the threshold in the golden sunlight. He smiled at her and said, 'I have been searching for you.'

Thérèse held the door firmly. 'With whom do you wish to speak, Monsieur?'

The man smiled again. 'With you, Madame.'

'I am afraid,' Thérèse said frigidly, 'that I do not receive uninvited guests.'

The man shifted his position and she noticed that he was wearing an old pair of canvas shoes. He was bareheaded, and his age might have been anywhere between thirty and fifty.

'I think it would be advisable for you to let me in, Madame,' he said, still smiling. 'I bear an important personal message from His Majesty the King.'

'The *King*?' repeated Thérèse, astounded.

Involuntarily she stepped back a pace and the man was in the kitchen, standing by the table. He bowed to Clothilde, who remained motionless, her needle poised.

'Poor ladies,' he said, 'to be so easily tricked.'

Rage filled Thérèse. She strode to the door and pointed to the courtyard.

'Out!'

The man looked at her and she glared back at him. He looked at Clothilde, and suddenly appeared to crumble. He slid to his knees and took her rigid hand in both of his own. He looked up at her with pale blue eyes full of tears.

'Save me,' he said.

CHAPTER ELEVEN

His name was Lucien. And the tears he shed were real and desperate while Thérèse stood at the open doorway, frowning and trying to think what to do. She wished more than ever that Henri were there.

'You must go,' she said, with slightly less conviction. 'Whoever you are and whatever you want, we cannot help you.'

'Save me,' he said. 'Hide me, the way you have hidden others.'

'We have hidden no one.'

'I know that you have,' he insisted, weeping against the folds of Clothilde's skirt. 'You and the one-armed man are famous for the work you do.'

Deeply perturbed, Thérèse leaned against the doorframe and said, 'We have hidden no one, but if such was our practice we would be fools to accept any strange cur who whined at our door.'

'Thérèse . . .' murmured Clothilde deprecatingly.

'War teaches one to speak bluntly,' muttered Thérèse. She folded her arms and glared at the intruder.

'And the war has taught me a great deal,' he said, still on his knees. 'My family were arrested and shot by the Uhlans in reparation for some deed of which they were totally innocent. My poor mother had passed her seventieth birthday.'

'And for what reason,' demanded Thérèse, 'did they see fit to spare you?'

'I was away from home. And on my return I was greeted by the sight of — of . . .'

'Try not to distress yourself,' murmured Clothilde, giving him her handkerchief.

'. . . their bodies lying in the mud where they had fallen. I dug their graves, one after the other.'

'And what do you propose to do now, Monsieur?'

'I am going to Holland,' he told Thérèse. 'I have heard that certain people know of the best routes to take, and once there I plan to join my compatriots fighting on the Western Front. I will never rest until I have helped to kill every Boche that crawls.'

His pale eyes narrowed and his face drained of colour. For a moment both women were startled by his expression of bestial hatred.

That man would murder, thought Thérèse, *and drink his victim's blood.*

As if he were aware of her silent observation he buried his face in Clothilde's skirt, then withdrew it from the dark folds and gave her a trembling smile.

'I may stay, Madame?'

'No,' replied Thérèse, 'you may not. This is an ordinary law-abiding home and we have no interest in the tribulations of others.' She held the door by its latch. 'I bid you good day.'

'I will not go.'

Her expression hardened. 'Perhaps you would prefer to wait until my husband returns. He is a man of jealousy and suspicion.'

'He is a man who risks his life for others.'

'His jealous manifests itself in the form of violent rages.'

'He helps people escape to Holland.'

'What you have heard is a lie,' Thérèse said steadily. 'And I advise you to leave before he arrives home.'

The man stared at her with his strange light-blue eyes for a moment, then said gently. 'My name is Lucien.'

'Get out,' said Thérèse. 'Whatever your name.'

The man Lucien gave a deep sigh, smiled at her sadly then walked through the door. Out on the cobblestones he turned and stared back through the kitchen. Abruptly Thérèse slammed the door and shot the bolt.

'Merciful God . . .' she said, wiping her face on her forearm. 'I thought we would never be rid of him!'

'Despite your extreme incivility . . .'

'Me — uncivil?' Thérèse returned to the table. 'Well, he provoked me. And furthermore, who is he?'

'He said his name was Lucien.'

'Very well. And *what* is he?'

Clothilde raised her large eyes. 'The world is full of poor unfortunates.'

'It is also full of stool pigeons,' Thérèse said. 'Greco has already told us that the Boche are disguising secret police as Belgian deportees.'

'Yet he seemed so . . .'

'These days,' Thérèse said harshly, 'people are frequently not what they seem.'

They said no more, and Clothilde continued to sew quietly while Thérèse set about preparing the evening meal.

An hour later Yvette banged on the door and rattled the catch while Thérèse unbolted it. She came in quickly, holding Albert tightly by the hand.

'The man—' she whispered. 'Did you bolt the door against the man at the gate?'

'He is still there?' Thérèse demanded.

'A big man with strange eyes. He is sitting in the dust with his back to the gatepost. I almost had to step over him.'

Thérèse drew a deep breath. 'Did he say anything?'

'Yes,' replied Yvette. 'He said he was waiting for you to change your mind and let him in.'

Thérèse decided that it was time to tell Yvette and Clothilde of the remarks made by the Widow LePage.

'It seems,' she said, 'that our secret is not as well guarded as we imagined. People must be talking, and the outcome could be fatal.'

Worriedly they discussed what to do, glancing at the clock and wishing that Henri would return.

'Why does the stupid creature have to hang about outside?' fumed Thérèse. 'Nothing could be more dangerous.'

'If he is really from the secret police,' said Yvette, 'why did he come alone? And when one considers it, he is not behaving very cleverly, is he?'

'That also worries me,' Thérèse said. 'He seems so child-like that one cannot accept it.'

'He appeared to be deeply distressed,' ventured Clothilde. 'It would be sad to turn an innocent sufferer from the door.'

'I will go out and speak to him,' resolved Thérèse. 'I will try to persuade him to go away, although with luck he may already have gone.'

'No, Thérèse—' Yvette said quickly. 'He is a big man and he could kill you.'

'I also think it would be unwise,' Clothilde said.

Thérèse shrugged, and they rebolted the kitchen door. Uneasily they waited.

Albert had been put to bed and supper was on the table when Henri arrived home. Clustering round him, the three women asked if he had seen the man at the gate.

'Man?' He looked tiredly from one to the other. 'Which man?'

They told him, and it was obvious from his expression that he had seen no one.

'Are you sure?' urged Thérèse. 'In the dusk it is difficult to see.'

'I saw no one,' repeated Henri. 'I came down the village street and it was deserted. There was no one at our gateway and no one in our courtyard.'

They sat down to eat, and it was a tremendous relief that Henri was home. Thérèse told him so.

'It is strange,' she mused, 'when I think how well we managed without you in the early days.'

'You have become soft,' he teased.

Under the table she gave his leg a jab with her sabot. 'I have not yet grown so soft that I cannot administer a few bruises to my husband's person—'

'I declare before God that I married a monster—'

Yvette's scream rang out sharply. Startled, Clothilde dropped her fork and the three of them turned quickly in the direction of Yvette's pointing finger.

Against the dark kitchen window the face of the man Lucien was pressed like a pale, round cheese.

'I know you hide people,' he said.

'Where did you hear this?' Henri sat opposite him at the kitchen table while Yvette silently handed round mugs of weak coffee.

The man Lucien repeated the story about his parents and again avowed his intention of escaping to Holland in order to join the Belgian Army on the Western Front.

'I will kill and kill and kill!' he said, and bestiality flickered in his eyes before being extinguished by the obsequious, eager-boy smile.

The pale blue eyes of a Boche, thought Henri, watching him. *And French spoken with an authentic middle-class Belgian accent.*

Somehow a decision had to be made. To accept him would be risky. To deny him, to leave him to hang about the village drawing attention to the convent, would be worse. Placing his one hand palm down on the table, Henri stared hard at the man and said, 'We believe your story. You are welcome to remain here provided you obey the necessary rules for your safety, until you are escorted on your way to the border by a reliable guide. I take it that you have an identity card and a work permit?'

The man shook his head.

Henri frowned. 'That makes things difficult. Might one ask what became of them?'

Lucian spread his hands and smiled happily. 'I lost them.'

'That, Monsieur, was extraordinarily careless.'

'I beg you,' replied his companion. 'Call me Lucien,'

But he was appalled when they showed him the hiding-place in the thickness of the wall.

'In *there*?' He hesitated at the entrance, peering through the carefully cluttered cupboard into the darkness beyond. 'But am I not allowed to stay downstairs with you?'

'No,' Henri said firmly.

'I could help the ladies.'

'The ladies,' Thérèse said laconically, 'are accustomed to helping themselves.'

Sighing, he allowed himself to be incarcerated.

Downstairs they debated the subject of Lucien ceaselessly, and after the first twenty-four hours had passed without incident, became increasingly convinced that he was as Clothilde had suggested, merely one more confused and unhappy creature uprooted by the vast machinery of war. The next consignment of *parcels* was not due to arrive for another two days and the women took it in turns to carry his meals; each time he greeted them with a pathetic gladness and delayed their departure for as long as possible with a torrent of eager conversation.

'It is terrible to have only a candle flame for company,' he mourned when Clothilde took his evening soup.

'One is never without the company of God,' she told him gently.

That same evening they were alerted by a smell of burning, and it was Henri who suddenly pounded off upstairs, cursing himself for a fool while he tore aside the contents of the cupboard and pulled open the door.

A dense cloud of smoke rolled out. Blind and choking, he encountered the inert body of Lucien lying on the smouldering mattress. The candle was out.

With the aid of Thérèse he dragged Lucien out, hauled the mattress to the nearest window and hastily bundled it through. It fell into the courtyard in a disintegrating heap of blackened straw.

'You fool! — you fat-gutted moron!' roared Thérèse, and drenched the recumbent figure with a pailful of cold water. He stirred, groaned, smiled an apology, then lapsed into unconsciousness.

It was four hours before he recovered.

'Yet despite his foolishness,' said Yvette, 'one cannot help liking him just a little.'

Grudgingly Thérèse agreed. 'Nevertheless I shall be more than relieved when he departs with the next consignment.'

'Unfortunately he will have to remain a little longer,' Henri said. 'He has no documents, and it takes time to notify Namur so that they may provide them.'

Thérèse sighed.

Monsieur Groult came that evening with some material for the next issue of *La Voix*. He also brought some disturbing news: the large house in the village that had once belonged to a retired Brussels notary and which now sheltered two refugee families, had been requisitioned by the Boche. According to rumour it was to be used as a local head-quarters for the secret police.

Henri and the three women looked at each other, but there seemed nothing worth saying.

While the hiding-place was being restored and prepared for the expected visitors, Lucien was allowed to remain in the kitchen with Clothilde. He sat at the table watching her at work repairing convent linen, and after a little while volunteered to turn the handle of the sewing machine. She accepted his offer, and later showed him the chapel. Silently he followed her down to the High Altar, where she genuflected before beginning the task of polishing the great candlesticks and then replacing them on the crisp white Altar cloth together with a jar of carefully arranged wild flowers.

'But when it rains,' he said, glancing up at the open roof, 'it will all become spoilt again.'

She smiled.

With the arrival of the three new escapees Henri insisted that Lucien remain with them in the hiding-place. He went, but within a short space of time was back in the kitchen, standing large and obsequious beside Thérèse, who was washing clothes. She rounded on him, and told him to go back at once. He scraped the toe of his worn canvas shoe on the floor and said that he didn't want to. It was dark in there, and the other men unfriendly.

Exasperated, she told him that he was a great big child, and immediately realized that she had inadvertently put her finger on the truth.

Far from being a stool pigeon or a German agent, or even an ordinary civilian driven by the war to a state of be-wildered uncertainty, Lucien was in fact a child inside a man's body. And like any other child he had a wilfulness, an insouciance that was far more difficult to deal with than any form of wickedness. For one thing, thought Thérèse, wicked people are not normally lovable.

Afraid that he might cause further gossip if they turned him out of the convent and he hung about the village, Henri and Thérèse decided not to insist that he remain cooped up in the hiding-place with the other men. If he could be persuaded to conceal himself, all well and good, but failing that he was to be allowed in the convent kitchen provided that he was never left alone. And with any luck his forged papers should arrive from Namur and he could then be sent on his way.

Lucien had been at the convent for a week when the four German baggage wagons arrived. White with summer dust they rumbled down the main street of St Louis les Bois and came to a halt outside the house that had belonged to the notary. Soldiers began to unload boxes and sacks and wicker hampers. Watched discreetly by the villagers they carried iron beds and straw mattresses into the house, then wooden tables and kitchen chairs.

Towards evening the wagons withdrew, and the villagers waited uneasily to see what would happen next. For two days the house remained deserted except for sentries, but on the following night the street was woken by the chugging of motor vehicles.

Early next morning they learned that they were German ambulances and their passengers convalescing soldiers. They saw them in the notary's garden on crutches, in splints, in bandages, and their faces were hollow with fatigue. The villagers continued to watch them coldly, waiting for the first sign of interference. None came. The orderlies and the two or three German nurses were engrossed in their duties while the convalescents seemed content to sit at peace under the trees. Sometimes a group of them would remain in the garden until quite late, their white bandages gleaming in the dusk while they sang German folk songs to the melancholy accompaniment of a mouth organ.

'They are homesick,' Yvette said, once.

'And pray, whose fault is that?' demanded Thérèse.

Another week passed before Greco appeared with a set of forged papers for Lucien.

'D. has made arrangement for him to be received at the usual house, along with the others. He asks that you set off tonight.'

Henri nodded, then told him of the Germans' arrival in the village.

'They cause no trouble,' he said, 'but they increase the risk, and I own that I will be very glad to be rid of the man Lucien. We all find his presence strangely unnerving.'

'Where did he come from?'

'I know not. Each time he tells a slightly different story.'

'He is the only escapee not to have come from us. Are you sure you can trust him?'

'Not entirely. We make it a rule never to leave him alone.'

'He is a strange man,' Greco said. 'And in these days of privation, how does he remain so plump?'

'Alas, I have no answer to that, either.'

Greco smiled, then patted Henri's shoulder. 'Courage,' he said, 'and by nightfall you will have him well on the way to Holland.'

Lucien was splitting kindling wood in the kitchen when Henri went to tell him the good news. He looked up, grinned, and then returned to his task.

'Think, Lucien,' exclaimed Thérèse, who was gutting a wild rabbit, 'within a week you may well be in Holland!'

Lucien up-ended another small log and divided it into neat sticks. He appeared absorbed.

'You had better rest now,' Henri said, 'for we leave this evening and will be walking until dawn.'

Lucien added the sticks to the pile he had made.

'Forgive me,' he said gently, 'but I have changed my mind. I wish to remain here.'

Henri blinked. Thérèse turned round from the table, the rabbit lying limp in her hands.

'You do not understand,' Henri said quietly. 'It is no longer a question of choice. Your papers have been prepared and your continued presence in this house is dangerous. You must go.'

Crouched on his knees, Lucien ran his big thumb along the blade of the hatchet. He ran it back again, and his smile was that of a loving child.

'You cannot make me go,' he said, and with sinking hearts the Aubels realized the truth of his words.

They decided not to argue, but went about the preparations for the long walk in silence.

The men hidden behind the cupboard were warned of their imminent departure, and were allowed downstairs to stretch their legs and receive a briefing from Henri.

As always, he travelled at night and slept hidden from the roads by day, and in the event of their being caught they were to pose as casual labourers looking for harvest work.

Thérèse and Yvette prepared a little food for them to take and they all waited for the long summer day to melt into the cool of night.

Lucien watched the preparations with interest but gave no sign of changing his mind. Casually Yvette asked him whether he enjoyed walking and, equally casual, he replied that it depended on his destination.

'Holland is a fine country,' Thérèse said meaningly. 'From there, one can reach England.'

'I shall stay here,' he said. 'I prefer it.'

'Does this mean that we are to be saddled with him for ever?' Thérèse asked despairingly. She and Henri were leaning on their bedroom windowsill shortly before he left, watching the stars appearing in the aubergine sky.

'I will get in touch with D.,' Henri said. 'Perhaps he can tell us how to solve the problem.'

'He frightens me,' Thérèse whispered. 'I am ill-equipped to deal with halfwits.'

He touched her thick black hair with his hand and impulsively she imprisoned it in both her own. Then she opened his palm, tilting it towards the dying light and examining it closely.

'What a strong, safe hand it is.'

'It must do the work of two.'

'Does it become very tired?'

'Sometimes. It depends on the work.'

'What type of work does it prefer?'

'This,' he said, and his fingers inched their way along her arm, reached her shoulder then moulded the back of her neck. He kissed her mouth, and melting with sudden desire she felt the fingers moving up her neck and gently removing the pins from her hair. It fell past her shoulders like a dense curtain.

She moved her mouth away. 'I cannot bear you to go.'

'I must.'

'I am afraid . . .'

'Oh, my lovely woman,' he said, 'you have never known the meaning of fear in your life . . .'

* * *

The summer heat had intensified, and each day seemed to bake the dry earth a little harder. By eight o'clock on the morning following Henri's departure the cobblestones in the courtyard were already hot to the touch and the whole world seemed locked in a sultry inertia.

Perhaps it was the weather that made little Albert unusually fractious. He hung around Yvette's skirts and grizzled until Thérèse became impatient.

'For the love of heaven, child — go out and play!'

Yvette turned on her. 'Leave him alone,' she exclaimed, 'he is nothing to do with you—'

'Nothing to do with me?' repeated Thérèse, astounded. 'And after all I've—'

'Go on — go on!' cried Yvette, abruptly losing her temper, 'tell me how much you've done for me, how much I owe to you—'

'Be silent!' roared Thérèse, her face crimson. Albert began to howl.

Lucien appeared, shambling through the door like an overgrown bear.

'Dear ladies,' he said, 'you are distressing the little boy. Allow me—'

'Leave my son alone and mind your own business—' shrieked Yvette.

'Yvette — Lucien—' began Thérèse, then halted. She looked from one to the other, then ramming her bare feet into her old sabots, marched out of the kitchen door.

She went out of the gate and into the street, and the sun was like a savage blow on the head. With her sleeves rolled up and the anger strong within her she made her way to the healing solitude of the farm.

And a little before midday Yvette went in search of Clothilde. She found her in the cellar beneath the kitchen, at work on the latest issue of *La Voix*.

'Clo,' she said, 'will you take a turn as Lucien's jailor while I go for a walk with Albert? It must be the hot weather that makes him so tiresome.'

Clothilde removed her pince-nez. 'Of course,' she said. 'There is little more I can do until I receive the article Monsieur Groult is writing.'

Yvette thanked her, hesitated, then said, 'Thérèse and I have had a quarrel.'

'What about?' enquired Clothilde, gathering papers together.

'About nothing, in truth. We just found ourselves shouting, and now I feel very miserable.'

'Blame the heat,' advised Clothilde. 'My dear Maman always remarked on the extraordinary affiliation between the weather and the state of one's nerves. And the outbursts of Thérèse are soon forgotten.'

'She is worried about Henri,' Yvette said. 'It is as if she senses trouble.'

Clothilde remained silent, but led the way up the stone steps. When they reached the kitchen she asked where Lucien was and Yvette pointed through the window.

He was lying on his back under a tree in the orchard, his large body spreadeagled in sleep.

'He is unlikely to cause you trouble,' she said. 'He sleeps like a pig.'

Albert ran up to her, then began to protest when she washed his hands and face and combed his bright yellow hair.

Clothilde watched her set off, holding Albert by the hand. She remained in the doorway for a moment, shading her eyes and staring at the motionless figure of Lucien.

Thérèse meanwhile sat alone on the edge of the well in the old farmyard, staring moodily at the green jungle that engulfed it a little more each year. Instead of offering comfort the place only increased her depression, and once again she felt overwhelmed by the endless drag of the war.

A year ago she had been fool enough to imagine that working for the Resistance would hasten the day of victory. But now she knew better. Despite the hardship and the risk, the war would go on for ever and she was destined to spend the rest of her life shut up in a ruined convent with two wearisome women and a child, forever worrying about a husband who was seldom there.

She picked up a stone and hurled it savagely.

And neither had Yvette recovered her equilibrium. She lay on the bunk in the hut that had once belonged to Jean-Baptiste and it was impossible to imagine his return. Two years since she had last seen him, there were whole days now when it was impossible even to recall his features.

Most probably he was dead. And they would never be married. And who would care? Certainly not Thérèse.

Outside the hut, little Albert ran through the woods laughing.

* * *

Lucien remained locked in sleep beneath the damson tree, and Clothilde peered at him for the umpteenth time and wished that either Thérèse or Yvette would return.

Inactivity always annoyed her, and despite the heat she had planned to call at Monsieur Groult's house to collect the article for *La Voix*. It had to be typed and duplicated, and time was running short.

She walked up and down the kitchen, then peered at Lucien again. He was now lying on his belly with his head on his arms, and although she called his name he made no answer.

How selfish Thérèse and Yvette had become! Merely because of a silly argument they had both turned their backs on their responsibilities and had left her alone in charge of a strange man. Her resentment grew.

Obeying a sudden impulse she smoothed her hair, buttoned the cuffs of her blouse and slipped out of the door. She gave a last quick glance at the sleeping figure of Lucien then hurried through the gate in the direction of Monsieur Groult's house.

It was the last time that she would walk alone in the sunlight.

CHAPTER TWELVE

Under the damson tree a fly alighted on Lucien's hand. Rising from the depths of sleep he brushed it away. It circled his head and then returned. He opened one pale blue eye and watched it. Stealthily raising his other hand he brought it down with a crack and the fly was dead.

He yawned and sat up. Across the orchard the convent courtyard was deserted, the kitchen door closed. There was no sign of the three women. He stretched lazily then stood up, and was on the point of calling them when something caught his attention. Standing motionless, he watched a German soldier walk stiffly across the courtyard and knock on the kitchen door. No one answered.

Lucien watched through half-closed eyes. The German went to the window and peered through it, framing his eyes with his hands. He went back to the door and knocked again. No one came.

Of course not. And standing by the damson tree Lucien pictured the three women hiding in terror, watching from a dark corner as the Boche sought them through the window. The thought of their plight filled him with excitement.

As the German soldier continued his reconnaissance Lucien began to walk towards the courtyard, his big body moving smoothly and quietly through the trees. The German tapped a brisk tattoo on the window pane and Lucien imagined the women shrinking back in terror. Yvette, he imagined, would be weeping with her little boy in her arms.

Passing through the wicket gate he began to move across the courtyard, his canvas shoes making no sound. Unaware of his presence the German returned to the door and opened it. Lucien watched him hesitate for a moment, then cross the threshold. Smiling, he followed him.

The kitchen was deserted, yet it was full of the women's presence. The sewing machine on the big scrubbed table spoke of Clothilde, the jar filled with wild flowers epitomised Yvette, and as for Thérèse . . . ?

He paused by the brownstone sink, his ears alert for the German who had walked through to the hall. A large iron pan filled with prepared vegetables stood ready for cooking and by the side of it lay the old kitchen knife that Thérèse always used. It was a wicked knife. Small, discoloured, and with a short stubby blade that had been sharpened to a thin point. His smile increased. Now that was Thérèse! He picked up the knife and held it concealed in the palm of his hand.

And now the excitement turned to a different feeling. He remembered about wanting to go to Holland to join the Allies. He remembered about his family, and he remembered the faces of the three Belgian women who had now become for him a kind of corporate mother-figure.

He met the soldier face to face at the foot of the staircase. The soldier drew in his breath with surprise, then smiled and held out his hand. He was a middle-aged man and held his body carefully, as if it were sensitive to sudden movement. He began to say something in halting French, then his expression changed when he saw the knife.

'The women,' Lucien said, 'are under my protection.'

The German took a step forward, then paused. He stood searching for words. 'Do you live here?'

'Yes. Furthermore, I am going to kill you.'

The German opened his hands. 'I am unarmed.'

'So much the easier.' Lucien gave a sudden giggle. The German moved towards the stairs.

'I am unarmed,' he repeated. 'I have friends here.'

'A Boche has no friends.'

With the knife out-thrust Lucien followed the German. The German gripped the balustrade and began to retreat backwards up the stairs. His movements were awkward. With his free hand he again indicated his lack of weapons. Lucien giggled, then sprang.

The knife slid between the soldier's ribs. He gasped, and fell back on the stairs. Lucien grabbed his ankles and pulled. Noisily he slid to the bottom, his head bumping on every stair.

'I am a friend.' He stared helplessly up at Lucien, his hand hovering over his chest.

Insane rage blinded Lucien. He wrenched the knife free and stabbed again and again.

'That one for Thérèse! — that one for Yvette! — and that one for Clothilde!'

The soldier's eyes glazed even as Lucien watched. Fascinated, he knelt down and traced the line of the man's eyebrow with one finger, then lightly flicked his cheek. No response. Like a child with a broken toy he flicked harder, willing the dead man back to life. Then he saw the blood on his fingers, felt its warm smooth stickiness, and horror filled him.

With a cry he scrambled to his feet and ran blindly into the courtyard. The scorching sun beat a blood-red retreat on his skull and he stumbled, then regaining his balance bolted back through the orchard and scrambled through the broken wall.

Sobbing, he fled away over the high sandy plateau that stretched into the heart of the Ardennes.

Greco was bicycling towards St. Louis les Bois, his boots thrusting hard at the pedals and his head bent low over the handlebars. Behind him the two-wheeled trailer bounced and rattled.

He was on the way from Namur, carrying bad news from D.

The German police had arrested Papa Vilain in Brussels and the old man's wife, presumably in an effort to save him, had told them of a one-armed man somewhere in the Dinant area who formed an important link in the escape route to Holland. So far as D. knew, she had said nothing about his connections with *La Voix des Ardennes*, but it was a matter of prime importance that all resistance work at the convent should cease, at least for the time being.

He pedalled faster, and the broiling sun brought lurid images of death. Civilians convicted of subversive activities were generally shot by a firing squad. Sometimes they were hanged. Neither appealed to him.

Out of the country silence he became aware of the steady chug-chug of a motor car on the road behind him. He glanced over his shoulder and saw a large limousine raising a cloud of dust on either side of its arrogantly glittering headlamps.

He tried to increase his speed even more. He had already noticed the car a short distance from Namur, and had wondered about it uneasily. Only Germans had motor cars. Especially the secret police.

The road dropped down until it ran parallel with the river and he entered the outskirts of Dinant. Obeying a sudden impulse he turned down a narrow side-street, swung into another one then turned in his tracks and took the rough back-road that led through the woods to St Louis. The sharp stones were cruel to his worn tyres but at least the car would be unable to follow him.

Three kilometres along the road a little waterfall splashed from the rocks. Dismounting, Greco cupped his hands and drank, gulping the water quickly and desperately then splashing some over his perspiring face. He rode on again, and at the entrance to the village slowed his speed and endeavoured to conform to the role of indolent street musician.

The place seemed deserted, lost in a hot summer dream. A few convalescent soldiers at the notary's house lay asleep in canvas chairs under the trees. Increasing his speed again he turned through the broken gateway of the convent then jammed on the brakes and came to a juddering halt. Outside the kitchen door stood the limousine that had followed him from Namur.

The uniformed chauffeur was holding a revolver.

'Inside,' he said, jerking his head at the door. Greco obeyed, his ill-co-ordinated limbs shaking.

The kitchen was deserted and the chauffeur prodded him into the hall where a shaft of sunlight fell across the body of an elderly German soldier. He lay on his back, and the front of his army shirt was crimson with blood.

Two men in civilian clothes stood looking at the body and opposite them Thérèse and Yvette huddled close together, Albert half hidden between their long skirts. Their faces were ashen. Thérèse looked up slowly as Greco entered, then looked away again.

'Who is this man?' One of the two civilians wore a monocle.

Greco watched Thérèse moisten her lips. 'I have no idea,' she said in a low voice.

'Come now,' said the other man. 'You seem not to know anyone. Does that include the German soldier lying stabbed to death on the floor?'

'I have never made a point of fraternizing with the enemy,' she retorted with a flash of the old spirit, but Greco noticed that she kept her eyes averted from the murdered man.

The monocled civilian gave her a level stare. 'Do you also deny knowing a one-armed man who goes by the name of Auguste Bourget? I have evidence that you have fraternized with him to a considerable degree, over the years.'

Thérèse clamped her lips shut and continued to stare at the floor.

'Answer me.'

'I have nothing to say.'

'He is your husband. And he is a criminal.'

'That is untrue!' Yvette cried. Thérèse nudged her to be silent.

The other German removed a cheroot from an inner pocket. He lit it and stood smoking reflectively.

'We know all about you,' he said to Thérèse, 'so it is quite useless to pretend ignorance. We know that your husband, the one-armed man, both hides and escorts Belgian workers out of the country. We know your contacts, in fact we already have most of them under lock and key.'

As his shocked mind slowly began to function again, Greco thought of Henri on the way home from Louvain. It was vital to warn him, and with a sudden wild leap he hurled himself at the chauffeur and knocked the gun out of his hand. It went off, the bullet smacking into the ceiling.

Dimly aware of Yvette falling to her knees to protect Albert, he sped past her and out of the convent.

The bicycle and trailer stood where he had left them and he leaped on to the saddle, turned in a circle and careered out of the gateway. A shot whined past his ear and he crouched lower, the ground flashing beneath his legs.

With no more than a confused idea of taking the general direction of Louvain in the hope of preventing Henri's return he sped down the village street. Two more shots rang out, the second one slapping into the trailer. Villagers rushed to their doors and a dog ran along beside him barking hysterically.

Shaking the sweat from his eyes he saw two grey uniforms ahead. Slowly and deliberately they stepped into the road and he realized that they were sentries from the German convalescent home.

It was too late to do any more. With a kind of tired fatalism he watched them raise their rifles. Two bullets found him simultaneously and he lay sprawled in the lee of the overturned trailer. Surprisingly there was no pain, and he floated away on a handful of notes released from the torn gut of the organ.

* * *

In an effort to find courage and strength Thérèse closed her eyes. When she opened them again, Clothilde had appeared in the hall. She saw the colour drain from her face and her hands fly to the high-boned collar of her blouse.

Compassionately she watched her huge eyes take in the two civilians and the inert body on the floor, then turned her head away as she heard Clothilde give a little cry and fall on her knees. She touched the man's short grey hair, then looked across at Thérèse and Yvette.

Remembering, Yvette burst into tears. Aware that the two Germans were watching them with interest, Thérèse fought to control her own emotions.

'And who have we here?' enquired one of them. 'What is your name and where do you come from?'

As if she hadn't heard, Clothilde knelt by the man they had called Fritzy, holding his hand while the tears rolled down her cheeks. She wept soundlessly, locked alone in a private and terrible grief.

'Who is this woman?'

Swallowing hard, Thérèse said in a harsh voice, 'She is a spinster seamstress from somewhere in Dinant. I do not know her personally. She undertakes small commissions for us now and then, mending linen, repairing clothes and suchlike. She calls about twice a year.'

'And she walks in without invitation?' enquired the man with the monocle.

'In all probability,' replied Thérèse, 'I failed to hear her knock.'

'And in addition to patching and darning she assists Belgian workers to evade their responsibilities?'

'She does not.'

'She hides Belgian workers.'

'That is a lie.'

Clothilde released Fritzy's hand and placed it by his side. With a gentle little movement she closed his eyes.

Then she stood up, looked unflinchingly at the two German civilians and said, 'I murdered him. And my name is Clothilde Toussant.'

211

After that, events moved swiftly.

The chauffeur reappeared with the sentries from the convalescent home, and after a rapid consultation with the two civilians fetched a motor bus and herded Thérèse and Yvette into the back of it. Albert was allowed to remain with them, and they were driven off.

Clothilde was treated differently. Holding the door of the limousine open for her, the monocled civilian bowed ironically as she gathered her long dark skirt about her and sat down on the elaborately buttoned seat. The back of the car was open to the late afternoon and she rode to prison with the scent of August in her nostrils and with the Chief of the Secret Police by her side.

Dinant Jail was a small building close to the river, a high circular wall separating it from nearby cottages. Thérèse and Yvette were pushed into a cell, and their relief at remaining together was so great that for a while they failed to notice the evil-smelling old vagrant who sat motionless in the corner.

Exhausted by the strange events of the day, little Albert fell asleep on his mother's lap.

'What will they do to him?' whispered Yvette, once more on the verge of tears.

'Nothing harmful,' Thérèse said. 'Whatever our future, he will not suffer.' She spoke with more conviction than she felt.

Their thoughts turned to Clothilde.

'But what happened?' demanded Yvette. 'How did Fritzy suddenly appear, and how on earth did she come to kill him?'

'It was not Clothilde.'

'Then who? Not the two men, or the one who drove the car — they would not kill one of their own kind in such a way . . .'

'No,' said Thérèse. 'Think again. Where, for instance, was Lucien?'

Yvette drew a sharp breath. 'I had forgotten him!'

'What happened,' said Thérèse slowly, 'is that Clothilde was down in the cellar at work on *La Voix*, Fritzy arrived at the notary's house as a convalescent and came to call on us. Lucien saw him and decided like a fool to kill him.'

'But why would Clothilde tell them that she did it?'

'I know not,' muttered Thérèse. 'Unless she was trying to protect us.'

They fell silent, watching the old vagrant scratching about in her rags.

'But she cannot continue to tell them that she killed Fritzy,' Yvette cried suddenly. 'Merciful God, they will execute her!'

'I know,' Thérèse said numbly.

Dusk was falling when the cell door was unlocked and a warder brought in three tin bowls of watery soup and three hunks of black bread.

'My little boy also needs food,' said Yvette.

The warder gave her a sour look. 'I have no instructions about a child,' he said and shuffled out, bolting the door behind him. But within a few minutes he returned with another bowl.

When they had eaten Yvette took off her skirt and tried to make a bed for Albert. He lay between them on the hard wooden bench, puzzled but not particularly alarmed by his new surroundings. Curled trustingly against his mother he fell asleep again.

They spent the night staring into the darkness and wondering ceaselessly about the true situation, and for Thérèse the most anguishing question of all concerned the whereabouts of Henri.

'And to think,' Yvette whispered towards dawn, 'that only a few hours ago you and I had a quarrel. What a waste of precious time . . .'

They held hands across the sleeping body of Albert.

* * *

The long walk towards Louvain had gone well. Henri and his party encountered no patrols, and at their destination their hostess had greeted them with an unexpectedly fine dish of jugged hare.

After a while he wished them goodbye and God speed and then set off again, having decided to break the return journey by calling on D. in Namur. The problem of Lucien was a pressing one, and he needed the advice of the man he had come to like and trust.

He walked by starlight, moving swiftly and silently down the lonely tracks and lanes, and he reached the outskirts of Namur when the sun was climbing in a peerless blue sky. It was still shady in the narrow street where D. lived and he glanced up at the windows of the tall dilapidated house. They were closed.

Glancing round he hurried up the steps and rang the bell, giving the customary signal of two short jabs and one long. He waited for the sound of D.'s window opening above his head.

Urgently he rang again, and when the door opened he was disconcerted to find himself confronted by the old woman who acted as concierge.

'The Monsieur has gone,' she said.

'The — the man on the third floor—' he stammered.

The old woman shrugged. 'Gone,' she repeated, then moved aside. 'See for yourself.'

With his heart thumping he ran up the familiar stone stairs. D.'s door stood open. He halted abruptly, then very slowly walked through it. The room had been ransacked and he slumped against the wall while his eyes took in the sickening mess. Chairs had been overturned and the floor was strewn with papers. Shaking, he bent down and picked one up but it proved to be nothing more incriminating than a laundry list.

Standing there, a loneliness came over him the like of which he had never known before. He might have been the last man left alive. It was an effort to pull himself together and go downstairs again. The concierge was lingering in the hallway.

'What happened, Madame?'

'The German police came.'

Although fearful of appearing too interested, it was vital that he should learn as much as possible.

'How strange. I wonder whether my friend was at home at the time?'

She shook her head. 'He left shortly before they came. I met him on the stairs and he said that he was going to visit a relative in the country. Three hours later the Boche arrived. They rushed upstairs and broke open the door of his apartment. I heard them shouting and throwing things about. They seemed very angry when I was unable to tell them where Monsieur had gone.'

Were her eyes as innocent as they seemed? It was difficult to tell how much she knew, and there was no time for further questioning. He thanked her and left the house.

He made straight for home, covering the twenty-five kilometres without any sense of physical fatigue. The only feeling of which he was conscious was the nagging fear in the pit of his stomach.

It was four in the afternoon when he approached the village, working his way circuitously to the edge of the plateau that rose to one side of it. He lay down in the dry sandy grass and anxiously scrutinized the one street with its patched and broken houses and its shattered church. The convent lay almost directly beneath him, the courtyard deserted, the wicket gate to the orchard hanging open.

The air of peacefulness brought reassurance. It was quite possible that the secret police had not had time to discover any connection between D.'s apartment and the convent at St Louis les Bois. He stood up, ready to hurry down the narrow track that led to the orchard when the German soldier walked out of the kitchen door. He was wearing braces over his grey shirt and he was carrying a couple of chairs. He set them down on the cobbles, then returned indoors. He reappeared, his arms piled with a miscellany of objects and heaped them by the chairs. Two more soldiers joined him, one of them carrying Clothilde's sewing machine.

Incapable of movement Henri watched them pour paraffin over the collection of things and then set fire to it. There was no hint of malicious enjoyment in their demeanour; the only impression they gave was that of three ordinary men going quietly and efficiently about an ordinary everyday task.

A dense cloud of smoke rose in the still air and stinging tears blinded the man who stood watching.

He remained up on the plateau until nightfall and he could think of nothing to do. At last he went down into the village where a few dim squares of light had appeared in the occupied houses. Conscious of hidden eyes watching he turned in at Monsieur Groult's gate. The old man was sitting in his kitchen, alone in the dark.

'What happened?'

'The secret police followed Greco from Namur. They shot him in the street. They went to the convent and apparently found a dead German soldier. They took Thérèse and Yvette away in a motor bus. Clothilde was taken separately. We saw her driven off in the big German limousine with the two civilians. It was as if she had been earmarked for a special destiny.'

'Who was the dead soldier?' His voice was quite calm.

'No one knows. Except that he was a convalescent from the notary's house.'

'Have they been here?'

'No,' said the old man. 'Not yet.'

'Someone has betrayed us and now everything is finished.'

They sat in silence for a while.

'They have taken everything,' Henri said. 'Even my wife.'

'Perhaps there is still hope.'

'They have taken my wife,' Henri said.

They parted, silently clasping hands, and Henri walked up the street towards the convent. His footsteps rang on the broken roadway, paused for a moment then unhurriedly continued. He walked through the shattered gateway, crossed the courtyard and opened the kitchen door.

A civilian wearing a monocle looked up from the bare scrubbed table, the only piece of furniture left in the room.

'So,' he said. 'The one-armed man. Come in, we have been expecting you.'

* * *

They had taken Clothilde to the prison at Namur.

She was in solitary confinement, but the Flemish wardress in charge of her was kind, and tried to make life as comfortable as possible for her. Extra titbits of food were greeted with little enthusiasm, but when she fulfilled the request for a notebook and pencil Clothilde's eyes lit up with pleasure.

Still impeccably neat in her dark skirt and high-necked blouse she sat on the edge of the bunk bed under the small barred window and began to write.

> *The course of my life lay in the hands of God from the moment of my birth. He alone in His wisdom can direct my footsteps through the turmoil and confusion of human frailty and lead me to a state of grace. I have no fear. I am willing to accept the role He has ordained for me.*

She seemed to be living in a strange, trance-like state, and three days after her arrival at Namur she was taken to see the Kommandant and the Chief of Police for the Province. She stood in front of them with her head erect and her hands folded.

'Your name is Clothilde Toussant?'

'Yes.'

'You are — or were — a dressmaker from Dinant?'

'That is so.'

'And since the war you have been living in the Convent of the Little Sisters of Mercy at St Louis les Bois?'

'Yes.'

'Why?'

'Because my home was destroyed in the shelling.'

217

'And because a deserted convent in a remote village was an excellent place from which to carry out certain subversive activities?'

Clothilde said nothing.

'You are accused of spying,' said the Chief of Police, rustling the papers on his desk, 'of harbouring Belgian conscripts, of producing and circulating propaganda with a view to promoting unrest and undermining the good relationship that exists between Germans and Belgians. You have also confessed to the murder of a German soldier, number 740832 Rifleman Johannes Schmidt.'

'I have never been a spy,' she said.

'But you admit to all the other charges?'

'Yes.'

The Chief of Police stared intently at her for a moment, then said, 'You will face a military trial in Brussels on a date to be arranged. In the meantime you will remain in solitary confinement, and anyone who attempts to communicate with you will be severely dealt with.'

Back in her small cell the air was close and stale. She paced up and down, six steps to the bunk bed, turn, six steps to the door . . .

Hidden under her single blanket were the notebook and pencil. She took them out, and clipping her gold pince-nez to her nose re-read what she had written earlier. Then she sat down, turned to a fresh page and began again:

Dear Thérèse, It is extremely doubtful whether you will ever receive this letter, but it is very pleasant to write to you nonetheless. I do hope that things are not too bad for you and Yvette and little Albert. I think of you, and pray for you constantly. I also wonder about certain other members of our family.

For myself, conditions could be very much worse. I have a small cell with a single bed, a tin plate for food and a mug to drink from. (The meals are regular and quite adequate.) There is a small window opposite the door but unfortunately it is too high to see out of. Today I was taken before the Kommandant and another man who questioned me, and I learned the real name of our friend whom we called Fritzy. It was Johannes Schmidt. How strange it is to think of him as Johannes, or as Monsieur Schmidt!

She paused for a moment, then continued:

But the real purpose of this letter, dear Thérèse, is to explain to you what happened on the last day. Yvette asked me to remain with Lucien while she went for a walk with Albert. I promised. And then I broke my promise. I went to the village to call on a certain friend, and left Lucien alone. Fritzy — Johannes, that is — came to call on us from the notary's house and Lucien, no doubt thinking to protect us, stabbed him. Poor Lucien. He stabbed him, but I was the murderer because I betrayed a trust.

How strange are the ways of God. Once before that man's life was in our hands and he offered us friendship. But now he is dead because of me and I am content to pay the price.

She stopped writing and fumbled in her skirt pocket for her handkerchief. She blew her nose. Then taking up the pencil again, wrote hurriedly:

To die for him is a small thing, because I loved him.

CHAPTER THIRTEEN

In Belgium the summer of 1917 ended in a torrent of rain. It came in from the North Sea and swept over the ravaged Flanders plain to where the giant armies were still locked in hopeless combat.

Tanks were used for the first time at the battle of Cambrai and during a week's hard fighting in November the British advanced five miles, only to withdraw under renewed German pressure.

Morale was low, for people were tired of heroism; children cried themselves to sleep with hunger and Belgian women, gaunt and haggard, queued patiently for a demi-kilo of potatoes. There was no American aid now because the Americans were no longer neutral. They had entered the war seven months ago.

The friends from the convent at St Louis les Bois were still in prison, awaiting trial. Early in October Thérèse and Yvette had been moved from Dinant to Namur, where they were placed in separate cells. Much more distressing was the fact that Yvette was separated from Albert, and the building rang with her screams when they took him away.

But they didn't take him far. He was lodged in the prison infirmary where the orderlies were reasonably kind, and where he was allowed to see his mother every Sunday afternoon for twenty minutes.

Thérèse was housed on the same floor as Yvette, in a cell where the gloom of late autumn filtered thickly through a small barred window. Unable to come to terms with close confinement she paced the floor hour after hour, her wooden sabots clacking a steady metronome beat between the door and the wall. Every now and then she would stand motionless, straining her ears to catch the slightest sound from outside.

Sometimes the silence drove her to a frenzy and she would beat on the door with clenched fists and shout the names of Henri, Clothilde and Yvette. No one ever answered, and as her frenzy increased she would hurl abuse at the Kaiser and General Ludendorff and any other German to whose name she could lay tongue, until her voice was hoarse and her fists bruised with hammering.

But as the days crept by and there was no sign of the trial she spent more time lying on the narrow bunk bed and thinking bitterly of the future. Even if they escaped with their lives they would face years of imprisonment.

It was two months before they told her that Henri was in the same building. Initial relief that he was at least alive brought the tears to her eyes.

She asked if she could speak to him. They said no. Could she be allowed a sight of him then, a fleeting glimpse? They told her that it was out of the question, whereupon she lost her temper, shook her fist and swore at them. She was thrust back into her cell and put on a diet of bread and water, which wasn't all that much worse than the ordinary fare.

But if Thérèse was denied a glimpse of Henri, Henri discovered that once a week he could catch sight of Yvette. By standing on his bunk on tiptoe he could just see in to one of the quadrangles of the prison, and on Sunday afternoon he recognized the figure of Yvette walking across the patch of muddy gravel escorted by a wardress. She was wearing a grey prison dress and her bright yellow hair was hidden beneath an unbecoming mob cap, but it was undeniably Yvette. Overcome with joy he watched her enter the building opposite.

He waited for her to reappear, and flexing his aching toes was rewarded by another glimpse of her twenty minutes later. This time, he thought she walked more slowly, and there was a dejected droop to her shoulders.

Cupping his hand to his mouth he bellowed through the window, 'Courage, Yvette . . . !' But she was too far away to hear.

Lying on the bunk and staring at the ceiling he wondered where she had been, and what for.

And he wondered for the millionth time if she was anywhere near Thérèse.

* * *

The good-natured wardress who had given Clothilde the notebook and pencil took pity on her still further and persuaded the authorities to provide her with some sewing as a further means of passing the long hours.

She was sitting on her bunk repairing some prison linen when the door was unlocked and a short man in a frock coat came in. He was carrying a briefcase.

'Mademoiselle Clothilde Toussant,' he said, 'I have been engaged as the counsel for your defence.'

She looked at him in surprise. 'But there is nothing that I wish to defend.'

He smiled, as if at the charming innocence of a child. 'I think, Mademoiselle, that there are certain matters I should explain to you.'

'By all means,' she said courteously, and indicated the neatly folded blanket on the bunk. 'Pray be seated, Monsieur.'

Opening his briefcase, he brought out a folder of papers.

'The German authorities,' he said, 'have prepared the dossier on your case.'

She expressed polite interest.

'And also on the case of your friends from St Louis les Bois.'

She flinched. 'Have you news of them?'

He looked her straight in the eyes. 'Mademoiselle Yvette Mazy and Madame Thérèse Aubel are awaiting trial for being accessories in the crime of aiding and abetting the escape of Belgian deportees, and of preparing and distributing literature of a seditious nature. Monsieur Henri Aubel faces even graver charges.'

He read in her eyes that he had succeeded in disturbing her calm.

'Monsieur Aubel,' he told her, 'is accused of treason.'

She looked away, then said in a whisper, 'I am prepared to die. Is that not sufficient?'

'My dear Mademoiselle,' the notary said harshly, 'the fact that you apparently have no interest in survival is neither here nor there. The Germans are not in the habit of conveniently heaping the sins of others upon the head of one sacrificial victim. When it comes to squandering human lives they have never shown the slightest tendency to economise.'

'I understand,' she whispered.

'In view of this,' he said, a little more gently, 'it would be as well if you would give me all the help within your power.'

'I will do whatever I can.'

The notary produced a blank sheet of paper and a pencil.

'To begin with,' he said, 'perhaps you would tell me quite truthfully about everything that happened at the convent in St Louis les Bois from the time that Monsieur Aubel returned from the Belgian Infantry. I understand, for example, that he went to Brussels and contacted the Resistance Movement there. That he established an illegal newspaper called *La Voix des Ardennes* and—'

'He had little connection with the newspaper,' she said. 'I was mainly responsible.'

He frowned. 'In what way?'

'I did all the typewriting.'

The notary took a large white handkerchief from his pocket and wiped his forehead. 'Mademoiselle,' he said, 'it is difficult to believe that you are as naive as you appear. Are you really incapable of appreciating the difference between instigator and accomplice?'

Clothilde said nothing.

'Our case is already a poor one, and needs all the help we can give it. Surely you have some sympathy for your friends?'

Clothilde folded the piece of linen she had been repairing and placed it on the foot of the bunk. She removed her pince-nez.

'Until the war came,' she said, 'I had never known the happiness of a real friendship. I had acquaintances, but nothing more. But with the coming of Thérèse and Yvette, and then Henri, I learned to love and to trust. And although none of them showed a deep concern for spiritual matters, I found—' her voice trembled slightly, 'I found that for the first time in my life I was living hand-in-hand with God.'

He looked at her questioningly.

'They taught me the meaning of tolerance,' she said.

There was a pause, then the notary said, 'Tell me about the German soldier who was found murdered.'

'I killed him.'

'Mademoiselle, are you sure?'

She inclined her head.

'The stab wounds were very deep, and had been inflicted with a force unusual for a woman.'

'I am strong,' she said. The notary looked at her thin spinster body and made no comment.

'Will you swear to me that you are not lying to protect your friends?' he said at length. 'If I am to help you at all, it is essential that I know the truth.'

'I am guilty of his murder,' she said quietly. 'And I am willing to pay the price.'

He gathered up his papers and replaced them in the briefcase. He stood up, then walked to the door and knocked for the wardress to open it. While he waited he looked across the cell at Clothilde.

'*Why*?' he asked her helplessly.

'Because my purpose in life is finished,' she said, and he went away haunted by the radiance of her smile.

* * *

The trial was held in Brussels, and German military police stood with fixed bayonets as the prisoners were escorted into the Parliament House.

Walking down the long corridors between two escorts Henri tried to remain impassive while he looked eagerly for Thérèse. It was now four months since he had seen her.

They came to a halt outside a pair of ornate double doors and his eyes flickered over the group of civilians already waiting there. With a sinking heart he noticed Papa Vilain. He looked small and very frail.

'Henri . . .'

She was standing quite close to him, wearing a black coat that didn't belong to her. The weeks of solitary confinement had drained the colour from her face, but she was smiling.

He tried to reach her hand, to touch her, however fleetingly, but a guard noticed his intention and pushed him further away. There was nothing he could do but stand and look at her, and try to send her messages of hope and love with his eyes.

When the double doors were opened they all filed into the court.

It was a lofty room, its former splendours harshly lit by bare electric light bulbs. He took his place with the other defendants, sitting between two men both of whom were unknown to him. Yvette he suddenly noticed on a bench in front, her bright hair making a splash of sunshine in the surrounding drabness. She was, he thought sadly, the youngest person there.

Clothilde was brought in last. Tall and thin and impeccably neat she sat in the space reserved for her, isolated from the rest of them by the frowning profile of two uniformed guards.

The three judges wearing tasselled epaulettes and military decorations sat at a long table facing the accused Belgians, and there were many other uniformed officers present, their function in the trial unknown to him. Raising his eyes he saw that there were more of them in the public gallery, some of them accompanied by well-dressed women who were staring down into the court through field glasses.

The trial began, and his sense of unreality increased when he realized that it was to be in German. Blankly, bitterly, he watched the proceedings, and although an interpreter translated into French it was a foreign, guttural French, the sound of which merely added to his resentment.

It took a long time to read out the charges against the eighteen civilians who stood accused of crimes varying from the distribution of forbidden literature to that of murder.

One by one they were called, and listening intently Henri was at last able to establish the extent of the network's collapse. Five men and two women were accused with Papa Vilain, but there was no sign of D. Evidently he had escaped in time. With the exception of two vaguely familiar faces he knew none of the accused outside his own immediate circle, which made him realize how well the organization had maintained its anonymity.

The prosecutor was a hairless officer whose relish for the job was depressingly apparent. He shouted and thumped his thick pink fist on the dossier of incriminating evidence that lay on the table in front of him, and his hatred for the prisoners in the dock seemed to reach culmination point when an elderly, black-clad woman was shown into the box as a witness for the prosecution. It was Madame Vilain.

'You say that you suspected your husband's involvement with the so-called Resistance Movement as far back as 1915. Why did you not notify the German authorities sooner?'

'I preferred to wait.'

'For what, Madame?'

She hesitated.

'You very sensibly preferred to wait, Madame, until you were in a position to furnish us with the maximum amount of incriminating evidence?'

She inclined her head. 'That is so.'

The prosecutor gave her what passed for a smile, then said, 'And tell me, Madame, do you recognize any other of the accused?'

Her cold gaze moved along the rows of faces, paused, then came to rest on the face of Henri.

'The man with one arm,' she said. 'I have seen him before. He called at my husband's shop and offered to become a member of the Resistance. He agreed to open a new channel of communication in the Ardennes area.'

'And the scene of his subsequent operations was in fact a village called St Louis les Bois?'

Once again she inclined her head in assent.

So the traitor from within had been Marthe Vilain. He stared across at the heavy face under the black straw hat and wondered what grotesque form of reasoning had compelled her to betray her own husband to the enemy.

Then it was Henri's turn. He stood to attention.

'Your name is Henri Aubel?'

'Yes.'

'And you come from a small farm on the outskirts of St Louis les Bois?'

'Yes.'

'And in May 1916 you called at the house of Georges Vilain for the purpose of joining the so-called Resistance Movement, knowing that all such organizations were strictly forbidden by the German High Command?'

'Yes.'

It went on and on, and the only thing he could do was to persist in a stubborn denial when the prosecutor came to the parts played by Thérèse, Clothilde and Yvette.

'These women helped in the production of an illegal newspaper?'

'They did not.'

'They hid Belgian deportees?'

'They did not.'

The hairless prosecutor thumped his fist. 'You are a liar! A liar and a traitor to your country, and I would remind you that the penalty for treason is death!'

Henri was dismissed, and the court was adjourned until the following day.

* * *

Clothilde was the last defendant to be called. She stood gripping the wooden rail in front of her and answering the prosecutor's questions in a small clear voice.

Henri listened with growing amazement.

Yes, she had been responsible for the production of the illegal newspaper *La Voix des Ardennes*. Yes, she had hidden deportees at the convent, mostly without the knowledge of the Aubels or Yvette Mazy. She had done these things knowing them to be punishable by death, and her only regret was that she had jeopardized the safety of Monsieur and Madame Aubel and Mademoiselle Mazy. They were innocent. She alone was guilty.

Further along the row of prisoners Thérèse rose to her feet and began to protest. She was thrust back in her seat by one of the guards. Henri also stood up, but his voice was drowned in the call to order which was loudly reiterated by the interpreter.

Swiftly the trial came to its conclusion with the prosecutor reading out the sentences recommended under Paragraph 90 of the German Penal Code, the three judges listening impassively as he called for the death penalty for both Clothilde and Henri. The lightest sentence demanded was for five years' hard labour.

The court was cleared, and the prisoners driven back to St-Gilles Prison. Henri caught a glimpse of Thérèse and

Yvette being herded into a prison bus, but of Clothilde there was no sign.

The next day was Saturday, so they were obliged to wait until Monday before the sentences were confirmed.

Once more assembled in the marble splendours of the Parliament House they learned that both Yvette and Thérèse had been awarded ten years' imprisonment for aiding and abetting in the production of seditious literature, and for assisting and conniving in the escape of Belgian conscripts. Henri's role in the affair had been carefully reconsidered in the light of confessions made by the prisoner Toussant and his sentence commuted to that of life imprisonment.

As if in a dream they heard the sentence pronounced on Clothilde.

'Todesstrafe!' And as in all cases involving treason it was to be death by firing squad.

* * *

The year 1917 crept to its melancholy conclusion, and at first light on 8 January, 1918, the chaplain of St-Gilles was admitted to Clothilde's cell.

Neat and composed, she knelt on the cold stone floor to receive Absolution, then she gave him a note addressed to Thérèse, which he promised to deliver. She also gave him her notebook, which he undertook to destroy.

She looked round the cell to make sure that everything was in order. Her bed was folded, and at the foot of it lay the mending she had completed the evening before. She removed the little gold chain from her neck that held her pince-nez and laid it beside her thimble and scissors and reel of cotton. She smoothed her hair, and said quietly, 'I am quite ready.'

A few flakes of snow were falling as they drove across Brussels to the Tir National, the firing range that stood in the Place des Carabiniers. A prison matron helped her from the grey military motor-wagon, and with the chaplain at her side she walked under the armed escort through the stone corridors and out on to the range.

The execution squad was already in place when they tied her to the wooden post. They blindfolded her, and in less than two minutes it was all over. The shots echoed and re-echoed before dying away, and while the chaplain prayed for the peace of her soul a German army doctor examined her and pronounced her dead.

The snow fell faster, muffling the footsteps of the stretcher-bearers who carried her away.

Thérèse and Yvette were sent back to the prison at Namur but Henri remained at St-Gilles until the following April. Three weeks after his arrival he was allowed to see Thérèse, in a room where they were separated by a wide table. The jailor in attendance warned them against trying to touch one another, but he allowed her to pass Clothilde's letter for Henri to read.

'The chaplain at St-Gilles gave it to me,' she said.

He unfolded it slowly because of his one hand. It was a short letter, but in it he could hear the voice of Clothilde. She sent her love to them all, she asked them to remember her sometimes, and she thanked them for sharing their lives with her. The letter ended with a quotation from St Francois de Sales:

To live according to the spirit is to love according to the spirit:
to live according to the flesh is to love according to the flesh:
for love is the life of the soul as the soul is the life of the body.

'She loved Fritzy,' Thérèse said. 'And he came back to see her on the day that Lucien killed him.'

He folded the letter and returned it to her. Fleetingly their fingers touched.

'They say that she died very bravely.'

'Having conquered her fear of life,' replied Thérèse, 'the fear of death was an easy matter.'

He watched her wipe the tears away on a square of dingy calico provided by the prison authorities. She blew her nose, then looked at him from the other side of the table.

'It is springtime,' she said. 'And this time next year we will be planting our fields.'

'You really believe?'

'Yes,' she said. 'I believe.'

* * *

For the war machine was running down at last, and in the second Battle of the Marne the Germans were unable to withstand the force of the attacking armies and they began to retreat. In the east, the Bulgarian front was the first to collapse, and in Palestine General Allenby launched a final and victorious attack against the Turks.

And in October the Germans left Belgium.

On a cold afternoon in November Yvette Mazy rang the bell of a tall house in Namur. An elderly woman in a dark uniform dress opened the door and invited her inside. She led her to a closed door and said, 'He is waiting for you in there.'

The room was cold and sparsely furnished. On a high-backed chair surrounded by a sea of polished linoleum sat a small fair-haired boy with his feet resting on a neatly tied brown paper parcel.

He considered her gravely. 'Good afternoon, Madame. Are you my mother?'

'Yes, Albert,' she said.

They studied one another, each trying to bridge the fifteen months' gap in their relationship. She wanted to embrace him, but was afraid.

'What was it like in prison?' he asked finally.

'Not very nice. But I was with Thérèse — do you remember Thérèse?'

He shook his head, then leaning forward pointed to his feet. 'Look,' he said, 'I am wearing boots with real laces.'

'They are the finest boots I have ever seen,' she said, then held out her hand. 'Come, Albert, I think we will go home now.'

He picked up the parcel. 'Where is home?'

'A place called St Louis les Bois,' she said. 'Where you were born.'

The work of rebuilding began, and until the farm was ready for occupation Henri and Thérèse, Yvette and Albert stayed with Monsieur Groult, and then one day without any warning Jean-Baptiste returned. He was wearing an old army greatcoat which hung loosely on his thin frame and his face was hollow with fatigue.

He found Yvette doing the ironing in Monsieur Groult's kitchen, and after all the years of waiting it seemed ridiculous not to come straight to the point.

'Dear little one,' he said. 'If you still love me will you please marry me?'

She scrubbed her fist against her wet cheek. 'When?'

'Do not start ironing another shirt,' he said.

By the following spring the restoration of the farmhouse was almost complete, the rooms repainted and the furniture arranged to Thérèse's satisfaction.

'Orphans?' repeated Henri, inspecting the bedrooms. 'How many have you in mind?'

'There are seventy-five at the place where Albert stayed.'

'I think it would be more prudent to start with one,' he said.

'Two.'

'Two would get into mischief.'

'One would be lonely.'

So they started with four, and the venture was such a success that by the end of the year they had a round half dozen. There was Armand, Emile, and Léon; and on the girls' side Marie and Madeleine — all of whom the war had deprived of homes and parents. And finally there was the baby, a sensitive, luminous-eyed child who was listed in the orphanage register as *Result of illicit union between Belgian woman and German soldier.*

'She has nothing in the world, not even a name,' said the matron. 'And all because of a momentary animal indulgence.'

'Perhaps that was not the way of it,' Thérèse said, slipping her finger inside the baby's hand. 'Perhaps they really loved one another.'

The matron snorted. 'Love? Who with any degree of responsibility could love her enemy?'

'I know someone who did,' Thérèse said.

So they took the baby, and because of how things had once been they christened her Clothilde.

* * *

Thérèse and Henri are both dead now. They lie in the churchyard at St Louis les Bois, close to Monsieur Groult and not far from Greco and the LePage twins.

Yvette is now an old lady of eighty-two, and after Jean-Baptiste retired from the staff of Louvain University they came back to the village, where they bought the notary's house.

Little Albert has become a charming and rather portly Brussels businessman and is married to Madeleine, one of the war orphans adopted by the Aubels. They have four children, one of whom has now become a representative in the European Parliament.

And everything in St Louis les Bois is quietly flourishing. Occasionally a summer coachload of tourists finds its way up the steep road from Dinant, but there isn't much to see. Unless you know what to look for, that is.

Like the small brass plaque set in the wall of the convent chapel: *In Memory of Clothilde Toussant, who Served God here. 1914–1917.*

'Perhaps,' said the Little Sister of Mercy who showed me round, 'someone will decide to write her story one day.'

THE END

THE JOFFE BOOKS STORY

We began in 2014 when Jasper agreed to publish his mum's much-rejected romance novel and it became a bestseller.

Since then we've grown into the largest independent publisher in the UK. We're extremely proud to publish some of the very best writers in the world, including Joy Ellis, Faith Martin, Caro Ramsay, Helen Forrester, Simon Brett and Robert Goddard. Everyone at Joffe Books loves reading and we never forget that it all begins with the magic of an author telling a story.

We are proud to publish talented first-time authors, as well as established writers whose books we love introducing to a new generation of readers.

We have been shortlisted for Independent Publisher of the Year at the British Book Awards three times, in 2020, 2021 and 2022, and for the Diversity and Inclusivity Award at the Independent Publishing Awards in 2022.

We built this company with your help, and we love to hear from you, so please email us about absolutely anything bookish at:

feedback@joffebooks.com

If you want to receive free books every Friday and hear about all our new releases, join our mailing list: www.joffebooks.com/contact

And when you tell your friends about us, just remember: it's pronounced Joffe as in coffee or toffee!

ALSO BY JUDY GARDINER

STANDALONES
MY LOVE, MY LAND